Deadlights

By Hugo Yelagin

Published by Parisian Phoenix Publishing, Easton, Pennsylvania USA

Cover Image: Bauder-Isaac Killian

C O N N E C T with the publisher:
ParisianPhoenix
ParisBirdBooks
parisianphoenix

Prologue

One Dreamless Night

"Uncle… Alexander…?" a tiny voice whispered.

Was that… Maxwell?

Alexander had only cracked the bedroom door, but even so, something was not quite right about the boy's room. There was a… miasma about it. And it smelled horrible inside, all damp and humid. Like rot. Not to mention that the boy himself was… Well, worse for wear would be putting it lightly.

"Maxwell?" he asked his nephew.

The boy, only seven or eight, with his head of ginger hair and cracked spectacles, stood upright, out of his bed, in the center of the room, the bags under his eyes darker than the very darkness he resided in. Though by looking at him, Alex didn't think Maxwell should have been out of bed at all.

Maxwell breathed through his mouth quite heavily, and there was… This terrible noise which came from his throat each time he inhaled. A noise in between stridor and suffocation, emanated from deep within his throat with each and every labored breath.

Alexander rushed to his nephew's aid. Maxwell's glassy eyes did not react as his uncle spoke.

"Nephew? Maxwell, what is going on here?" Alexander asked. "Are you… Well, are you…"

Alexander wanted to ask if the boy was all right but decided against it. There wasn't much point in asking, Maxwell very clearly was not, in any sense of the word. Alexander instead chose to ask a much more important question:

"Maxwell, does your father know that you're sick?"

Blankly, the boy shook his head.

"Follow me, Maxwell," Alexander said as he grabbed the sickly boy's hand.

Slowly, as to not outpace his exhausted, morbidly ill nephew, Alexander led Maxwell from the door of that sickly, mephitic bedroom of his. But soon enough, his nephew's continued wheezing with every step, made it abundantly clear that the boy couldn't even handle walking in his sorry state. Poor bugger...

"Would you like me to carry you?"

His nephew nodded, vacantly, and barely conscious. As soon as Alexander had scooped up the boy, Max was practically asleep. He probably would have fainted if upright any longer. Then, with the delirious child in his arms, Alex descended the staircase of the manor, towards the unthematic music and the lavish, colorful party awaiting them at the bottom, neither of which should have been happening considering the literal decay of the host's own son.

"Maverick!" Alexander bellowed, upon reaching the bottom of the staircase.

The music, the laughter, the banter, it all stopped. People in exquisite masks stared at Alexander, holding the sickly child in his arms. The room drew still and silent. He then placed his eyes on his disgruntled brother Maverick, creeping his way through the crowd. Maxwell's father.

"Maverick, explain yourself! Now!"

"Alexander, please." Maverick crooned in his particularly dismissive, fork-tongued voice, the same probably used by the snake in the garden of Eden. "We have guests over. Could we perhaps take this to a more... You know what? This won't be but a moment, everyone! Continue with the party, your host is just dealing with some family matters at the moment–"

"What is the matter with you!" Alexander screamed. Maxwell coughed, sputtering black dust from the recesses of his throat. Guests moved away, like they were scared of him, scared of a sick child... "He is sick! Your son is ill! And you throw a party!"

"Alex!" his brother crooned once more. "It's just a little mold poisoning! Maxwell will be fine. He's lived through worse. He has... a strong immune system. This is ridiculous, Alex! Lighten up a little! Enjoy. The. Party."

"You put him up there, knowing his room was killing him!"

"Well, where else was I supposed to put him? He can't be down here, infecting everybody else now, can he? Be reasonable!"

"You. Are. Insane." Alexander hissed. His brother did not seem insulted.

He wanted to hit Maverick so badly, but... not here. Not in front of all these sniveling sycophants, who did nothing, watching the dispute with what looked like morbid curiosity. Alexander forced his way through the crowd.

"Since she died," Alexander muttered bitterly, "you've gone mad, Brother."

Alexander opened the front door.

"I can assure you, Alex," his brother hissed, smirking. Smirking, at something like this. "If I were mad, my madness would be all my own."

Alexander closed the door behind himself, ignoring Maverick's protests, still holding Maxwell, his brother's only son. Maverick clearly could not provide for the boy. Alex would have to care for him now, after witnessing the barbarous treatment of Max dealt within his own home. Seeing the way Maverick had still smirked, while his only son was in this condition… Ugh… It made him sick. It wasn't just Maxwell's room. Everyone inside that house was sick, in some way or another. Even his brother.

"Uncle Alexander…?" Maxwell wheezed. "Where are we going?"

"To get you to a proper doctor," he assured his nephew.

Still carrying the boy, Alexander walked towards the carriage which had brought him here, to the middle nowhere, at what remained of their family estate. What was left of the Corvid family home, a lavish manor with no real family within it, a luxurious, starlit courtyard, run rampant with weeds and vermin. A family home that could have been a beautiful place… If the will had only said his name, rather than his brother's. Maverick didn't deserve it. He didn't deserve anything that he had.

"The doctors can help you," Alexander said quietly to the boy.

"Will I be… okay?"

"Whatever happens Maxwell…" he said, transporting the nephew he would now care for towards some place far, far better than this.

"One day, you may think of all this as just a very, very bad dream."

Chapter One

The Road to Damnation

Maxwell Corvid could not remember his dreams.

Lying in bed, at his college dormitory, Maxwell often found himself drifting to a place where he was not quite awake, but not quite dreaming either. This had happened every night for as long as he could remember. Really, it was who he was, and he had decided long ago that there was no point in really changing it. Not really worth the effort.

Besides, if Maxwell couldn't remember his dreams, they probably weren't worth remembering.

So, despite waking in the middle of the night soaked in sweat and panic, he didn't even know what had terrified him to begin with. He really didn't think he wanted to know, but... What were his nightmares about? Deep down he wanted to experience one, or more accurately, remember one, just to see what they were like. Just to see what he was so scared of.

And as he sat there miserably on this equally miserable coach ride, half-asleep and heading to a place he hadn't seen in almost fifteen years: he couldn't help but wonder if he was finally getting his wish.

This all felt like a bad dream. His first bad dream in years, his first dream in years actually, good or bad. Being trapped in this rickety wooden coffin of a stagecoach, lagging down a long, winding dirt road, it certainly would have made for a chilling setting. The fact he didn't wake up to his familiar dusty and decrepit dorm room though, now that was an unusually potent shock to his system. So potent he had almost forgotten what had happened for a split second.

But eventually, his memory finally returned. With that memory, came a realization.

He probably would never see that dormitory at Miskatonic University ever again.

"Ah, so you *were* awake. Your father always said you didn't sleep easy. Trying to get away from your new responsibilities so soon, Mr. Corvid?"

The banker across from him had been so quiet that Max had almost forgotten he had been skulking around at all. The man's choice in attire didn't help. Although, it was startlingly appropriate for a time of mourning, if you could call what Maxwell was doing "mourning." A black suit with yellow pinstripes and matching top hat made his observer almost invisible against the dim wooden walls of the stagecoach, the man blending into the passing shadows cast by the trees outside. The man had better camouflage than most animals. The only sign he was even there was the stench of smoke wafting from his dying cigarette and the faint glow of that ornate silver lighter as he lit another one, after grinding the first into ashes.

"No," Max replied groggily.

He stretched his arms. The banker blew a puff of smoke in his direction. Maxwell cleared his throat before he continued, an attempt to cleanse the smoke from his airways. He fanned the cloud away from his face and absent-mindedly cleaned his glasses fighting the thin layer of film on the lenses.

"The bump woke me, actually."

Suddenly, he remembered. That unusual shock wore off, and now Maxwell only had a regrettable tingling. Technically, he had agreed to come, yes, although when on the steps of the university, he hadn't known exactly what he was doing. Uncle Alexander had made this dejected arrangement for him.

A memory returned to him, one shrouded in smoke in the most literal sense. One where this particular banker had stepped from his rickety carriage, and Maxwell initially feared the man might be escaping a fire based on the thick haze streaming from the windows. With the smoke perpetually surrounding the executor, the man offered his hand. Max had reluctantly taken it, and… and well the rest didn't really matter.

It all blended together anyway — this trip, a mixture of uneasy sleep, and the drowsy waking world. Maxwell rubbed his eyes, as they teared from the fuggy air that unwantedly made it into his lungs.

"Well, it's good you're awake anyway. We have a lot of paperwork to get done now, don't we?" the banker said, in his sleazy way. "After all, it's been three weeks since your father died, and we've barely started!"

The man opened a large, brown briefcase on his lap, revealing a stack of yellowed paper almost as thick as the university's textbooks. After straightening the dog-eared edges, the banker flicked through them, still puffing away at his cigarette, before handing around a third of them to Max. And they were, in fact, heavier than they looked.

"Don't worry," the banker assured Max. The man took his cigarette from his mouth. He then released a long, satisfying exhale. "Half of these are just the backups. We wouldn't want there to be any mistakes now, would we?" he said. "I'm sure you have much better things to do than sign these silly formalities. All forty-seven of them."

"Oh good," Max replied sarcastically.

With a grimace, Maxwell unenthusiastically accepted the stack. He normally had to squint to view the fine print, let alone now in the dark, with the unhelpful, dim glowering of the sunset behind him. And it didn't help that everything in the carriage was smoke screened.

As Maxwell inspected the forms, the banker passed his little stick of cancer holding it to Max's face like a treat for a dog. Max could somehow still smell the man's breath on it. It smelled like dried meat, like something left out in the sun for too long. What Max might be smelling the banker's lungs, black as charcoal and regulating his petrol-pumping heart. Or, on the other hand, Max could have smelled the fake niceties and the forced small talk in their breath. The familiar smell of customer service.

"Care for a smoke?"

"No, thank you," Max answered. "Trying to quit."

"And what brought that on?"

"Studies show tobacco turns your lungs to mush. Trying not to end up like my old man. The man couldn't walk for the latter half of his life, and he was coughing out black stuff on his deathbed," Max said. "Didn't really care about his health too much. Well, he actually didn't really care about anything much. But I don't want to end up a vegetable, not just yet."

"Now, now, your father really cared about his relationship with the bank," his new "friend" informed him. What was his name again? Max's memory was foggy.

The banker returned the cigarette to his mouth, billowing smoke to the side once again. As the banker leaned over, Max could finally get a good look at his face in the light cast by the descending sun. He had long, frizzy brown hair, which looked almost liked a charred version of a French magistrate's wig, and wore black lensed spectacles over his face, which reflected the glow of his cigarette perfectly. However, all Max noticed about the sleazy executor was the smugness of his grin and how much he reminded Maxwell of the very cigarettes he smoked. He was quite young. In fact, they were around the same age. The banker had skin the same color as the brown paper wrapping. His breath reminded Max of chimney soot. It hung in the air, almost as black as motor car exhaust. His skin was dry and flaking. His suit was rumpled, scruffy, and hardly fit him, being about five sizes too big. Just about the only thing in good health about the man was his teeth, which were blinding white. The banker flashed him a smile from behind his black-rimmed glasses. Then, he coughed into his elbow before resuming the conversation. Now just what was his name!

"Despite the rumors, your father was a good man, honest! It's a shame really, that… this… had to happen. Real shame."

Maxwell could beg to differ, but he didn't want to talk more than required. Every comment led to small talk. And then small talk led to conversations. And Maxwell wasn't in the mood for conversations at the moment.

He should have been studying. He should have been anywhere else. He wished he could bury his nose in his textbook and avoid the man's words. But no. It was quite important that he remained cordial in his conversations. Doubly so now that he had that article in the paper written about him.

"We wouldn't want all of the wonderful things that he left you to go to waste," the banker continued. "Mr. Corvid gave me… I…I mean he gave my father, Otto, very specific instructions in the event of his… well, his passing. They were very good friends, you know. I'm hoping we can continue that legacy between families, the two of us. Told you before, but I'm Percival Crane, here on behalf of Otto. You can call me Percy."

"As you've said three times," Max mumbled. Though he did need that reminder.

"Have I given you my card? The one for the Crane and Sons banking branch?"

"Don't bother."

"Come again?" Percy said. "Didn't quite catch that."

"Nothing, sorry, just clearing my throat," Maxwell replied. "Used to fresher air is all."

The banker seemed a little disgruntled from Max's remark, before immediately washing that feeling off with a smile. The man wiped his hand on his suit, before holding out to Max. Now, the hand probably contained more filth than before.

Maxwell shook the banker's hand, but then immediately wiped it on his own trousers. He had learnt that when it came to handshakes, he just had to get them over with fast.

"I wasn't aware that Mr. Crane had another son," Maxwell said. "Did he remarry again?"

"Well, it's been a long time since you've seen him. You started your first year at university, when, almost five years ago now?" Percy responded. "He had many wives, and many children, but sadly, most of my brothers left the business and poor sister…"

Percy took the cigarette from his mouth and held it between his fingers.

"Well, you know the story from the papers," Percy said. "Are you sure you don't want to reconsider that smoke? I assure you, it's only the good stuff. Nothing less, for a Corvid."

Percy once again placed the cigarette to his lips and inhaled.

"I always try to make a good first impression. Only quality, for you." Percy rambled. "That's actually why I saw to this little excursion myself, instead of sending somebody else to—"

"No, thank you, to the cigarette, I mean," Maxwell said. "I try to… Well, I'm just not really a smoker."

"Really?" The executor reached into his pocket and frowned.

Percy took out a small cardboard box, it's red and white packaging faded and dulled. Only a few stragglers remained in it, which meant the man had run low on his favorite pastime. Percy shook the cardboard, as if it might have more. No luck. He returned his gaze to Maxwell, his wide, cheap smile growing all the wider and cheaper.

"Judging by your reputation from the paper, Mr. Corvid, I would have assumed you indulged in these sorts of things. Things that calm the nerves, I mean," Percy said. "I thought it was why they expelled you, from Miskatonic. Because of your… Well… Your… Well, I'm sure you know…"

Of course, Percy the Chimney would mention that.

It wasn't his fault.

They had told lies about him in the article. He didn't have a "neurotic reputation," at least he didn't think he did. And it hadn't been an "outburst." He had exposed the truth about that school. And they had expelled him for it!

It was absurd.

"What are you implying, Percy?"

"I'm not implying anything Mr. Corvid, and I do apologize if that struck a nerve in you, didn't mean to offend. And if you want to state your case, set the record straight with me…"

The banker leaned, his face tightening and his lips cracking into that all too familiar face-splitting smile.

"Be my guest," he said. "Change my mind. Go on. And don't spare the gritty details. You're among friends here. Or, well, one friend."

"It was the school's fault, not mine," Maxwell replied. "I'm not a looney. Many of us at the school were sick, dying. What did they expect us to do? Die quieter?"

"Tell me more about this 'sickness' then." Percy mocked him, toying with the word "sickness" in his mouth like it was chewing gum. "Come on, really sell the pitch."

"It was mold," Maxwell admitted. "Really dangerous mold. I hate mold—"

"Yes, yes," Percy interrupted. "Your uncle informed me. I did a little digging, it's actually not that hard to find out why Maxwell Corvid would hate mold, considering he almost died of it as a child. Go on, skip to the good part."

There had been no reason for Percy to interrupt him rudely like that. But despite the banker's demeanor, begrudgingly, to prove he wasn't mad, Maxwell continued. Max felt like he was being prodded and picked at, like a specimen in a lab. He hated that feeling, the feeling that people were studying him instead of listening to him. Because Maxwell felt as though he might have been the only person in the world sometimes with ideas worth listening to.

"Mold grew on everything: the textbooks, the ceilings. Hell, you could find it under the floorboards! That school was more mold than wood! We were all breathing that, and nobody cared!"

"Mhm." The banker said absent-mindedly, slowly losing interest.

Max could see it, the way his eyes were lulling around the cabin, looking at anything but the speaker. Maxwell… realized that he was getting far more worked up over this than he should be. He had actually almost stood upright in the carriage! How silly of him… It wasn't helping him keep the allegations of lunacy away by any means. He sat back down, embarrassed.

"That university probably had more disease than the entirety of the city," Maxwell sullenly remarked. More to himself than to the banker. "So I'm not crazy. People just love to make up stories about me, that's all. Miskatonic just wants to shut me up. That's why I'm here. The only reason that I am here."

He breathed in the dried-out air again. His throat felt dried out.

"Ah, okay," the banker said casually, staring out the window at the boring countryside, entirely disinterested now. "Yes, that clears everything up then."

"Yes," Maxwell replied. He straightened his collar. Percy had shrunk into the shadows once again, except for the glow of a new cigarette. "Yes, I believe it does."

Eventually, the banker resumed conversation, as much as Maxwell would have preferred the silence.

"Well, I didn't mean to insinuate anything Mr. Corvid," Percy said. "You have to believe me, but I don't really care why they booted you from that crummy, stuffy old school. The academics are all dreadfully boring, if you ask me. I'm an artist at heart, a creative type, Dad used to say. Would you believe me if I said I even did acting school for a few years? Eventually, I had to take up the torch though, I'm sure you know how these things go. I think we understand each other perfectly. Two peas in a pod."

"Yeah… Sure, Percy," Maxwell muttered. "That's right. Two peas in a pod."

Max barely paid attention to the man's words, as he pretended to be preoccupied with the paperwork. He knew he had to get a start on this stack of papers at some point, even if he was just feigning his interest. None of it made any sense in the light, and they might as well have been written in another language in the dimly-lit light of dusk. He could read the fine print upside down and backwards, and it would vex him all the same.

There was another uncomfortably long silence, as the banker waited for Max to start a conversation… like he wanted to do that. Eventually, the banker resumed his constant prattle, given enough time.

"Make sure to sign all of those. In quintuplicate, of course," Percy said. "The last thing we would want is for your precious time to be wasted by repeating this whole process."

"Crystal clear," Maxwell remarked.

In reality of course, things were not crystal clear, literally or figuratively. Nothing was ever crystal clear. Maxwell could barely see the forms, nor his shadowy executor either. So yes, things were the furthest thing from crystal clear.

But on the bright side, after sitting in this smoky, stale carriage for hours, the fresh, country air would taste like candy.

Maxwell lowered the forms and rested his head against the grimy window, hoping to escape the infectious ennui of fine print. Outside stood nothing but dying trees as far as the eye could see. There was nothing on the estate that he was traveling to that he wanted, or cared about. The sooner he could get out of here, and back to his studies at a new school, the better.

"Terribly sorry for your loss, by the way, Maxwell," Percy said. "He was a good man. I never met him of course, but from what my father told me he seemed decent. Sickly, but decent nonetheless."

"Sure,"Maxwell replied. "Either way, he was a shitty father."

Percy gave a raspy chuckle, before coughing obnoxiously. Maxwell didn't even cast him a glance. Percy couldn't see through the smoke clinging to his face like a swarm of gnats.

Percy Crane knew everything about Maxwell's father, even if by reputation alone. Maverick Corvid was practically as famous as the boogeyman. Perhaps even more so. Famous for plenty of things, all disgusting or mysterious, sometimes both, that Maxwell didn't want to be associated with. But the reputation of the Corvid name followed him around like a black cloud. No wonder his professor jumped at the chance to be rid of him.

"And of course, since he's dead now, and you're listed as his closest living relative," Percy continued (it seemed Percy endlessly had more to say), "the debt he accrued falls to you, unfortunately, of course."

"I'm aware," Maxwell snapped.

"And you're aware of the magnitude of the funds we've loaned him to do who knows what with?"

"Yes," Maxwell said.

"Of course you are. You're signing the paperwork, right now," Percy said. "Take your time, Maxwell. Wouldn't want there to be any mistakes, the bank values its customers' time above all. And Mr. Corvid? There's one last thing I'd like to admit, and considering we're friends and all, I should probably come clean. I'm, in fact not—"

The coach jostled again, this time more violently. The jolt forced Percy's mouth closed.

"Are the roads always like this?" Max asked, ignoring the previous comment.

"Yes, well, usually they are a little rough," Percy answered, "but this is just…"

A gunshot interrupted Percy.

Max pressed his face against the smudged glass. Percy did the same on his side. A hobbled shape tumbled past the glass. Blood stained the soil as a body somersaulted away, as their driver crumpled into the dirt.

This was no longer just a coach. It might *really* be his coffin.

"Percy!" he exclaimed. "What the Hell is happening? Percy!"

The cigarette smoke still swirled in the carriage. The banker's voice took on a new tone, one which was far angrier and savage, as if the man released years' worth of stored emotions. Like he was billowing out the toxic smoke stored inside. At least he had knocked off that cheap customer service routine.

"How the fuck am I supposed to know!" Percy replied. "You're a smart guy! Figure it out!"

Without a driver to control them, the horses accelerated in terror, Percy shoved past him, struggling to balance as the coach swayed side to side, wheels spinning faster and faster. The carriage veered from the old dirt road into the woods. Percy unbolted the door, bracing for impact as he wobbled towards the hatch.

"What are you doing?" Max screamed.

"If you want to stay here in this deathtrap, that's fine by me," Percy said. "But don't lump me in! I'm leaving!"

Percy lifted his feet to jump but froze just before they left the ground, hesitating for a moment before he did actually jump for it. Max had half a mind to push him out, but before he could even think to, the banker was gone. Before Maxwell could even do anything, Percy rolled to the forest floor like a rag doll. The horses roared at full speed now.

Next, the coach's wheels gave out. Then, the axles completely snapped. The horses whinnied in panic as they ran faster into the dense forest, completely without guidance. The coach wheezed and groaned. A dust cloud threatened to envelope him, sawdust mixing with the remaining smoke.

Everything was sideways. There was this little voice inside his head, a hushed voice, that deafened the world around him as everything faded to black.

A voice that sounded… familiar, in a way.

"WELCOME HOME… LITTLE… BIRD…"

Chapter Two

Wolves at the Door

Maxwell Corvid had never really been able to remember his dreams.

And he had tried everything to fix that. But obviously, no methods ever worked.

Dreaming didn't come naturally to him. If he did happen to fall asleep and drift into some far-off place conjured by his imagination, he couldn't remember it. And so ironically, it was his dream to remember his dreams, if that made any sense.

In short: Maxwell Corvid didn't dream. Not ever. It was just the way it was.

So, when something absurd happened, regardless how unlikely or improbable, he could barely distinguish the difference between dream and reality.

Because Maxwell had never experienced a dream — not in a long, long time at least, he didn't know what they were like. Meaning of course, that anything could have been a dream, and he wouldn't know it. But from what he had heard, dreams were supposed to be absurd. They were supposed to be ludicrous, fantastic, and sometimes even scary, which were of course the ones which haunted you the longest. And this stagecoach crash ticked all of the boxes.

Though unlike people waking from a dream instead of finding his eyeglasses on his bedside table, he found them shattered on the splintery floorboards. Instead of waking peacefully to his unkempt dorm, he woke to the discarded carcass of the stagecoach, a corpse of twisted metal and broken wood, at home with those unnumbered dying trees that gave the Corvid estate its particular unsavory appearance. Instead of his lumpy pillow under his head, something oozed back there… a trickle of blood.

Head spinning, Maxwell groggily rose, dusting the wood chips from his hands and the filth from his clothes. With everything lopsided, he couldn't tell if it were the coach on its side, or his fractured view from his newly bashed-in skull. He could see without his spectacles, but not when everything hurt. Everything still ached, stung, or might have been bruised. His head must have gotten the worst of it. Even though off-balance, stumbling and stupefied, he was in one piece. Barely.

He never should have come back. He never should have returned to this awful place. He should have steered clear of family matters; it was so much easier that way. But he was here now, wasn't he?

Hopefully whoever decided to rob the carriage would be happy with taking his meager possessions and whatever Percy had. Though, speaking of Percy... Maxwell angled an ear towards outside the carriage. The banker was talking to someone. And judging by Percy's horrified tone of voice, it was someone very, very bad.

"Oh, oh yeah, of course, we can figure somethin' out," Percy stammered. "Come on now...D-d-don't be unreasonable here! We can do business however you see fit... uhh... I wanna say, sir?"

While muffled, it was still the unmistakable, oily voice of that even oilier banker. Each word waterfalled it's way out of his stupid mouth dripping with insincerity. Groveling didn't suit him in the slightest.

But neither did his baggy clothes, so maybe Percy didn't value appearances. Maxwell could say the same. Finally, something they agreed on, without Max having to lie through his teeth.

Luckily, the coach hadn't completely overturned, even if it was a bit crumpled. Max haltingly stepped towards one of the grimy windows. He took a fleeting glance. He could barely witness two silhouettes in the distance, the setting sun cast long shadows behind them both. One held what looked like a shotgun. The other was a trembling facsimile of a man, obvious Percival Crane, at his brave best.

Percy dropped to the ground, clawing and scrambling up the legs of the gunman's heavy boots like a stray cat. And suddenly, Maxwell could only think of how short Percy was. The brigand tried to shake Percy off but he clung like a parasite. The brigand then dragged Percy through the mud, making his rumpled, ugly trash bag of a suit even dirtier and uglier.

"You... you want money, yeah? Well... well, I don't exactly have much on me right now," Percy babbled. "But — But, I have friends that could be well interested in your services. You're a weird one, aren't you? Quiet, too, I can respect that. I, in fact, know someone that a person of your... profession... might wanna meet pretty badly."

The brigand remained silent. Percy did not.

"I knew you'd be reasonable. You sure look like you'd be a real professional at this sort of thing," Percy said. "And I'm also pretty sure we can work something out, make a deal—"

CRACK

Percy screamed as the butt of the shotgun slammed into the front of his mouth. A single incisor flew from his face, a bloody trail arcing behind it like a demented rainbow. More muffled screams rippled through the air. The banker flopped over into the mud, clutching his mouth with his hands, blood dribbling from his mouth, as he clutched it, rolling back and forth.

Wincing and gritting his own teeth at Percy's plight, Maxwell turned. With morbid curiosity, he eventually returned to the diorama of gruesomeness playing out in front of him, but of course, only through his fingers.

For the first time since he had met the banker, he felt sorry for the poor sap. But what could he do? If he were to shout out in defiance, he would be most certainly found. Then, something worse could happen to him. Maxwell looked again in time to see the brigand grab Percy's collar and hoist him from the ground.

Percy stiffened, his joints seizing, and even the blood dripping from his mouth paused. Everything stood still, even Max's own thoughts. Not even the crows had the audacity to caw. Percy raised a quivering hand… and pointed.

Slowly, Percy's hand passed the treeline. Max followed the banker's finger, as it pivoted, like the needle of a compass. It led… Slowly, the banker's terrified eyes met his own. And then a third pair of eyes, shining, yellowed eyes, the brigand's eyes, bore into him as well.

The brigand slowly turned towards the coach. Maxwell darted down from the window, Maxwell's respirations increased, as the footsteps crunched closer and closer, louder and louder. Maxwell slumped below the cracked windowpane, amidst shards of glass and wood as the brigand approached.

Maxwell's heartbeat pounded in his ears; his stomach flipped, warning that he might vomit. He gagged at the stagnant, sickening silence. But it wasn't silent. Each footstep brought that highwayman closer and closer.

Maxwell forced his shaking hands to reach for the nearest piece of jagged glass. Holding it close to his heart, he knew it wouldn't do him much good against the hunter's shotgun, but he needed something to tether him to reality and add to the likelihood of his survival. However small that was…

Maxwell gripped that glass so tightly that it cut his own palms, but he was so scared, he barely noticed. He sweated so badly; the glass became slippery. Blood leaked from his hand onto the shard like a used scalpel.

God, what was he doing? Maxwell dropped it, and it clattered. It didn't really matter anyway, once again, it wouldn't do him much good. He clapped his bloodied hand over his mouth and held it there, as if the brigand could smell his breath. The stench of iron suddenly overpowered everything else.

Why had he ever left the university? Why couldn't he go back, lie in his uncomfortable bed, stare blankly at the ceiling like he had so many nights before?

A large shape blotted what was left of the sun coming through the window. Maxwell didn't dare breathe. The brigand must have been right outside. Whoever 'they' were.

A hushed, almost inaudible whimper escaped Maxwell's mouth. Max closed his eyes and waited, hoping for the brigand to pass but they never did. They instead lingered. Maxwell heard heavy breathing, as he watched the brigand's cooled breath dither over his head before it dissipated, much like Percy's smoke. The brigand paused. They tilted their head and scanned the surroundings robotically. They watched for what felt like hours, breathing steadily through their mouth, in and out, in and out, over and over and over again.

This was what nightmares were like, he reasoned. Would the brigand ever leave? Did the brigand know Maxwell was there? What the hell were they doing? Were they going to kill him, rob him? Or were they just going to stand there?

While Maxwell could only see their shadow slowly retreat from the confines of the window frame. A small relief from caustic pressure came with each crunching step, as the brigand walked away from the coach wreckage. Each squelching step in the mud offered further repose. Maxwell still didn't dare breathe, but he did, at first shakily, and then more confidently. The unwanted yet familiar scent of petrichor tormented his sense of smell. Maxwell had always hated that smell, not because it was odorous or fetid, but because it reminded him of this place.

But now, Maxwell couldn't get enough of it.

Peeking out the window, Maxwell realized nobody was there anymore. Not even Percy remained, perhaps he had crawled to some remote corner of the estate to lick his wounds.

Maxwell exhaled. He would rest for a moment. Yeah, that sounded good. For now it seemed he was safe. He felt tired, except for the lingering adrenaline. Not in an actual, sleepy way, no, God no, but in an exhausted way.

Maxwell peered to the other window of the coach. It had surprisingly remained intact after the crash. He examined himself in the reflective glare of the setting sun. He almost couldn't recognize himself anymore.

His glasses were lopsided. His nose had stopped bleeding, though he hadn't noticed it. The back of his skull burned. Bruises covered his arms, legs, just about everywhere like hives. He noticed all of this in the reflection of the other window, the one across from him, the sun's glare providing just enough light so he could see…

…his reflection.

He could see his own reflection in the window. Which meant…

If Maxwell were in fact looking at himself in the reflection, he might have noticed the pair of ghastly yellow eyes shining back at him. He would have noticed the leaves and sticks woven through a rats' nest of hair, and a large black trench coat. Maxwell might have noticed the fact that this brigand, this highwayman, wasn't a man, but a *highwaywoman*. She had never left the window. She just stood dead silent, not even breathing.

But Maxwell hadn't noticed any of that. And now, Maxwell wasn't exactly focused on running away either. He did what any cornered animal would do in a situation like this. What any animal would do, if the lifeless eyes of a hunter, or rather, huntress, were locked with their own.

He pleaded for mercy. Just like Percy.

"H-hello there…"

Maxwell calmly waved from the other side of the shattered glass. The highwaywoman stood outside the carriage, but Max was close enough to notice her stench. Her skin was as pale as a corpse. But Maxwell could barely see her face between the layers and layers of grime caked upon it, not to mention her curly black hair hiding half of it. Yet despite all of this, Maxwell could only focus on one trait: her eyes. Glowing, yellow eyes that glinted in the dusk.

They were distinctly yellow, a bright and vibrant shade. This was unlike anything he had ever seen, and not a symptom of jaundice. These weren't bile-shot, they couldn't be, not with skin like hers almost whiter than ivory. They glowed a bright, radiant shade of yellow, practically shining like those of a cat, no, brighter than any cat he had ever seen. And they were focused directly on him.

"You're his son, aren't you?"

Her voice was lower than he had expected, and monotonous, with an accent buried deep in there somewhere, Scottish maybe?

She barely moved her facial muscles when speaking, mumbling her words, like she was half-asleep. It took him a moment to process what she had said. Once Maxwell deciphered her speech. He nodded furiously.

She knew who he was! He was saved! For once, his family's shitty, aristocratic reputation would save him!

"Yes! Yes, I am!" Maxwell said, the only time he had ever been eager to tell someone his last name. "I'm Maxwell Corvid, of house Corvi—"

The highwaywoman interrupted him with a growl, a literal animalistic growl emanating from somewhere deep in her throat.

He had never once, not once, in any of his conversations, been growled at before. Not by anybody. Because it was an incredibly un-civil thing to do. But this woman, she had just… she had just *growled* at him. She had quite literally *growled*, like some kind of animal. He half-expected her to foam at the mouth like a dog after that.

"O-okay then, I…I see you've probably met my father. Alright, well—"

The huntress cut him off with a single hand-motion.

"I know who you are." She spat. "And that means there aren't any introductions for you, Corvid."

Maxwell's reflexes were far from sharp. So he watched, helplessly, as the brigand loaded two shells into her shotgun. He watched as she aimed down the sights. And then, he watched as she pulled the trigger.

Unsurprisingly, growing up in a quite civilized part of society, Maxwell had never actually heard a gunshot before. And though his uncle had offered to take him hunting, or have him learn to shoot competitively, he had never had much interest in that sort of thing. He had assumed that it sounded and felt as the storybooks described it, louder than thunder, more deadly than lightning. A sound that needed no introduction. The sound of ubiquitous despondency and death.

Maxwell could confirm the storybooks—they were right.

Maxwell ducked, clutching his ears as the first buckshot flew over his head, shattering what remained of the window. The glass didn't rain so much, as most of it was already on the floor.

Maxwell barely made it, ducking just under the shot in the nick of time and covering his head. Looks like his reflexes weren't as bad as he thought they were. He wanted to stutter something out, but no words came from his mouth, just a jumble of incoherent noise. He had to scream over the tinnitus in his ears.

A low growl emanated from the huntress once again, as she began the reloading process once over, nothing but a gentle click. When she moved from the window, it terrified Maxwell all the more because now she could have been anywhere.

Maxwell scrambled upwards, bowing his head to avoid hitting the ceiling of the coach. Run. He had to run. The realization dripped slowly into his brain. But where could he even go? Everything was moving too fast, faced with a mural of so many equally terrible options.

The brigand's large black boots reappeared under the wooden doorframe. She approached the inside of the cabin. Before he had time to think, a gunshot erupted once more.

Crows took off overhead, fleeing the coming bloodshed as the buckshot from the hunter's shotgun ripped right through the door. It grazed Maxwell's clothes with shrapnel, which obliterated the section of the coach.

Maxwell threw himself out the window, onto the muddied earth, not a second too soon. The brigand, and the barrel of her gun, peered through the hole she had made in the door. She reached for the handle. He landed in mud, glass, and his own pandemonia. A dreadful mix, to be sure.

The next gunshot was like a starter pistol at a sporting competition, Maxwell sprinted faster than he ever had. Fear was a great motivator after all. Possibly even the best. He could barely hear the heavy footsteps of the brigand over his own. She pursued him into the treeline, again reloading her gun. Turning around for a second, he lowered his head in anticipation, covering his ears. The brigand snapped the muzzle of the gun closed and...

Another gunshot rang out as he reached the forest's shadowy embrace. This one went straight over his head and into the underbrush. Leaves scattered everywhere as shrapnel pierced the veil of the forest's canopy. Maxwell rushed towards the treeline as the buckshot cleared a path.

Panting, he pushed his glasses up his face. The sun finally vanished. The sky turned to night, not that he could really tell underneath the thick woodland leaves that smothered the forest regardless of the time.

Maxwell noticed that the brigand had slowed, as if hesitant to step into the patch of trees... He hid behind a narrow trunk, hoping for enough shadows to cloak him?

With those strange eyes, he wasn't exactly sure... Maybe, like any predator, her vision would be limited to movement.

Her boots stomped the undergrowth of crunching leaves. She had arrived in the unsettling peace of the woods. Each breath she took was louder. The woods fell quiet before her. She was close. In fact, her unique scent, which Maxwell recognized as bourbon mixed with dirt, was so pungent and smothering that she could only be in one place really:

Right behind him.

A mangled mess of profanities and fragments of sentences filled his mind.

There was one smell around him that he was suddenly beginning to notice, and he hadn't noticed it before because, well... there were other matters that seemed to be more important. For instance, the huntress about to chop him up and turn him into bait for her next catch.

Amidst the delirium of these last few minutes, Maxwell had forgotten earlier concerns. But now, *now* he noticed something, something not as fetid or strong or foul as her smell, it was definitely there... hiding amidst the chaos.

Blood.

Maxwell squinted in the last of the dull twilight... Around him, staining each leaf in a particular line, was blood. He knew exactly whose blood, too, given by the stagger zig-zagging through the underbrush. Percy. It would only make sense. He had been the only other one here. Any pisspoor hunter would follow a trail. Especially a trail as obvious and half-brained as this one.

The highwaywoman calmly rose to her feet, without a word. She stepped through the leaves, her breathing slowly fading into obscurity and another distant sound of the forest.

Luckily, she seemed distracted by Percy's blood. But now that Maxwell was alone, could he assume that she had forgotten about him? Moved on to easier prey?

When Maxwell finally moved again, he walked opposite Percy's trail. He almost felt bad doing it, but the banker had done this to himself. Max was not going to bail him out. Why should he? Really, why would he help Percy in the first place? The man had done nothing but cause him inconvenience and indirectly needle him since he got here. And like he said, even if he was a family friend, Maxwell didn't even consider himself a part of his own family. Not anymore. Truthfully, Max just wanted to return to the coach and wait.

Somebody would come along eventually, right? They would, wouldn't they? His uncle would find him in a matter of time or at least try to find him in a timely fashion.

But where was the coach?

Maxwell hadn't run that far into the woods. But now it looked like it stretched on for miles. Which direction had he run again? A few moments ago, Maxwell had spotted the wreckage of the stagecoach through the treeline, but the darkness had grown more complete.

It was getting dark out as well…

A pit opened in Maxwell's stomach. It dropped, down, down, downwards.

Well, in any case, he would have to find his way. That was, regrettably, his only option. He couldn't have gone that far, could he? Maxwell didn't think his legs could even carry him that far, that fast.

Maxwell had already established this wasn't a dream. That was obvious by the bruises and the cuts stinging all over. And besides, it wasn't like he had dreams anyway.

But then again, it had always been his dream to experience a nightmare.

So, maybe his dreams were coming true.

Chapter Three

A Rude Awakening

Maxwell could remember... the lecture hall. Yes, yes, the lecture hall had been there.

And... Well, that was about it.

Had he been... asleep? Out here in the woods? How long had it been? After what had happened earlier, with the brigand and the banker, it was a wonder how he even had gotten to sleep at all. Well, not exactly a wonder. He supposed he had been tired...

Besides, he should have been ecstatic, if not for his current situation. Even if a minor, foggy detail, he remembered something, something from a dream he had just been having. Maxwell remembered more about that dream his mind had conjured, than he did all of his studies. There, in the dream, it had taken place in the University's Lecture hall... There had been paper ripping in the dream, right? And he swore that somebody had been talking, right in his ear the entire time... but he couldn't remember a word of it. Someone had said something important to him, he was sure of it... And it was still there, rattling around in the back of his mind... Just too far back to remember.

And then, he lost it.

Simply opening your eyes could change your outlook. One minute, the lucidity of a make-believe story enraptured him, and the next, he returned to the estate, in all of its inglorious putridity. He had gone from Miskatonic University to the woods. Both equally uncomfortable places, though, at least one had a library. A library, where despite the uncomfortable reading chair, he could still feel safe from the glowering countryside beyond.

Anywhere was better than this place. No matter how uncomfortable that library armchair, he would always prefer the lantern-lit halls of Miskatonic over the roots of a tree, a bed of dirt, and a mattress of crunching dead leaves. At least at Miskatonic, his antagonists dealt their damage to his head with languor, rather than a shotgun.

Maxwell had woken in a peculiar burrow of sorts, sheltered under roots of a large tree, a moss-covered tree no doubt far older than he.

Maxwell supposed he had crawled into this hole to avoid the rain, and the cold, although it wasn't doing a very good job of either. The roots dripped with the wind brushing them into his face. Now that Maxwell had woken, he would probably never remember what he had heard in that dream.

Maxwell could still feel the lukewarm breath on his face. Or at least, he thought he could still feel it. And, that was a first for him, even if it was a side effect of the gentle rain that had begun to fall. The cold mist falling on his forehead had woken him in the first place.

This, remembering his dream, may not have excited some people, but Maxwell, well, Maxwell was ecstatic. He believed that he had forgotten how to dream a long time ago, so this was completely alien, in a weird sort of way. Maxwell had uncovered a new talent, as silly as that sounded. He had to record this somewhere… It was… It was revolutionary! At least, to him. Revolutionary was a strong turn of phrase, but it truly was from Maxwell, considering he hadn't dreamt in… well, a long time. He had to write… He had to write it…

Where was his pen?

Matter of fact, where was anything?

The forms Percy had given him had gone missing. So was the pen he used to sign them. He rummaged in his satchel. Nothing. Hardly anything was left in there. He remembered bringing his textbook, a handkerchief, some other supplies… and now all of it was gone. All that remained now was some loose lint, some leaves that had haphazardly fallen in from above. Had he, maybe, misplaced things? Dropped it?

It was raining now. Not a heavy rain, a misty rain, well, almost a misty sort of rain, but not quite real mist just yet. When he left town with Percy, he had recognized a darkening sky. A storm chasing them. Not anticipating the ambush and the extended travel time, Maxwell had assumed he would reach the manor and be asleep under its roof before the storm arrived. But now, he feared the worst. The evening's setting sun had long since slunk behind the clouds which smothered the stars, telltale signs of the oncoming thunderstorm. And a bad one at that.

It was strange. He couldn't remember a single thing since the crash. It was like his head had been on autopilot this entire time.

Where had he passed out? How long had it been since the chase? Maxwell couldn't remember. Not since the brigand had pursued him into these blasted woods. There was always still a possibility that he could run into her again, she could use a name, he supposed. She had hunted him, much like a hunter would an animal, even using the same weapons, hadn't she? So he would call her something like the Huntress. Yes, until he learnt the name of his pursuer, the Huntress would do nicely.

Wait…

Was she still hunting him? Had she caught him? Was that why he was down here, in her… in her lair maybe? Maxwell surveyed the strange cove of hollowed out earth below the tree. He moved his head slowly, deliberately. Predators couldn't see prey, if they moved slowly. His gaze lingered and studied each section of this makeshift shelter checking for anything that might be a sign of life, a signal that someone squatted here. There were no signs of life. Even the tree was dead. The warren was no home anyway. Only big enough to lie down in, and even then the roots of the tree above scraped against your face. This was silly…

No. Don't be stupid Maxwell, that… that wasn't possible. He definitely would have remembered that. Really, how long had he been asleep? How long had he been beneath the roots of this blasted tree?

Maxwell stood up and hit his head against this little warren. The roots clung to him, begging him to stay. Then, after muttering a swear under his breath, crawled to the exit of the hole, the earth getting under his fingernails, almost mud, but still not quite, more like a clay. Upon reaching the outside, the estate wasn't much better.

Only at the Corvid property would a muddy hole in the ground be more inviting than the actual estate. There were just these trees for miles, the same dying species of tree, repeated, over and over. Their leaves coated the ground like a battlefield. And their voices, the hissing of the wind through their branches, was like a dirge for all of the leaves scattered below.

Everywhere looked the same in those backwoods. It didn't matter if he had passed out near the crash, or several miles from it. In the end, everywhere looked exactly the same. He wished he could go back to the dream. It was probably so much easier there. He wouldn't know, after all, he could barely remember it. But he longed for the safety of the lecture hall over this. Even if it wasn't in fact, real.

Maxwell emerged from the burrow, rubbing his bleary eyes, and adjusting his crooked glasses. It was strange doing his routine for waking up under rain and not just the roof of Miskatonic's dormitories. He would have given anything to be back in his dormitory right now. It was better than… this. In his room at Miskatonic, his familiarity overpowered the fetid walls with their scurrying rats. He had taken everything he had for granted, and looking back on it, he had it pretty good back there in Miskatonic, well, except for the mold covering the walls, and choking the air.

What had he hoped to achieve with his crusade? He knew they would not listen. In the end, it just caused his untimely expulsion. He should have left when he had the chance, instead of risking his health by staying. He should have never bothered to inspect that supply closet. He never should have complained about his itchy skin. He shouldn't have delved beyond the sickly, yellow wallpaper.

Because when Maxwell pulled those supplies out of the science lab closet and found what lurked beyond, he hadn't liked what he had found festering beneath the surface. The governing board would rather expel him, and call him a "nutcase," rather than face a routine health inspection.

Honestly, if Maxwell survived this ordeal of a trip home, he could find another school that didn't trigger his Mycophobia, quite as much as the moldering prison he had spent for four years at Miskatonic.

The wind blew sour. It should have blown fresh air across his skin, because, well, after the stale air of the burrow, the wind *should* offer fresh air in comparison. But, somehow, the wind… But somehow, instead of fresh, the wind felt the opposite. It felt acrid, astringent, maybe even pickled, with the very foulness of the estate itself carried on the breeze, developing into a gale. Whatever leaves gripped to the trees, they drifted and billowed, before gently fluttering to the ground. If it weren't for the distant thunder rumbling in the distance, Maxwell would feel like one of those leaves, falling deeper and deeper not to the ground but into his own self-pity. He knew he should be thinking about how he would hide from the storm, or that dream he had just had, but… He couldn't. He couldn't get his own expulsion out of his head.

Before he had been called home, Maxwell had done good. The mold of the university slowly poisoned both staff and students, and the building itself was the disease itself and a victim. The mold wound its way through the insulation and the pipes, just as illness traveled through the human body. Maxwell had made the right decision, taken the right actions. The medical college should have been shuttered as a health violation. The condition of the facilities precluded its stature as a place of healing.

Maxwell did not flinch at the distant rumbling thunder. Even with the wind increasing and the leaves swirling as if the estate taunted him, it barely mattered. Maxwell was too lost in his own head now, and when he got like that, stuck, this time sinking into the muddy memories instead of literal muck, he struggled to recenter. So Maxwell sat there, slumped against the warty and gnarled trunk of the tree. Maxwell sat wet, cold, and utterly sinking deeper and deeper, away from the outside world.

Goddammit, what had he been thinking? Why the hell had he done this to himself. For fuck's sake! Active: Maxwell would overthink everything — it's what he was best at, so why didn't he take a minute and do that? Why couldn't he have found the fatal flaws in his own plan? He wanted to go to sleep and forget about all of this: the school, his family, the estate, the hunter, just escape it all for one night. He should have finished this excursion quickly, and continued searching for a new school by the start of the summer… What was he doing!

In fact, why couldn't he have stayed at Miskatonic, lying on his bed and staring at the ceiling. Why couldn't he allow the disgusting stuff to take root and eat away in his lungs.

He could take it a step further. Why didn't he stay with his father, in that ugly house on the hill, and have that same exact mold, that black, putrid gunk, drift into his mouth and rot him like a carcass from the inside? It would have been so much easier… And—

Was… was that paper?

It was quite difficult to revive Maxwell Corvid from one of these "slumps." Once he descended into mental quicksand, he could rarely be pulled out. But rarely was, in fact, *not* impossible.

From the corner of his eye, he watched an ordinary leaf drift by. But it wasn't, was it? It had a vibrant glow to it. Nothing white and pristine existed in this place; nothing remained pure and untouched. And so, when he took a second look at the "leaf" he uncovered what it truly was.

A sheet of paper laid amongst the leaves.

He bent over to pick the sheet up. It was a sheet of paper, after all. When he flipped it over, he realized that maybe his dream had been more important than he had first thought. Paper ripping… right?

He had gotten his hands on one of Percy's forms! After having to re-read them so many times, he would have recognized them anywhere. He had placed them in his satchel for later, back on the coach.

Over all the fine print, someone had scribbled a picture. Maxwell pulled the paper closer to his face but couldn't exactly discern the image. Maxwell thought it might be a face, but… It was far too damaged by the rain for him to make it out. And to top it all off, in the corner of his vision, another sheet fluttering a few yards away. Then another. And another. And another one… at least he had figured out what had happened to the contents of his satchel.

Following the pages could in fact, lead him back to the carriage! His bag could have been open this entire time, making a convenient, and literal, paper trail for him to follow. And, of course, the puzzle of how they managed to fly out of the satchel, kept his mind from dwelling on Miskatonic. He picked a sheet up, placing it in his satchel. Then, walking a few paces, he picked up another. While yes, he could have just left them out in the rain… But if worse came to worst, they would make good kindling.

He picked up another, then another, each with what looked like a signature on the dotted line. Not his signature… but, maybe Percy's? One sheet blew against a tree, more clumped against a few of the branches, others he had to rise on his tiptoes to reach, and others he had no hope of reaching at all. He supposed that for all the misery the estate had caused him, it finally decided to help him by leaving a literal paper trail. How thoughtful…

Maxwell collected each sheet, each one ranging from soggy to sopping, shoving them into his satchel, some melting together and transforming to a thick, papery pulp. If he focused on his work collecting the contacts, Maxwell believed that he could get through anything. He had collected eight pages already!

Focus on that. Just focus on your work, Maxwell! Focus on your studies! Block the world out, and everything will be fine!

Until the world decided to barge in again.

Last time Maxwell checked, and of course, he didn't check often, the estate had never weathered any natural disasters. Once in a blue moon, a minor hurricane would approach. The estate had survived the earthquake better than nearby towns a few years back.

And so you could imagine Maxwell's surprise when he almost walked off the edge of a cliff into what looked like a chunk, bitten right out of the earth.

What in the hell was this? Well, he knew what it was. It was a sinkhole. Maxwell imagined a massive earthworm tunneling into the rock and feasting upon its core. Maxwell felt like an ant in its wake. He was almost like an ant in this imaginary worm's wake. Enormous! It could have swallowed the manor itself! Why the hell was it here? And why in God's name had he almost walked right off of the edge and into it.

After shuffling back a few paces (and you would too if you almost had fallen to your death), He couldn't even see the bottom! It was just blackness, black as a starless night sky, and impossibly deep. Though that wasn't the weirdest part of the sinkhole. The crater appeared to breathe. Air flowed in, and out, at a steady rate like a heartbeat. In, and out. In, and out.

Max seized one of the stones lying around the edge and threw it into the dark abyss. It never hit the bottom. Or at least, over the sound of the rain, rain now coming down a trifle harder, Maxwell never *heard* it hit the bottom.

There was no way this had happened without the papers hearing about it. His family estate was remote, the actions of his father reclusive, but even then, this was front page news. This was recent, this catastrophe! Would the bank have known of this giant crater? Of course they did! Why else would they have such fervor to unload the property. And his father had to have known, because a massive crater is exactly what his father would bequeath him, a good-for-nothing hole for a good-for-nothing son.

Maxwell caught a whiff of smoke. He wheeled around, alarmed by the combination of smoke and rain. The underbrush rustled underbrush.

"Now," a familiar voice said, followed by a cough. "I know this all looks…"

Maxwell turned his neck ever so slightly to confirm the owner of the voice. Percy coughed twice more.

"…pretty bad on my part."

The banker tugged at his collar. He walked to Maxwell, skulking about in the shadows. This was a recurring motif with the pencil-pusher, wasn't it? The skulking. Like he was constantly guilty.

Though, granted, this time he *was* in fact, guilty.

"You sold me out," Maxwell told him, as if it wasn't obvious enough.

"Relax. Wasn't anything personal Max, honest! Survival of the fittest, all that jazz."

Percy's suit and hat seemed a bit cleaner, as if the rain had washed some of the muck. Not all of it. It would be a miracle if that suit would ever be clean again. Though the thing that had changed most about the man wasn't his attire: it was his face. That smug shit-eating grin he had worn like a badge of honor: it seemed far more forced. Was that sweat rolling down his face or just more rain? It looked like that facade becoming harder and harder to maintain. Some would say that the man was even more obnoxious to be around now. Maxwell couldn't say the same.

"Enjoying the sights?" Percy said, in his typical, condescending, wordy way. "Well my friend, I was gonna take you on a tour of a property, but this, this is new! Weird, huh? Happened just out of the blue."

Percy snapped his fingers.

"Just like that!" the banker finished.

"For the record, you're not my friend." Max said, rubbing his temples, mostly to avoid eye contact with Percy. Percy's grin, stuck halfway in between a smile and a frown, his cracked lips contorted and pulled taught, offered an expression just toothy enough to keep his cigarette between his teeth. "You ratted me out. Left me to die. Not something friends do."

"Come on Max," the banker crooned. His voice lost its calm, no longer a collected variant trained to maintain the version of itself used for customer service. "You said it yourself, we were thick as thieves back in the coach. It was just business, that doesn't have to affect our friendship! And besides, if we're not friends, then what am I then?"

Maxwell wanted to punch him. You have no idea how much he wanted to. He wanted to strangle the banker, until his face turned blue and those overworked lungs of his finally stopped breathing. But that would be horrible. And contrary to what the papers said, he was not horrible. So he exhaled, and simply said:

"A banker."

"Now that is true!" Percy agreed, stepping closer towards him. Percy's smile had vanished. Beneath the brim of his hat, Percy displaced a grimace—as if someone had taken his toothy smile, ripped it off and replaced it upside down."That, that I can understand. Finally, you're talkin' straight."

The banker was even talking differently now, clipping his G's. The act was fading. His customer service voice was slowly mutating back into the one he used for regular conversations. But the smoking, well, that wasn't an act, as it turned out.

You could actually count the seconds when Maxwell looked away, and when Percy lit himself a new cigarette. He kept flicking the lighter, over and over again,. Click. Click. Click, click, click, click, click, it was driving Max crazy! Could he spend five seconds without another dose of carcinogens? This went past addiction into something else, this was practically mania.

"Could you *please* spend five minutes without a cigarette, Percy."

"Stupid thing, never fucking works. I'm sorry, can you repeat that? I can't hear stupid questions," the banker said with a snarl. Percy had finally snapped.. The banker turned, frantically rubbing the tip of the lighter on his pant leg, as if trying to dry it.

"Have you seen the Huntress again?" Maxwell asked.

"Who?"

"Shotgun lady? You know, the one who did that," Maxwell pointed to the gap in his perfect smile.

"Oh, oh her. Ah, shit. Thought she was after you… HAH! I got it! You're not dying on me today, you little shit!" Percy cried to his inanimate lighter. It weakly barely mustered enough flame to light his cigarette.

Stiff silence hung in the air for a long time. Not a bad thing. Maxwell preferred listening to the rain versus Percy's boring ramblings. The rain kept getting louder, having progressed from a mist to a storm over this *tête-à-tête*. Just as Maxwell went to clear his throat, Percy cleared his. And thank god, because Maxwell hadn't wanted to start another conversation.

"*Ahem*. Look, we're havin' a… rough night." Percy stated, in what could almost be read as an apologetic tone of voice. "Sure you don't want to reconsider that smoke from earlier? It actually *does* help a whole lot."

"Helps with what?"

"Relax the nerves, feels great… And, come on, it's great for socializing."

The banker snickered at his own joke, but Max was unamused. Maxwell could barely tell if the banker was trying to be courteous, or trying to poke fun at him like everyone else had. Maybe both? Regardless, the moment he didn't hear Max laugh, the banker stopped his sniggering all on his own. The rain was pouring down harder now. Percy turned to look at him, but they could barely see each other through the rain. The banker raised the cigarette to his mouth once again, illuminating the lower portion of his face. He guarded the smoldering tobacco from the rain and the wind with his hand. He passed the little torch in Maxwell's direction and held it there. Much less mockingly now. It was hard to tell when the banker was being genuine.

"So. Still not interested then I take it? I get it, I get it, we would have to share, and you're a germaphobe or somethin' like that. This is my last one though, so last chance. Going on one…"

Maxwell kind of felt obligated. He needed to try it again, at least once. It might be the last time he ever got to, if the Huntress caught up to them. His last taste of the finer things, and it tasted like expensive cigarettes…

"Going on two…"

The banker seemed surprised when Max took the slim stick of tobacco. Maxwell was surprised, too. He had smoked before, but that had been a long time ago. He remembered hating it. Maxwell raised the damp, flaccid cigarette to his mouth. Percy waited in smug anticipation for Max's reaction. He didn't have to wait long. Max's face said it all.

"So how is it? Even better than you remember?"

As soon as Maxwell inhaled the foul vapors, he gacked and wheezed the smoke in a familiar coughing fit. It transformed his throat into sandpaper. Burning sandpaper. The banker laughed, a hiss of a laugh, like his lungs strained against the effort. It was so much worse than Maxwell remembered it, but he didn't give Percy the satisfaction of saying that aloud. Max coughed again, but pretended like he was clearing his throat.

"How the hell can you do that for hours?"

"What, the coughing? Believe me," Percy said, smirking. "You get used to it. I guess smoking isn't for you. Can I have that back now?"

"Yes. Take it, please. That stuff is disgusting."

"Tobacco's an… *acquired* taste."

Thunder rumbled in the distance and lightning cracked in the shrouded panorama of the background. Percy's spectacles reflected it, as they did his cigarette. The banker rambled about something, but Maxwell didn't catch what. The wind picked up. Blowing leaves everywhere. Percy desperately held his hat as he spoke, both him and the wind, now screaming. And if you wanted to know which won the shouting contest between the banker and the estate: it was the estate.

"Y'see, the secret is to just not have any pride in the first pl—"

Percy's top hat blew towards the crater.

"Ah shit!" Percy exclaimed. The wind plucked the tophat Percy had been wearing since Max had first met him right off of the banker's head. It fluttered away on the wind, joining the leaves in the angry and frantic dance of the storm. "Get back here!"

The hat, now lost in a torrent of rain, went down, down, down, right into the pit. It belonged to the sinkhole now. The wind helped that gaping pit inhale another meal.

"God… damn it… Well, I guess you owe me another hat. It was on your land. I'll just add it onto that debt you owe. Oh, come on, don't look at me like… Oh. Heh."

Was… was Maxwell really that reliant on his glasses? Was he… seeing correctly? Percy continued speaking, not truly grasping what had happened. But soon enough they both came to the realization. As strange as it was.

"Well, I guess the jig is up then huh?" Percy chuckled.

Percy Crane had noticed that *her* hat had flown off.

Chapter Four

Smoke and Mirrors

If you were smart, smarter than Maxwell Corvid at least, you might have charted the inconsistencies that sprouted like weeds around the rather conspicuously inconspicuous banker, Percival P. Crane.

First off, Percy wore baggy oversized suits that hung on "him" like hand-me-downs. Bigger in this case meaning both older, and more on the heavier side. Someone like Otto Crane.

Secondly, Percy Crane always wore black-rimmed glasses so that nobody could see any hint of his face behind that smoggy cloud of smoke, except for that unenchanting smile.

Thirdly, there had never been a member of the Crane family named Percival and therefore, certainly nobody in the Crane family named, nicknamed, or referred to as "Percy." And while it was quite a large family tree (Otto Crane was not known for keeping it in his pants), most in that line were practically more famous than the members of the monarchy. Otto Crane was the furthest thing from humble about how proud he was of each of each of his sons, and while Maxwell didn't follow celebrity drama and had no interest in politics, the names Rodger, Randal, and Clyde Crane were just a few descendants of the Crane's that he could remember off of the top of his head.

So, it was strange then, that the name Percival Crane had never even been put in print. And for a family as famous, and simultaneously infamous, as the Cranes, the new heir to the banking franchise should have been front page news. Even he, who once again had no interest, would have at least heard about it. Even he read the paper, after all. And since he read the paper… Now, snippets of articles he had read featuring the Crane's were all beginning to flood back to him. Very strange snippets.

And then finally, perhaps there was a memory of this tiny article from the paper he had read in the lecture hall one day… He hadn't really cared at the time, but it had lingered in Max's head, resurfacing as a distraction during the most mundane lectures. The article spoke about the Crane family's missing daughter. A daughter who, quite frankly, nobody had ever heard of, considering her many other, more successful, and male, siblings, which were all doing something or another to promote the Crane and Sons business. Besides, in the world's current climate, it was… frowned upon… to have a daughter inherit the business, especially one as large as Crane and Sons.

Maxwell didn't care to keep up with someone else's family drama, not when he had plenty of his own to deal with. But Maxwell hadn't vetted Percy, as he couldn't keep track of the Crane family brood: there were too many Crane siblings to count. Plus, the name Percy sounded familiar. Maxwell thought he had read about a Percy Crane, but the clipping hadn't been about Percy. The article mentioned another member of that sprawling bloodline, a little girl.

"Penny…" Maxwell whispered. He hadn't meant to even say the name out loud. It had escaped, evolved into the spoken word without his approval. "Penny Crane…"

It still took Maxwell a few seconds to fully piece what was happening in front of him together. Then another few, then a few more. But before long, he did come to his conclusion.

Perhaps Otto Crane, a man particularly famous for his talent to… bend the rules, had bent the name, and the rules, of his own company. Or perhaps his daughter had bent them for herself. But one thing was for certain:

Penny Crane was not allowed to inherit the family business, by some upper-class, imaginary social standards.

Percy Crane, on the other hand…

"You're the Crane family's missing daughter, aren't you? You're Penny."

"And? What about it? Come on, pipe up!"

"Percy," or, well now, Penny muttered something to herself, through bared teeth, before she reached for her lighter. They both knew that there were no more cigarettes. So she just flicked and fidgeted with the lighter absent-mindedly, as she turned away. Maxwell, he was ashamed that he hadn't deciphered her ruse sooner and Penny, she seemed livid that he had ever been discovered to begin with.

Penny paced backwards and forward, back and forth, her face twitching and convulsing, going through a range of different expressions like she was trying to put on a face which showed she wasn't bothered, while she very clearly was. Her glasses slipped from her face and hit matted, decaying leaves. She bent down to pick them up, but for all he knew, she may not have needed them, just being a part of the disguise. And, mind you, it was a pretty good disguise. It had fooled him. In between the smoke and the glasses and the hat, mixed with the darkness of the coach, he would have never known who she really was, if the hat hadn't flown off of her head.

Maxwell wasn't quite sure what to say. If "Percy" had all been fake... everything from the name to the suit... was it all right to assume this entire ordeal was real to begin with? The huntress, the crash... Was any of it reality? Or was it just another scam, something which the Crane family were known for pulling. It just felt... awkward... standing here, not commenting on it. More awkward than usual. He had to try and say something, didn't he? Yes, yes he had to try and say something.

"Well," Maxwell started, taking a hesitant step towards the banker, if she still in fact was one. "I must say I am intrigued by the idea of a woman banker."

"Heh... Intrigued..." Penny said. The dramatic spark in her voice had left her, and now all that was a smolder: like a burnt-out cigarette. "Yeah, sure. 'Intriguing.' That's what I am, aren't I? I'm "Intriguing.'"

She was this enigma, this piece of lost history, staring him right in the face. So... it was a little intriguing. But it didn't really matter how intriguing it was. Was he... safe? Was this another trick? One more layer? He didn't want to sound too skeptical, especially not while she was... Well, for a second Maxwell mistook it for a cough, maybe a laugh but no... Penny, she was crying. That was... unexpected. He wasn't really sure what to do now. This wasn't a situation he really found himself in too often, this was practically new. Oh, oh dear. Uhm... what was he... how was he going to...

Now, usually, he would just ignore this... display... and move on with his day. Especially for someone like Percy Crane. But the façade had come off. And something told him that this wasn't Percy anymore. It was Penny.

Against his better judgment, Maxwell approached the shivering husk of a person he had thought he knew, against his natural tendency to hold grudges. He offered her a handshake. That was simultaneously the most, and least, he could offer up.

"If you would like, I can still call you Percy, and we can pretend this never happened."

"No, no, you know now Corvid," she said, kicking up some dirt, and sending bunch of leaves into the air and over the edge of the sinkhole, into the abyss. "God, Dad is gotta be so pissed up there right now..."

The banker's face suddenly changed, a switch flipping on somewhere in her head. Tears had been replaced with anger, as Penny stood, adjusting her posture, cracking and loosening her joints as if galvanized by the thunderstorm's air.

"Fuck! Fuck's sake, fuck, fuck! Shit! Fucking..."

Penny continued to swear, as she kicked the earth and the leaves, casting them into the sinkhole, and onto his trousers. He didn't say anything. Though you couldn't tell anyway amidst all the other muck.

"How could I have been so fuckin' stupid!" she yelled, with one final kick. "I'm a screwup. I'm a total fuckin' screwup aren't I? I'm totally bloody useless, just like how Clyde said... I just had to pretend for a few hours, how did I already muckle the whole bloody thing up!"

He cleared his throat but decidedly didn't say anything else in response.

"Look if it's any consolation I—"

"Don't! Just... Just don't! I don't need pity, I'm... I'm gonna be fine. It's all gonna be..."

In an instant, Penny whirled around and thrust an accusatory finger in his face. He took a step backwards, but each time he did, she just took another one forward.

"It isn't pity for God's sake, Perc... Penny!"

He repeated to reinforce it. But while he was doing that, she had just leaned forward, and spat on his shoe.

It was about this time that Maxwell realized Penny or Percy or whoever had just been just rude and made uncouth remarks at him all night, not to mention leaving him to die at the hands of a shotgun to the face, lord knows how he had escaped that!

"Fine! Don't have any pity then Penny, not that it was- Hey!"

The banker had just shoved him. Now, he was certain. Certain that she was a miserable rat of a person, shouting orders above the rest of their filthy subjects working at Crane and company, as they all extorted and embezzled and fired and denied, a rat dressed in her father's ill-fitted clothes.

"You're the one who dragged us into this mess, Corvid!" she screamed. "You're the reason why I'm here! If your fucking dad hadn't spent all our—"

"Me? You think *I* dragged *you* into this? You showed up at my school! You wanted your money back! And you think it's my bloody fault we're stuck here? How about the crazy woman with the shotgun that you obviously set up!"

"You think I set that up Corvid? Didn't you go to university or some crap? Why would I let my front teeth get knocked out! You see this?" she yelled, flashing a now cracked smile. "Why in god's name would I ever, ever do something stupid enough to be in your head!"

They yelled, now more loudly, over the howling winds and the swirling leaves. Even the sinkhole joined, foul smelling air surging from it.

An orange light washed over Maxwell's face. He immediately jumped to conclusions.

"Are you seriously lighting another damn cigaret—"

"Maxwell…" Penny whispered. "I'm… I'm outta cigarettes."

A light burned through the trees and the rain. Orange light, refracting as if the raindrops were prisms sharing the flames of a nearby roaring fire. Maxwell almost instinctively ran towards the mysterious light for help but stopped himself. Because it wasn't a warm, welcoming light. He didn't know why but this light felt… cold on his face. Somehow it was emotionless. An empty gesture. It felt false, fake, like a piece of bait thrown into the jaws of a trap just to catch a cold, wet animal. What if it was… her? The huntress? Maxwell suddenly became much more cautious around the light, the false, empty gesture of a light.

Though it looked as though Penny Crane had other plans.

Before he could even blink, the banker had regained that familiar, sinister smile. She was able to switch to it remarkably quickly too. It was truly like watching someone flick a switch, and all of sudden, the lights lit up on her face, like he was watching an actor getting into character, putting on a forced smile before walking out on stage. Only Penny wasn't heading for any stage. She was waltzing right towards that blighted beacon shining through the trees.

The light made Maxwell's mind rife with this viscous pusillanimity, as it beckoned warmly, yet without warmth, little rays of yellow shining through the leaves and the rain. And as Penny glided towards it, Max's fetid cowardice was replaced with a reflux of anger, and frustration. The crafty executor controlled their fates now, depending on who was behind the glow in the trees, be it a potential savior or their shotgun-shooting stalker. Because since their time together, Maxwell had noticed many conspicuous and bizarre mannerisms of Penny Crane, one of which was the face she made as an idea formed in her mind. It was the face she was making right now, as she walked out onto her stage of leaves and mud, under a spotlight of that eerie glow and a curtain of rain.

Maxwell did try to stop her. There was an attempt made, at least. Maxwell lunged for her coat, though he missed her entirely. Though even if he hadn't missed, and even if he was loud enough for his voice to break through the storm, while still being quiet enough to not alert the lantern bearer, he doubted that Penny would have listened. He knew that he wouldn't listen to him.

It was not unfair to say that Maxwell Corvid didn't like Penny Crane too much. And so, if she wanted to get herself killed, it wasn't his problem. She was an adult. She could dig herself out of her own hole. The rational thing to do was watch and wait to see what would happen to her. To see if the light was real, or a trap. That was the rational thing. The logical thing to do. And he was nothing if not logical.

So, why was he still trying to run after her?

Turn around Maxwell. Turn around. Just *turn around.*

But he didn't.

"Now I do hope, I really do hope, you have taken care of our guests, haven't you, Julia?" a new voice said. A woman's voice. One that sounded almost pleasant to listen to. Hypnotic, in a way. Though despite its pleasantness, Maxwell darted behind the nearest bunch of bushes, to stay out of sight, while the voice continued to speak. "I would hate for them to feel unwelcome. You do know I organized this event specifically for their arrival. First impressions matter!"

Was she who was behind the light? The woman sounded nice enough. But it was just barely not right, out of place for a place so horrible. It felt too welcoming, too hospitable. Sickly sweet. Maxwell couldn't make a sound, he didn't want to, not with this mysterious woman close enough to hear even over the rainstorm, but he wanted to get out of here. Nothing about this felt right, not the light, not the woman's voice, not any of it. He gestured to Penny, who crouched down opposite from him, in another cluster of sparse shrubbery. With an irritated expression, the banker slapped his hand away. She continued to creep closer towards the voice, closer and closer, eavesdropping suddenly becoming riskier and riskier. It was like he was interrupting her while she was watching a stage play, the way she was invested in this, her ear tilted towards the voices, her breath held in anticipation.

"No, not yet," another voice added. Another feminine voice. One that mumbled, one with the hint of an accent. Was that… Oh God it was her, wasn't it? "They ran. Figures."

Maxwell clapped a hand over his mouth, not even caring if it had touched the estate's filth. Well, maybe caring a little bit. He knew that voice, the new one. This was the woman who had chased him at the crash… the Huntress.

"My my, such bad manners! And to think I even gave them the time of day to send an invitation! The nerve! The nerve on them! The nerve, the nerve, the nerve, the—"

"You didn't."

"I didn't what?" the kind-sounding woman said. Her words sounded like they were barely sliding through her teeth. Maxwell looked back at the sinkhole, only a hundred feet away. He shouldn't have gone towards the light in the trees, he shouldn't have followed Penny… He should have done something that made sense.

"You didn't send for 'em." The Huntress growled from the other side of the bushes. "That isn't one of your invitations. It's something I swiped off of one back there. One of them Corvids is back. And he's brought a friend."

"Oh hush, Julia! Of course I sent for them! I got him to send an invitation quite a long time ago now. And speak up, speak up! You mustn't speak with your head down, it's quite improper! I must say, maybe if you spoke with your chin up a little more you might not look so… pardon my language, but so… lower class."

Apparently, the highwaywoman's name was Julia. But before he even had time to process that, Julia groaned, a noise like a dog or a bear, and the feral nature of it snapped Maxwell from his thoughts. Penny stuffed a laugh. Maxwell hadn't even remembered that Penny was next to him until she had, he had been too absorbed in the conversation. Though maybe it was a little funny to hear this huntress he had been so afraid of scolded like a child. Or rather like a hunting dog.

"Oh, and one more thing, Julia, honey."

"Hm? Yes, ma'am?"

"Please escort our guests to the Corvid manor now, considering they were kind enough to finally grace us with their presence. And get them out of those bushes, they must be positively filthy! And I will not have them tracking mud through my floors, not on your life."

With ankles shaking, Maxwell thrashed out of the bushes, all thoughts leaving his head, becoming prey yet again. But where was there to go? He was in between the edge of the sinkhole, and the edge of the woods… The sinkhole filling one direction, and the barrel of a shotgun most likely filling the other.

And to make matters worse, the sinkhole was in the middle of a clearing, everywhere was open, there was nowhere to hide, nowhere to take cover, just revenant grass and the occasional twiggy tree getting thrashed around in the wind. Penny had done something similar and peered into the pit with eyes wide and trembling lips as if the only way to escape meant plunging down. Julia, he supposed he would now call her, finally stepped through the brush, shotgun in hand. She started 100 feet away at the tree line. But she moved quickly. Seventy. Sixty. Fifty feet. And his only options were to go towards her or jump into the sinkhole. There was nowhere to hide, nowhere to run… However, the woman who had been talking to her was nowhere to be seen. The light, the false light shining through the trees, grew dimmer and dimmer as it got further away, their mysterious hostess vanishing the same way she had appeared — out of sight.

Julia was still getting closer, and it was just now that Maxwell realized it was the end of the line. Penny reached the edge soon after him. It seemed she was out of ideas as well. His feet tottered on the rocky edge of the sinkhole. It's hideous, earthy mouth beckoning them closer with repeated ins and recurrent outs. Maxwell almost fell in because of the winds. Julia took one final step towards them both.

A shotgun reloaded. The storm continued to rage. Penny looked at him. With the tempo of his breaths still ever accelerating, Maxwell pivoted and faced Julia, which also meant staring down the business end of a shotgun, like the snout of some snarling animal. He tried again, like he had earlier, to plea.

"Could we please talk—"

"Sorry, lad. You don't get a say."

"Maxwell…" Penny whispered in his ear, turning to the uncannily alive sinkhole. "I'm about to do something really, really stupid."

"No!" He riposted. "No, absolutely do not do something stupid!"

Penny was gazing intently at the sinkhole. She was taking deep breaths. In. Out. In. Out.

"If I get hurt in any way I'm suing your ass to hell. It is your property after all."

Penny Crane calmly walked off the edge of the cliff.

Maxwell gasped. Julia's face shriveled into astonishment. After a few seconds, Julia recovered and kept him at gunpoint. Penny hit the bottom with a splash that echoed throughout Maxwell's mind.

A splash that meant water…

Maxwell steeled himself. He readjusted his spectacles. Took some deep breaths. In. Out.

And then Maxwell Corvid took his first step into madness.

Chapter Five

Dreams of Grandeur

How had he…

Did it really even matter?

By this point, after such a ludicrously stupid decision, Maxwell rejoiced that he was still breathing. Like all things, the novelty faded. Questions plagued him. He couldn't escape them, not even here, it seemed. So, he might as well start with the easiest:

Where was here?

Well, it definitely wasn't the bottom of the sinkhole. Neither was it the infamous fire and brimstone — or white fluffy clouds he had heard so much about. He knew where he sat but, it… Well, it couldn't be right. It simply couldn't be. This could not be real. Unless this was some cruel trick of an afterlife. And in that case, well played to whoever was looking down on him.

Unless the bottom of this sinkhole was remarkably well-furnished, this should be impossible. And even then, it was a stretch of the imagination. From the excruciatingly uncomfortable seating, to the dingy yet still agonizingly bright classroom, they had practically nailed the intolerable atmosphere of Miskatonic University's lecture hall.

"We'll start off with an easy one." A lethargic, oily voice said from the front of the lecture hall. Professor Weaver's voice. The man turned around to face the class from his position in front of the messy blackboard, his old bones creaking as they did so, his scraggly white beard scattering even more chalk dust all over the front of his attire. "Now, who here can tell me when the body contracts the melancholic breed of humors… Corvid, perhaps?"

The entire hall gazed at him, what felt like a thousand pairs of fixated eyes and scowling faces all jerkily spinning to face Max. "Corvid" snapped to attention almost as robotically as his peers had turned to stare at him. He tensed, not because of the question. Maxwell considered that juvenile. He needed a minute to soak in the situation, the environment, and he wondered — was he really here? Was he really in Mr. Weaver's anatomical class? He never considered himself religious, but given the circumstances... could... could this be the good place? Or... or the bad?

Mr. Weaver glared at Maxwell from the podium. Weaver, an ancient relic just barely clinging to what little life he could still suck out of his students, waited for Maxwell to stutter an answer. Maxwell knew he would prefer an incorrect response. As he had admitted before, Maxwell held grudges quite easily. In this case, Weaver's need for superiority gave Maxwell reason to hold a grudge and that grudge pushed Maxwell to succeed.

"I... I believe... It is fall, Sir. They secrete from the brain—"

"Yes, yes, I've heard enough. Correct as usual, Mr. Corvid, very well." His professor cut him off, grimacing as he usually did when one of his students got a question right. "Even if you slept through the lecture, you managed to get it correct. Lucky you. As Maxwell just stated, melancholic humors take the form of a thick, black bile resembling tar which will secrete from the brain during the autumn seasons and..."

The man would continue droning for another hour if he wasn't stopped, which of course he wouldn't be, and Max's peers would snicker through the obnoxiously mundane monologue listening to the professor's hopelessly conventional curriculum. Weaver wouldn't notice, of course. Weaver cared more about the uniform dress code than he did teaching. Stuck as a fossil, Weaver would explain in excruciatingly vivid detail the most archaic and now outdated procedures. Any question asked, he would answer with one simple statement, a string of magic words: 'Because entropy always wins in the end.'

Moments ago, Maxwell had been on his father's estate... What was this? Was that entire excursion... no. He shook his head, trying to shake the ridiculous notion that the entire thing had been a dream. His mind could not fabricate a story as complex and enthralling as that He hadn't had a dream in... Maxwell Corvid didn't dream. That was all there was to it. Except for maybe that one time earlier under the tree, before he had uncovered that Percy was really Penny... What had that dream been about? No! Stay focused. He tuned into the professor's mindless drivel while, more importantly, determining what was wrong.

"...H' ah or'azath. Ahh don't ymg' fhtagn?"

Perhaps Maxwell had heard wrong but that sounded like a sneeze or gibberish. Had Maxwell been daydreaming? Had he misheard? Maxwell stared to each one of his classmates, studiously scribbling down the inexorable information into their notes. But either way, the rest of Weaver's little cult members had clearly understood it. In fact, this had been the most attentive he had ever seen his peers. Most of them didn't really care if they passed or failed, knowing their affluent and influential families would just bail them out. Maxwell tapped his neighbor, the one on his right, on the shoulder of his impeccable smoking jacket which felt as soft and lush as it looked. The other student scowled in response, hurriedly scraping his pen across the page. No doubt afraid to miss something that might make his fancy family proud.

Maxwell probably wasn't exactly a popular figure in the school. Not since the scandal he had caused a little while ago, mold and all that. Come to think of it, he had been expelled, hadn't he? Yes, Maxwell had been expelled from Miskatonic... he was quite sure of that much. He turned his head towards one of his peers.

"...uh... Could I borrow your notes for a second?" Maxwell whispered to the other student on his left. He didn't socialize much with the others in his major, so he didn't know this man's name. He leaned closer, as the other man's mouth hung open stupidly. Max tried to force out words, but he was preoccupied with searching for drool. The stupid-looking student's bleary eyes stared at him sluggishly and Max wondered if they even spoke the same language. Maxwell repeated himself once more. "Hello? Excuse me, what did the professor say just now?"

"Shhh! The professor is speaking!" a female student in the row in front of him chastised, answering for her doltish friend to Max's right. She then returned her focus back to Weaver at the front of the room, her eyes glued to the husk shambling about in front of the blackboard. The student on his left, the slow-looking one, then hunched over his work, protecting it from prying eyes. Max felt as though he could hear his brain sizzling louder and louder the longer he sat here.

His peers wouldn't help him. As he figured. Maxwell fixed on Mr. Weaver, pushing his glasses up his face so he could see better. Had... had Weaver always looked that sickly? The poor man looked like a corpse fresh from the morgue- gray skin and a bit of... something... growing on his balding scalp. Max reassured himself that it was really, positively something else. It had to be something else, unless Weaver truly was a walking corpse which, in all honesty, could have very well been the case, due to his age and generally miserable, groaning disposition.

"...Mr. Corvid. Mr. Corvid? MISTER! CORVID!"

The professor's bellowing shattered the veil of vacancy smothering his mind, as usual for this class. Snickers permeated the room, as Maxwell straightened himself up once more, stopping his daydreaming to focus on the task at hand, Weaver still glowering from the podium.

Mr. Weaver, thought out of character, silenced the room with a single hand gesture. Then the geriatric cleared his throat, as the rest of his pupils sat in an unusual fervor of avid anticipation. They seemed so excited for some reason. Far too excited for Weaver's class.

Had... had the students also changed? Maxwell knew that the sluggish one next to him hadn't always looked that miserable, but he now had the same gray skin and black growths as Weaver. Maxwell's neighbor's mouth still hung open, but the eyes... his eyes were fixated on Maxwell — bright, yellow, jaundiced eyes, like a predator's. His once lavish smoking jacket was entirely ruined, drenched in some sort of black mucus, and his smell was awful! Like rotting fish... And it wasn't just the sluggish man, the woman, and even the other members of the class sat turned, transformed into vapid, slimy husks... waiting in utter silence.

"E-excuse me, Pofessor..." Maxwell asked, suppressing his urge to respond in the same tone he was spoken to. "Did you just call on me? I... I just answered."

"Yes. And did you expect that you were you done for the day, Corvid?"

The mutated students shifted in the seats, like one hypnotized mass, to face Weaver. The professor grinned. Like he was enjoying the lecture hall's transformation into... into a painting of otherworldly *ghouls*.

"Ahe ya. Ahh. Ah. Ymg'. Nafl. Fhtagn."

That just proved it, either Professor Weaver had had a stroke and now spoke only gibberish, or Maxwell had lost his mind. Only the latter option explained the nonsense language and the state of his classmates.

"Excuse me, Professor Weaver?"

"Ahh ymg' ah nafl fhtagn? ahh? Ahe ahlloigehye."

Maxwell's face flushed as he strained to understand the continued stream of nonsense words. He began to worry that he would never hear English ever again.

His professor repeated the question to him, still in gibberish. Maxwell answered by asking his own questions, to avoid the impossible situation laid before him. This had to be a dream. Was... was this what they were like?

This was supported by the uncanny condition of his peers and teacher. Panning around the room, his peers were becoming... blurrier. Their faces were warping, becoming these fuzzy conglomerates, unintelligible from one another. Even Weaver's face was getting worse. It was like they were all melting, noses becoming deformed and dripping down their faces, skin sagging and tightening in places where it shouldn't, and all the while the stink, that smell of rotting fish: was getting worse.

"Professor, I was actually just about to use the restroom. Could we maybe continue this another time?"

"If you must. But that would be throwing in the towel, Corvid. And as I always say, practice is only second to persistence."

Maxwell had never heard him say that, but the professor was not indifferent to inventing things with no rhyme or reason. Weaver continued.

"You may answer first, or do you finally acknowledge the fact you should not sleep through my class? After all, what I teach is very important to a young doctor such as yourself. Isn't that right, Mr. Corvid?"

"Maybe if you didn't give us so much homework to do, I wouldn't have to sleep through it in the first place, *sir.*"

"What was that Corvid?"

"If I must, I'll get some more sleep."

Smiling and exposing ill-fitted dentures, the teacher gestured to the door. Maxwell walked dejectedly down the stairs and out of the lecture hall. The class snickered. It was robotic, and forced, more like they were being forced by their puppeteer than actually laughing at him. Just like chittering cicadas. A faceless hive mind, of ridicule and debased hysterics. And this time, the professor didn't stop them.

Maxwell had never failed to answer Mr. Weaver's questions, despite the teacher's disdain towards him. If this resembled an ordinary dream, he was glad.

"And Corvid? Please fetch me more chalk from the supply closet while you're out!"

"Yes, Professor…"

Maxwell remembered the layout of Miskatonic perfectly even after being disowned by the school, despite the place being built with the purest intention of isolating its students and staff. Most people, even senior students and some faculty got lost amongst the winding passages. Maxwell knew every crack in the filthy floor tiling and the way the older bare walls had never known plaster. He had walked these corridors a thousand times, marveling at how a prestigious medical academy got away with this abhorred interior. Maxwell enjoyed one feature: the large Gothic windows, despite smudged glass overlooking which took up most of the right wall, which would have been glorious on a nice day, though Miskatonic rarely had those, the grounds being unkempt grounds and the wild and unruly surrounding woods. Then again, he supposed the reputation of the school had fallen since his father was no longer able to fund its development.

Of course he didn't have to actually use the bathroom, nobody really used them in the university. It was disgusting in there already, made even worse when everybody knew the custodians avoided cleaning them as well.

But regardless of the state of the school or its reputation, which had no doubt changed with his father gone, there were more important things than the state of the lavatory. Like what this place actually was. Because clearly, by his mutated classmates, this was not Miskatonic. But it wasn't... *not* Miskatonic either.

Maxwell turned a sharp corner, and suddenly he found himself someplace he did not recognize. It looked like the East Wing, but he had gone nowhere near the East Wing.

The East Wing was the part of Miskatonic which had been decommissioned. Within the hallways that had been condemned as unsafe, there was a different draft from under every door, a different substance flaking down from the ceiling, and sometimes on occasion you could find the periodic rat scuttling around the halls. Most people avoided the East Wing. But Maxwell found... comfort... in the solemnity sometimes.

What he did not enjoy about the East Wing, however, was the mold.

The occasional black fleck sprinkled down from the ceiling, like a tiny piece of marine snow falling to the bottom of the ocean. And said ceiling was saggy, and flaking, as if the building itself had a skin infection. The mold was still thriving it seemed, even after he had raised hell just to point out how toxic of an environment the east wing was, not to mention the rest of the dormitories and classrooms which had similar, albeit more minor contaminations.

The seat of the incident which had gotten him expelled stared him down from across the hall. He didn't want to go back after what had happened. The supply closet beckoned him closer, creaking open its door slightly (something it was prone to because of the draft within). Max ignored it.

Now was not the time to relive what had happened. If this was his new reality, he should not repeat previous mistakes. He kept walking, trying not to look at the supply closet. If he made it to the next hallway, it would be out of sight, and hopefully, out of mind. So, Maxwell turned the corner.

...Wait. Hadn't he already turned down this hall once before?

The entire university was familiar obviously, but this seemed a little too familiar. This was the hallway he had just walked, the east wing again. The supply closet remained there, smugly sitting at the end of the hall and complacently watching him avoid it. Maxwell turned the corner, only to arrive at the other end of the hall, staring at the back of his own head. The hallway remained largely the same, if not for some locked classroom doors or in some cases, classrooms boarded up entirely. The only door that remained belonged to the supply closet. Maxwell found himself still unwilling to enter. Maybe if left with no other options, then he might go in there again though, he wouldn't like it.

He walked around the corner again, and again, hoping for a way out but one didn't appear. It was just him, and the door. The door which he wouldn't enter.

Maxwell saw no way out of it. He pinched himself. Then slapped himself. Wake up, wake up, wake up, wake up! This was a dream, it had to be a dream, if it wasn't a dream then… then… then he didn't really know what to make of it. His glasses fell sideways, off of his face and…

His glasses… glasses, glasses, glasses… His glasses!

His glasses were fixed! How had he not noticed sooner! They had been cracked before the crash, but now, now they were back! He still had the twisted, discarded rims in his pocket. So now he had two pairs. And his clothes had been fixed up as well, going from disheveled to practically new. But if this was the dream… the question remained:

How the hell was he going to wake up?

Wait a minute, there was still something he hadn't tried yet. He very calmly walked over to the windows, which occupied more wall than the actual walls. Maxwell stared at the dark, gloomy countryside. He had established that this was a dream. It had to be. And the dream, for whatever reason, was keeping him in the school building, trapped, going round and round. It didn't want him to get out.

But there clearly was an outside.

Even though he was quite sure that this was all a dream now anyway, Maxwell still felt uneasy, performing such an act of vandalism. Like the professor was going to appear down that looping hallway in just a few moments, and chastise him no end, beginning a very tedious speech about how he, in all his years, had never seen such insolence, and so on and so forth.

Maxwell needed something to break the window. If he used his hands, he could break bones and/or receive some serious lacerations. He could not seize a chair from the neighboring classrooms as they all had locked doors. Even the halls of the East Wing were empty… except the supply closet. The same supply closet that taunted him from the end of the hall.

Maxwell crept towards the supply closet, pausing every few steps to beg his racing heartbeat to slow. He reached for the door, already feeling specks of mold as they flaked from the ceiling and tickled the flesh on the nape of his neck. Already feeling squeamish, he opened the door, tried not to think about what could be festering on the brass door handle, and reached for the cord that hung from the dusty lightbulb. It didn't throw much light as it flickered on, and maybe that served as a blessing. But he could almost still see the tiny, estranged patterns of the mold growing beneath the wallpaper, like little swirling whirlpools of decay. Even so, he picked up the scraggly broom that was leaning against the left wall, tearing it away from the molding spirals which kept it trapped. If the school's moldering foundations were similar to a disease, then the supply closet was the source of the epidemic. Without thinking any more about any of it, Maxwell slammed the supply closet door.

Holding the broom under his arm like a battering ram, Maxwell ran full speed towards the window. The first attempt ended with him rebounding off the glass dishearteningly. Then, on the second try, the glass presented with a small crack. Max readjusted his newly whole spectacles and charged again. And again. And again. The crack widened and splintered the glass.

He continued. Once more. And then again. This would work, this would *have* to work, hell, it looked like it actually would work. He continued charging into the glass, one, two, three more times, each thrust creating progress. Until finally, without warning, shards showered the air like glittering gold. Glass cut his face, his forehead, his arms, but it didn't hurt. Vindication was nothing more than a better kind of adrenaline.

Though what he discovered outside hurt his head more than the glass. Or what he had discovered in the... lack of an outside.

Where the outside was supposed to be, Maxwell found a void. What Maxwell had seen through the window — the forest and the countryside—-was all gone. It seemed as if the forest had just been painted onto the windows themselves. The gloaming wealds of Miskatonic had disappeared into a vast expanse of nothing but black, nothing but the cold and infinite void. In the center of the landscape, something stood erect against the backdrop of darkness, something tall and towering. Something that should not have been there. It stood there, motionless, barely perceivable...

Until it turned on the light.

click

It was something wearing a yellow cloak.

The moment that Maxwell noticed it, the thing in the dark, his hair began standing on end. He noticed as his body almost prickled in response, the air feeling just as galvanized as it had before the storm. Each breath felt as though it was charged, as if the smallest little exhale could suddenly have him struck by lightning at any moment. The yellow thing... the air around it crackled with electricity. It was an awful sensation. But not as awful as the sensation that came as the thing looked down at him, this great tall thing, taller than anything should have been, donning a matted yellow color. It wore an alewife hat, the same ones that fairytale wizards wore, which pointed against the sky, though this creature's hat had gone limp and flaccid.

The shadow cast by the headwear so dark Maxwell couldn't see the thing's face. The hat obscured its eyes. Despite a strangely human frame, covered by a yellowed cloak, the cloak rippled like skin. The occasional twitch of a muscle, the rare pump of a vein. But even if it was just a cloak, Maxwell didn't even want to know what could be beneath such a… wrong and… incorrect exterior.

Above the thing, illuminating its alien strangeness hung a lightbulb. This lightbulb on a string, which hung from nowhere, and swayed gently over the yellow thing's head. There was no power source. There was no sign that the creature had even touched the bulb to begin with, it just… it just was.

It sat there, staring at him.

The only motion that came from the thing emerged from its strange cloak-like skin. Maxwell stared into its eyeless face, and it seemed to stare back, as if the electricity that hummed from its body indicated the direction of its attention. He stared back into that empty face, not knowing exactly where to stare, considering its lack of eyes. Had it been looking at him this whole time? Had it been watching him from behind the window? What was it thinking? Why was it… where was it… Was it… was it the devil? An angel? Something… something else?

"H-Hello?" Maxwell stuttered out. Neither he, nor the yellow thing, were interacting. It didn't seem… interested in him. Not in the slightest. So, it was up to Maxwell to break the ice. "Hello, can you… hear me?"

No answer was returned immediately. Whatever it was, it wasn't up for conversa—

"LITTLE… BIRD…"

When it spoke, it did not open its mouth. If it even had one to begin with, underneath the veil of shadows beneath the thing's hat. The thing's words echoed and rebounded off within the walls of his mind. Its voice stumbled as if it struggled to communicate. Whispered words deafened him and drowned out Maxwell's thoughts. The voice didn't travel through the air, but instead, wriggled straight into his ears. Maxwell stepped backwards.

One foot passed back behind the other as Maxwell continued to retreat. He took one more step, and then another, and another.

"COMING BACK… TO ROOST…"

It was like his mind was being probed. He could feel it in the back of his head, searching and probing, jabbing and slithering, prodding and poking, re-arranging the thoughts in his brain. Maxwell shivered, as the thing explored every little nook and cranny in his head, that made him… him. He didn't like that feeling. And then to make matters worse…

It began to walk towards him.

It rose from its stillness beneath the bulb and shuffled, no staggered, closer and closer. Its movements proved as loud and as deafening as its voice, echoing throughout the void. It moved like it had trench foot. But the problem wasn't really the fact it was sluggishly marching him, it was really the fact that Maxwell couldn't do anything about it.

Maxwell tried to run, of course he did. But as he backed away further, he found it increasingly hard to run. Some invisible force was pulling him backwards, stretching his skin and his hair back towards the thing. And even if he could get away… the hallway would just loop into infinity, as the thing only got closer… and closer… and closer… Maxwell watched as it entered the school building through the hole in the window, contorting and stretching and warping its form, as it snaked its way inside. Then that horror intensified, as it stood in the center of the hallway, limping along robotically towards its goal.

It was only getting closer, and the way it was pulling him back, it was like he was trying to run through molasses. Maxwell had no other choice. It was the only thing close enough to him where he could hide… The thing said nothing, as he darted for the supply closet.

Maxwell lunged towards the supply closet door, flung it open, and dove inside, slamming the door as the creature inched his hand and foot into the space with him. Silently recoiling, its slimy fingertips slid away and retreated. Maxwell heard the door click.

Maxwell's panicked breaths and his heightened heart rate fell into an unholy anthem to this thing, this great yellow thing. It jiggled the doorknob. Maxwell clung to his side of it, his fingers tight and unyielding as he braced with all his bodyweight. Then the thing knocked. It knocked three times. And it knocked, and knocked, and knocked, until everything fell silent.

Maxwell caught his breath. Wake up, wake up, wake up, wake up, wake up, he begged himself. This was a dream. Or a nightmare. And so, he should be able to *wake up*. Maxwell studied his feet, his back pressed against the far wall of the closet. A damp, warm powder rubbed onto his hand. He wiped it onto his clothes, and but then realized — it covered one side of him already.

Mold.

Pulling on the light-string frantically, he discovered that mold blanketed his body. Mold, black with green specks, that tormented him every day at Miskatonic, spread over and across his body as if it were a colony of ants. The mold moved, writhed, wriggled, quivered, and nobbled him. The more he wiped off, the more he spread it. The walls of the supply closet came to life, pulsating with spiraling patterns. The bare wooden planks buckled from the filth. Maxwell couldn't breathe. The air itself was tainted.

Maxwell seized the doorknob, but now it was locked from the outside.

"ARE WE... CONNECTED? ...WONDERFUL..."

It was inside. The thing was inside the room, it rose from behind him out of the black spirals, out of the decay, its yellow body being created out of the mold itself. It was made of mold. No, it *was* the mold. Maxwell closed his eyes and pretended like nothing was wrong, but he could still hear the thing in his mind, its voice somehow worming its way into his head. He couldn't breathe. The mold was beginning to take dominion, the creature looming behind him as it's body was born anew out of rot and spores. Maxwell was helpless as the thing's cold, mucilaginous hand covered his mouth, each finger snaking its way up his nose, his mouth, his eyes, wriggling inside of him like he was filled with worms. It's skin carried the same horrid pattern as the decaying spores, black, dripping, filled with little green flecks.

"MY... NAME... IS... KYRIOUS..."

Maxwell didn't even know what he could say back to it, if the thing took its hand away.

"LET US RUN... AN EXPERIMENT... LITTLE BIRD..."

He could see through the thing's eyes for a moment, and it could see through his. It was like for a second, only a split second, they were one in the same. He looked down upon himself.

He was seeing things, hearing things, tasting, smelling, feeling things that he didn't know were even possible, so many things, all impossible, all equally awful. And it was all through the mold, this creature, this thing all made from the same disgusting *mold*. And he tried to scream, though his mouth had been taken from him, by... by Kyrious. It was like it was puppeteering him from the inside out, as he turned to one of his peers from the lecture hall.

"IT WILL... JUST TAKE... A FEW... HOURS... OF YOUR... TIME..."

Maxwell's eyelids closed. The lightbulb above Maxwell flashed and flickered. And then, the lightbulb exploded. The bulb detonated with a flash of golden, burning, intolerable light, a light that burned away the mold and melted it all down to ash...

And then... it all just sort of... stopped.

Kyrious and his awful, hateful, moldering nightmare... it just stopped.

Then all of that faded, as Maxwell woke up, his body, his senses, his mind, finally all his own again. But the thing's voice still echoed off the walls of his mind, even after waking, as water filled his lungs and panic filled his brain.

"LET US SEE... IF THINGS... CAN... CHANGE..."

"MAXWELL... CORVID..."

Chapter Six

Rock Bottom

Maxwell had never been so glad to wake up from a dream.

That towering yellow thing, the deteriorating, state of Miskatonic, everything he had just seen: all of that ceased to even matter, the moment that he opened his eyes. Reasons one through twelve as to why could be described in one simple word:

Cold.

Freezing water flooded his lungs, its searing frigidity urgently summoning him to consciousness. His skin burned with bitter cold, and his bones grounded to a halt. But most importantly, this was the most effective wakeup call he had ever had.

He was drowning.

Flailing helplessly in the icy black of underwater, Maxwell could have been swimming down, left, right, and he would have had no idea which direction he was going. But he was hopefully swimming up. Please let it be up…

Maxwell's lungs longed for air, his muscles ached and spasmed with shivers. In his fatigue and discomfort, Maxwell stopped swimming. Instead, he floundered with useless kicking and silent splashing. which did more harm than good. And so, he sank, down, even more down, sinking even more downwards, and eventually he imagined he would land in the silt at the bottom of this pit. Maxwell gathered his energy and offered one final push towards the water's ceiling.

Somehow, as he sputtered and gasped in sheer astonishment, Maxwell's head burst through the water's freezing embrace. He spewed water, choked as it came out of his lungs, and although he knew it was anatomically impossible, he thought he might be expelling water from deep inside his arms and legs. The chilling caress of hypothermia hugged his spine, but he wouldn't mind a hug about now, a real one anyway. It was still a shock to him he was even alive, after taking the plunge into this dark abyss.

Max finished coughing, and looked around the bottom of this crater, only to realize there was nowhere to really even look amidst the darkness. Still treading water but now with his head solidly above the brackish blackness, Maxwell finished coughing and took a deep, shuddering breath. He extended each foot, as if standing on tiptoe, and gingerly searched for any semblance of ground… But no luck. It was like he had sunken to the bottom of the seafloor. But even still…

"Ha ha ha! I'm alive!"

His words echoed off the walls of the sinkhole and up into the sky. He was almost sad when his echo finally left him alone, considering it was all he had to talk to now. But not for long, because his heart and chest soon opened with relief to the idea that he had survived. So, despite the grimness of the situation, with water still stinging and dripping from his nose, Maxwell rejoiced …. How long exactly that was unknown to him. But it certainly was a nice change of pace. Rejoicing for once. He really ought to do it more often.

After his minor and yet still dissatisfactory celebration, he began swimming. In what direction, he didn't really care. It wasn't like he could see where he was going to begin with, so he might as well have picked one at random. The sinkhole was huge. Bigger down here than it had looked up there, even. So, he supposed he would just swim until he found… something.

Maxwell knew it was silly, so incredibly silly of him, to be fixated on something as mundane as a singular little night terror even while swimming in the icy water, knowing any wrong stroke could lead to drowning but… Maxwell's thoughts still drifted and dwelled on the stifling, all-encompassing presence of… of that mold creature. What had it called itself again? Kyrious? Yes, that was it. Either mold constructed Kyrious, or it controlled and animated the spores — either made his stomach flip. Not that he had anything left in him to vomit.

After several seconds of swimming, it had already become monotonous to even describe how dark it was, because the word dark really didn't describe it well enough. But eventually, amidst the pitch-black backdrop, he noticed a tiny little light, bobbing on the surface of the water, quickly flick on. It glimmered very, very dimly, but still radiant in this endless watery abyss. Curious… Though also, quite… quite perturbing. He had heard some startling descriptions from some of his more biology-oriented peers about the bioluminescent things that patrolled the darkest depths of the ocean, things with too many teeth and not enough eyes. But the light was the only notable thing down here besides him, the cold, and the dark. And he didn't want to spend any more time alone with the cold or the dark.

As he swam closer, he came to a realization. And a rather humorous one as well. It was, in fact, a lightbulb. He was sure of it. A lightbulb! A lightbulb which, by all intents and purposes, should *not* have been currently lit. And it was in the water, at the bottom of a sinkhole, and not connected to any power source. Honestly, it was quite austere from a different perspective. As Maxwell had decided previously, any light was a blessing.

Maxwell reached across the cold water to tap the glassy exterior of the mysterious little light. As he did, the light began to glow brighter and emit a sort of hum. He pulled his hand further away, and it began to dim. Was the light… reacting? Reacting to him? Maxwell carefully cupped his fingers and batted the glass. The bulb bobbed away like a fishing lure or a buoy. He still had so many questions.

Maxwell reached out a third time and snatched the light. To his surprise, it had no wires. Its buzz recommenced and disrupted the eerie silence of the depths. Maxwell, nervous and tired, shoved the bulb in the breast pocket of his vest. It shone like a pocketed star, and even through the fabric of his shirt, the light brought some warmth to the cold waves. It also brought warmth to his chilled, wet skin. He prayed that it didn't burn through his clothes, God knows they had had way too much abuse pointed at them tonight.

Now that he could actually see where he was going with the help of the lightbulb, Maxwell was beginning to realize just how strange this sinkhole actually was. For one, as Maxwell slowly paddled his way through the aquifer. Suddenly, he noticed lights everywhere. And they all seemed to do the same thing: detect his movement, as if Maxwell himself was conducting electricity…

As Maxwell swam, he became more and more certain that the sinkhole led to, and that this definitely was, an underground lake. In the direct middle of the lake, surrounded by almost extinguished lights, in the direct center:

There was a jacket.

Penny's jacket — black with thin pinstripes, aimless, discarded, and crumpled. Though the banker herself, she was nowhere to be found. Like she had just disappeared in a literal puff of smoke. Had she just lost it? Shed it when she landed? There was no way she could have… no… no it wasn't possible that she could have… drowned, was it?

"Penny!" he screamed. Nothing but his own mocking voice returned from the darkness. "Penny? Are you okay?"

This time the echo of his own words mocked him, and the phrase "are you okay?" continued to mock him until it spiraled all the way upward to the surface. She… must have known how to swim… she had to have known how to swim…

What if she didn't know how to swim?

Maxwell wasn't even sure why he did it to begin with considering this was a woman he absolutely hated, but he dove beneath the surface of the water, the lightbulb now being not only thing allowing him search for the now twice-missing Penny Crane. It was as you would expect. Dark. Cold. Black. Cold. Had he mentioned it was cold? Because it was very, very cold. And then even colder still. He resurfaced for air.

There was still the jacket though, right? He hadn't even thought to investigate that yet, though it seemed like a rather obvious suggestion when he said it aloud.

After paddling over towards it, he noticed that the crumpled clothing next to him was missing that trademark hat she usually wore. It should have floated on the surface, shouldn't it? Yet it was nowhere around.

And Maxwell was quite sure that if he could call Penny Crane a companion, his companion would appreciate having their expensive pinstripe jacket back safe and sound. So, he brought it with him. There was no harm in it. It was all he had left to bring, considering the satchel no longer held anything of sentimental, or realistic value to him.

But why did he care so much?

Because despite the situation, and how much he had begun to hate the odor of second-hand smoke following him everywhere he went, he did know that there was only one thing worse than being trapped in the sinkhole forever, deep below the surface: Being trapped there alone. He would probably go insane without someone to talk to. And even if he didn't value Penny's company on the outside, deep down, somewhere he had to. Company was company, no matter how unpleasant, and he supposed that Penny wasn't exactly the worst company he could have had. Though it would be more interesting to speak to someone a bit more pleasant to be around.

Maxwell, so close to exhaustion his shoulders threatened to liquify, followed his light to what his feet detected might be a shore. Though far from one you would ever find on any idyllic beach. As he clumsily climbed to a rocky, jagged outcropping, the light in his pocket illuminated the huge, gaping maw of a cave.

Maxwell's legs quivered and complained as Maxwell brought himself to his feet. The Corvid Estate's topography included a variety of useless caves, nothing like contained silver, gold or anything his father would consider of value. The sinkhole had obviously cracked open this unexplored network across the property — one Maxwell's father would have never explored.

It was then that Maxwell Corvid took his *second* step into a world of madness.

Something he noticed about the maw of the cave, as soon as he set foot in it, was just how quiet it was. Just like the estate above, there was absolutely no life anywhere. If the breathing sinkhole was the body of some great and terrible monster, it had been fossilized long ago. As far as the eye could see, it was just stalactites resembling teeth, and the sharp gypsum jutting out everywhere being the crystalline bait that would lure so many would-be spelunkers into its jaws.

As Maxwell pressed further into the cave, goose pimples rose on his flesh, and even the light in his pocket seemed less pure. The flowstone looked like petrified waterfalls and massive white columns supported the ceiling, like massive Greek pillars on a temple. Maxwell breathed in stale air and soaked in the sense of everything being untouched. It made him queasy. It was entirely alien.

And then there was… the *slime*.

He wasn't quite sure how to describe it really. This *slime* was coating the floors, the ceilings, everything. He had heard that sometimes caves could be sort of gooey, occasionally even snowy, with a kind of bacteria biofilms growing within them, like a kind of lichen, but… slimier. This stuff was different though. You could just faintly see white sparkly flecks within it though: like stars in the night sky. It almost looked like… no, it couldn't be… could it?

Was it… *mold*…?

Well, it couldn't be mold, *exactly*. It wasn't powdery, it was thick slime, but it had the same color, the same white sparkles, hell, even the same smell as the disgusting stuff he had seen in his dreams. But how the hell was it down here? How was it growing on the stone? Mold couldn't exist down here. It had to be something else. But he couldn't shake the idea now that it had planted a seed in his head. That this entire cave was just… festering… with mold.

Maxwell walked to the wall, reaching towards what seemed like bile, but as he drew close, he gagged. He wiped the slimy sediment, feeling something underneath, something spongy and soggy. It almost felt like-

Maxwell unveiled a sheet of paper.

Maybe the cave wasn't exactly untouched. Considering it now looked as though somebody had been living down here.

It was only now that Maxwell realized that little light bulbs that hung from the ceiling on strings, clearly manmade. He was so used to daylight that he hadn't even been wondering where the rest of the light was coming from. There were towers of rocks, like somebody had been playing with building blocks. But most clearly of all, and most unsettling of all: the cave contained an alarming number of drawings.

As Maxwell pulled the soggy paper from the debris, he noticed that the drawings; they were everywhere. They plastered the walls, ceilings, floors, all displaying an almost childlike depiction of a portrait, and all buried beneath an ocean of slime. Only the pictures were… wrong. That was the best way to put it. He wasn't trying to bash on his mystery host's artistic integrity but this… art… was usually more often than not a random assortment of scribbles or finger-paintings. Maxwell thought they showed hellish depictions of people. Maxwell squinted to determine what the artist was *attempting* to draw.

Some faces had little to no mouths or eyes, others had much too many. Some had too many limbs, and others possessed an unnatural number of fingers. Some had ridiculous amounts of teeth. Some were too unspeakable to describe. Whoever had made them must have been proud of them, as Maxwell studied the arrangement of the lights around him and realized that the strings of lightbulbs that illuminated the walls did so in such a way that displays these works like they hung in… some kind of gallery.

Maxwell raced closer to the well-lit area of the exhibition. He had seen these before. When he had gathered the paperwork from the forest floor after the carriage accident. He hadn't thought about it much at the time with the other commotion, but seeing these crude sketches, Maxwell realized that whoever, or whatever, drew these sketches had been on the surface close enough to mark his paperwork.

At first, he thought he had discovered ordinary bits of paper, maybe yellowed bits of an old newspaper or a few loose-leaf sheets torn from a book. But no, upon closer inspection, he was able to decipher the words. Those words were possibly the most horrible he could have read at the time.

The familiar logo of *Crane and Sons Banking* was stamped on every page.

The artist had made every monstrous masterpiece from official paperwork.

Maxwell's paperwork.

Someone — or something — had erected this entire gallery highlighting artwork made on his paperwork within the last few hours. Maxwell frantically surveyed the room for any signs of how this could have happened in a few hours. He studied the walls, reexamined the art and pondered the ludicrousness of an art gallery in a sinkhole accessible by a frigid sea. There was no way any of this was happening. Right? Another dream maybe?

No, this was real.

A quick movement here, a sudden chill in the air from over there… had someone been… watching him? He readied the lightbulb in his breast pocket. He waved it sporadically, seeking to torch any unseen beast in his personal space. as one would do to protect against spirits or vampires. Had it always smelled like fish down there? His nostrils were suddenly invaded by the stench of fresh kippers or herring or maybe even sardines.

Maxwell didn't want to, but he couldn't help himself, he moved towards the tunnel before him and peered in. Like the main chamber, something had papered the entire tunnel with drawings and scattered loose-leaf pages. A little yellow light flickered in the distance.

A person, a small person, the silhouette of a small person, was slowly standing up in that light.

"Whoever's out there…" Maxwell said, his heart accelerating in his chest. "I know you are these. So just come out… Please…?"

The cave itself answered him with thirty or forty flapping, gnawing, ghastly answers— bats.

Bats crawled from every crack and crevice, haphazardly screeching and screaming their way through the cavern walls. Maxwell would be lying if he said he didn't jump and almost scream along with them. Some flew around him. Others flapped so close their wings brushed his cheeks. Some aimed directly for his nose and veered at the last second, causing him to throw up his hands in an effort to shield his eyes.

Then, Maxwell dropped his lightbulb.

It silently hit the floor, so it didn't shatter upon contact. In the glow of the manmade lightbulbs, Maxwell watched his bulb roll deeper into the corridor.

Somebody was down there. Waiting for him. Maxwell slinked down the tunnel, the very dark, very damp, very unstable, scary tunnel filled with scary drawings… He tried to be very, very quiet. But Each step he took grew exponentially louder. Black goop squelched under his feet. As he continued into the tunnel, he noticed a faint glimmer of what he hoped was his lightbulb. He followed whatever it was, and it grew stronger, glistening only a few meters from him, camouflaged and weakened by the sludge on the floor. Five steps away. Then four. Three…

Maxwell crouched, and slipped in the muck, falling to his knees. He crawled towards his lightbulb.

The smell of fish, of salt, of the distant ocean intensified. Of crab pots and all the slippery, insidious, snake-like things that lay beneath the sea. Why would it smell like that down here? Maxwell reached his hand out and placed it over the warm glass once again.

He hadn't expected the thing at the end of the tunnel to do the same.

A cool, smaller, and mucus-covered hand laid over his. Maxwell instantly recoiled backwards and scrambled to his feet. Overpowering noise reverberated throughout the tunnel.

Maxwell and the mysterious cave "monster" were both screaming at the top of their lungs.

Chapter Seven

Vanessa

She told Maxwell Corvid that her name was Vanessa.

That was last useful thing she had said.

His enigmatic, questionably artistic host was a young girl.

Once they had stopped screaming, Vanessa had conducted herself quite well in civil, polite, and most importantly, normal conversation. Though no matter how civil, polite, or normal she was, talking to Vanessa didn't seem to be getting him anywhere.

Maxwell had asked her about her age, and Vanessa had said she didn't exactly know it. Maxwell asked how she got down here. Vanessa said she didn't really know where "here" even was. Maxwell asked if she was with anybody, or if she had anybody to call to get them both out of there. She said, you guessed it: she didn't really know.

The only thing she knew was her name. No surname apparently, she said she didn't know that. Just, Vanessa. Apparently, that was all the universe thought he needed to know.

This girl, maybe eight- or nine-years-old by the looks of her, but she had gray, almost slimy skin, and blazingly yellow eyes, the same as a certain someone else he had met earlier on the estate. Her appearance looked rather… amphibian. Upon closer examination Maxwell noticed that she had webbed feet and black slime instead of hair, the same moldy substance that coated the rest of the cave. When she moved into the light, jelly-like pale spots in her "hair" sparkled and created stars. And Maxwell's nose told him that she was also the source of the fish smell.

It was all a big misunderstanding, in the end. Vanessa called him a monster, or implied that she at first mistook him for one, with his "weird eyes" and "strange red hair."

"Alright, let's try this again, Vanessa… Any family members? Any at all?"

He had been asking her the same couple of queries in different orders for what felt like the past ten hours, though it was probably only the last ten minutes. The caves felt like purgatory. But Vanessa didn't seem to think so. In fact, she had told him she quite liked it here, as evidenced by her macabre but still strangely happy pictures.

So far he had nothing other than Vanessa's name, as introductions usually went. He was beginning to lose hope she knew anything.

"Well, I have my Auntie Allison… but she's probably busy… I wouldn't want to bother her…"

Finally, he was getting somewhere. Took long enough.

Maxwell immediately began listening again, his brain snapping out of its numbness like he had been showered with ice-cold water. Though he had had enough of that for one night. Either way, he began to listen again.

"Well why didn't you say that before Vanessa!" he exclaimed. "Where is your auntie? How can we get in touch with her?"

"Well… She told me to wait here a little while ago… She didn't tell me when she was coming back and… and… and…"

"How long ago was a little while, Vanessa?"

Maxwell knew he shouldn't have asked that question the moment it had passed over his lips. Vanessa was beginning to tear up with weird, slimy, jellied tears glooping down from her big, yellow, fishlike eyes.

Maxwell knew that it was probably family drama, but just like the freezing water, he had had quite enough of that.

But at the same time, doubt crept into the back of his mind. A little family drama was one thing and leaving your niece in a hell pit was something else entirely. Vanessa heaved and sputtered, threatening to cry again.

"I don't… know."

Maxwell still wasn't quite sure on how to comfort someone in this state. But… maybe with Vanessa it would be a little easier?

"No, no… Don't cry! I'm sure it couldn't have been that long, I'm sure she'll be back. And until then, let's play a game, yeah?"

She sniffled again, he seemed to have her interest.

W-what g-g-game?"

"It's quite simple really. It's called questions and answers. I ask you a question, you give me an answer. See? Simple!"

"O-Okay…"

"We'll start whenever you're ready."

"A-alright… y-y-you can s-start…"

"Alright. Here's the first question. Have you seen Penny?"

"Who's... Penny?"

"Right, I haven't told you. Um..." Maxwell had completely forgotten to tell her who Penny was, the whole reason he was down here to begin with. He struggled to decide on how he could describe a member of the Crane family in the most pleasant way possible. "She's short, shorter than me, taller than you. Smells like smoke, has a bit of a temper, darker complexion than you or I... she's an um... friend... that I lost a little while ago. Yeah. Yes, a friend of mine. Oh And sometimes she likes to go by Percy. Maybe you met a Percy?"

Vanessa lit up like a shooting star in the night sky. Maxwell sighed. Hopefully this meant Vanessa had seen Penny and that Penny was alive.

"Oh, uhm..." Vanessa rubbed her temples, as an interesting little drama played out on her face, as if a spotlight of remembrance struggled to stay on the performers. "I think I did see her! She looked angry and she smelt like burning. Is... Is that... right

"Yes, that's exactly right, Vanessa! Hooray! You've won this round!"

In soft celebration, he waved his hands rather than cheer any louder concerned about the fragility of underground caverns. She giggled.

"And I have even better news," he said. She clapped politely in anticipation. "You've won... this."

He offered his hand to Vanessa. She looked confused or perhaps a little disappointed. Maybe she didn't even really know what a handshake was.

"Vanessa, what if we look for them both? Your auntie and my friend. Maybe together we could find the two of them, yeah?"

Vanessa considered his proposal. And like everything else she did, she hesitated to accept it. In the end, his persuasion worked, and she grabbed his finger instead of his hand. It was close enough, he supposed.

Her skin was cold, morbidly cold, and her tenuous thin skin possessed a viscous, frog-like texture, like one he had once dissected back at the academy.

"Okay..." she said. "I'll come with you."

Really?" he asked, sounding a little confused. He hadn't actually been expecting to get this far. "Didn't your Auntie Allison ever tell you not to... Well, didn't she tell you not to talk to strangers?"

Vanessa shook her head. Maxwell sighed.

"I mean, seriously?" he asked. "The most you know about me is my name!"

"Actually, you... You never told me your name..."

"Right, of course. Where are my manners? I'm Maxwell. Maxwell Corvid."

"How come you get two names when I only get one?" she asked.

"Well, it's because I have a surname, Vanessa. Are you sure your Aunt Allison didn't tell you yours? Everyone has one."

As soon as he said it, he knew his mistake. The familiar sight of water eyes and quivering lips unfolded before him. He should not have added that last part. A single tear splashed to the cave floor.

"Oh… really? Ev…everyone has o…one? Except f-for… except for…"

"No, no, no, no, no…. It's a good thing! It really is! That makes you unique! Think about it this way, you might be the only person in the entire world that doesn't have to bother with more than just one name on their paperwork! I don't even like my surname! Who needs them!"

She sniffled, wiped her nose on her sleeve, and then brought her dirty white dress to her face in an attempt to dry it. Maxwell shuddered He did still have Penny's jacket, but that was already covered in slimy mucus, considering the same stuff that had just come out of her nose coated every wall, the floor, and the ceiling. The slime served as the building block of everything here.

"What's … paperwork?"

"Something dreadfully boring that I don't have time to explain," he curtly said.

He sighed, now completely out of breath. She smiled for the second time since meeting him, even if fleeting, gone just as quickly as it had appeared. He didn't blame her, this situation was rather grim.

"So, Vanessa… shall we go?"

"Oh, uh, yes. Sorry Mr…"

"Maxwell. Just Maxwell."

"…sorry, Mr. Maxwell…"

"No, it's, uhm, just Maxwell, actually. No Mr. required."

"Well, your name sounded like someone else's… someone that my auntie used to know. Someone who she used to like very much… So I thought that maybe… Maybe I should call you Mr. as well."

He fell silent for a long time.

"Well, if it's absolutely necessary… Go ahead."

There was no harm in it, and so he decided that he really didn't mind. It was better than her calling him "Mr. Corvid." That would have been much worse.

Vanessa led him deeper into the caves, weaving through tunnels and between formations without a single pause. She scampered over rocks, darted into the new chambers and even in the darkness navigated with ease. The occasional bulb, half buried in muck or hanging from the cave ceiling on a string, threw enough light for Maxwell to keep pace with her. With the way she moved, no wonder people thought she was a monster at first.

"So, what kind of person was this… um…" he asked, while walking briskly to keep up. "This mister. that your auntie told you about?"

"Well," Vanessa started, stopping ahead of him in front of the next never-ending tunnel. The caves seemed to go on forever, and everything looked the exact same. "I didn't know much about him. I just knew that he was Auntie's favorite."

"Right… Did he have any name other than Mister?"

"No. Just Mister."

He only knew one person on the estate who would have been addressed by the title of "Mister" other than himself. And he prayed that Vanessa, or her aunt for that matter, would never have had any contact with Max's father.

The two of them continued deeper into the cavern. The passages grew more and more cramped. It did not phase Vanessa, she moved through the caves as if they had been made for her. She slipped between the cracks in the crevices and ducked under low ceilings. She had clearly done this a thousand times. How long had she been living down here?

"So, Vanessa, what kind of woman is your auntie?"

"Well…" Vanessa started. "Auntie Allison is…"

She stopped. Maxwell stopped. They both stopped, dead in their tracks.

Because the lightbulb had just flicked off.

Maxwell had suddenly just remembered how scary the dark was, now that his only way to ward it off had been snatched from him. Why wasn't it working? Why wasn't it turned back on yet?

"Vanessa? Vanessa? Are you still there?"

Her hand latched onto his, squeezing. Her hand tightly in his, she began to tremble.

"Vanessa?" He asked. "Vanessa, are you alright?"

"Mr. Maxwell… Be quiet… please…"

"Why should I—"

"Shhhh…"

There was very likely a reason he should be scared right now.

They stood for what felt like hours. There was nothing. The dark had stolen Maxwell's senses. Water dripped beside him. Vanessa released stuttered breaths. The darkness and the cold, stale air choked them from all directions.

"Who's… out there?"

This was a new voice. A voice Maxwell had never heard before. A voice with a distinct phlegmy, injured sound to it, as if the speaker's had been forced to gargle saltwater until the wound was pink and raw.

"I asked… Who's… out there…?" it repeated.

The voice sounded closer. Oh God, it was getting closer. Vanessa shook harder. Her respirations increased rapidly, her own lungs unable to keep up.

"Vanessa? It's going to be okay, alright?" he whispered barely audibly. He squeezed her hand tighter to reassure her. "Shhhhh… Everything will be okay. Trust me on that."

Her breathing slowed and her jitters did, too. Whatever was out there, trudging around in the dark, walked in circles aimlessly, if Maxwell could trust the echo of its footfalls.

"I… heard you…" said the gurgling and sleepy voice.

Squelching footsteps approached them now, slow and ambling. If Vanessa smelled like fish, this newcomer smelled more like… like…

…like eggs.

Rotting eggs. Like sulphur.

The entity on the other side of the darkness smelled like sulfur.

As the footsteps continued towards them, something crackled like static. A faint hum followed. As Maxwell realized he should recognize the sound, a gradual light illuminated his surroundings. Maxwell quickly tried to shove his free hand, the hand not clutching Vanessa, into his pocket. The lightbulb had resumed its shine, and he needed to stifle it.

His efforts were in vain. With a terrible screech something lurched from the darkness towards Vanessa. Like a moth, with arms outstretched the lightbulb which Maxwell fumbled with in his one free hand, a humanoid creature, dripping with slime and glowing yellow from his face, charged them. With claw-like hands, it reached towards them, but not them. The monstrosity lunged not for Vanessa, but towards Maxwell. Maxwell reflexively pinched his eyes shut but quickly forced them open, determined not to display cowardice with a child present. As his eyes reopened, Maxwell noticed that the creature did not aim for either of them but for the lightbulb still in Maxwell's hand.

Maxwell instinctively placed a hand softly over Vanessa's eyes to shield them. Though, Maxwell supposed she knew the face of this monster.

And she wasn't the only one. Maxwell thought it familiar, as if he had also seen it before. He did not recognize this creature from a dream or from the waking world. Maxwell recognized this creature from the confines of the page. Maxwell recognized this creature from a particular set of unsettling drawings.

Maxwell would have to tell Vanessa, if they survived this, that she had done a good job of portraying this horrific face, especially as a roughly seven-year-old artist.

Next came a gunshot.

The creature, the thing in the dark, whatever it was, dropped as the resounding muzzle flash lit the cavern much better than the lightbulb ever could.

Maxwell flinched. He moved his hands from over Vanessa's eyes, to her ears, still just managing to clutch onto the lightbulb. The creature writhed and wriggled on the ground with its human-ish body, arms and legs flailing about like mad. It sputtered and gargled, but Maxwell couldn't determine whether it was drowning in its own blood or if it normally sounded like that.

A new powerful odor suddenly permeated the stagnant cave. One of the outside world, known to Maxwell. And it wasn't smoke. This ruled out the reappearance of Penny.

The smell was of petrichor and whiskey. Firewater and spent gunpowder. The dirt under his fingernails. The neighbor's compost and of the polluted city river.

Maxwell knew that smell. It brought him full circle to the first terror of this whole absurd adventure.

Heavy breathing, labored breathing through the mouth, drew close behind him. In and out. In and out.

"Mr. Maxwell," Vanessa whimpered. "W-what h-h-happened?"

The barrel of a shotgun pressed against the back of Maxwell's head.

"So," Julia asked. "Who's the kid Corvid?"

Chapter Eight

Thrill of the Hunt

Maxwell couldn't remember the last time he had stopped thinking.

His mind had gone completely blank. It must have been a good ten seconds of nothing. Staring straight ahead, into the dark, and the myriads of dangers it could hide. The only thing that remained in those moments was the hum of the lightbulb, the soothing hum, ringing in his ears.

A knock against the back of his head for him to rejoin the present.

"Mr. Maxwell?" Vanessa asked. "Who's she?"

Even if Julia was a gun for hire… She wouldn't have the heart to kill a kid, would she?

…Would she?

"She's… She's… another friend of mine, Vanessa."

A long, deep, agitated growl emanated from behind his as the shotgun moved away from his head. But he also felt the shotgun barrel being taken away from his head. So, there was that.

Julia walked in front of him, towards the warm body of that creature. It was twitching on the ground. As Julia approached it, Maxwell peered in the direction from whence she had come. How had she entered the cave? Her clothes weren't wet at all…

"Vanessa, stay right here, alright?" He told her, leaving her side, just for a moment. "I'll be right back, okay? I just need to talk to my… friend."

Vanessa nodded, though in his peripherals, he could see her briefly reaching for him.

Julia bent to examine the corpse. It finally stopped twitching. Maxwell shuffled up behind her and felt the agitation radiating off of her, as she exhaled long and hard.

Maxwell peered into the creature's brain via a crater made where Julia had shot it. Whatever the creature had been in life, it was equally horrible in death. Its skin was pale, and its blood was black, filled with white flecks. Its face, also damaged by the wound, seemed distinctly human though warped. Like everything else in the cave, a layer of slime coated the creature, and he had the same thin amphibious skin...

Maxwell looked at Vanessa. The girl awkwardly stared as if she wanted to say something, but then stopped. Her mouth opened, but no sound emerged. When Maxwell turned back, he found huntress looking at Vanessa, too.

"So..." Maxwell said, "Julia was it, I... I believe?"

Julia grunted in response. He knew she could speak, so why wasn't she answering? In any case, Maxwell hoped it was a grunt of "yes" and not a grunt that meant "I'll shoot you the moment you're not looking." But in all likeliness, he felt it was both.

Julia scowled, shriveling her nose, like a bloodhound about to bare its teeth.

Julia struck him across the face with the butt of her rifle. Maxwell crumpled to the ground. Vanessa gasped. The girl took a step towards him, and then, upon hearing Julia growl, retreated three steps backwards.

Fuck. It hurt. It hurt really badly. His face was throbbing, and sore, his entire head spinning. Maxwell wasn't sure he had ever been hit that hard by anyone... He reached to touch his face, his cheek, where the back of the shotgun had bashed into him. He didn't think anything was broken... Though he had also never broken anything, so he didn't really know. It still hurt like hell though... He tried to get up but staggered.

"What the... hell... was that for?" he asked, clutching his bruised face.

"Idiot," Julia grumbled, ignoring the question.

Maxwell tried to begin the process of standing up, adjusting his spectacles and wiping away the sludge from the floor which had spattered onto his face.

"That was uncalled for, wouldn't you say?" he asked again.

"Oh, believe me," Julia said, her words barely escaping the corners of her mouth. "It was *very* called for, Corvid."

"It's Maxwell."

"You're going to be dead meat if you tell me what to do again."

"Still better than Corvid."

Julia shrugged.

"Mr. Maxwell?" Vanessa called from across the cave. "Is this your friend from before? The one you were trying to find?"

"No... She's a different friend. She's actually... probably... looking for Penny, too."

He turned to Julia.

"And what makes you think I'll help look for her?" Julia asked, quietly, so only Maxwell could hear.

"Because that's why you're down here, isn't it? To look for us?"

"I'm down here on orders," Julia replied.

"Orders from whom?"

She didn't respond. Unless you counted a particularly strong exhale, which Maxwell did not.

"Okay then, don't answer. Orders to do what? Can you answer that?"

Still no answer.

"Don't like those types of questions? Got it. How about a different question?" Maxwell asked. He stopped trying to be remotely polite. "What in the ever-loving *fuck*, is that thing?"

He pointed to that pale-skinned abomination, it's face nothing but black, white-speckled mush. Julia's eyes followed his finger, but then went straight back to him. Her face didn't change, but her bile-shot yellow eyes certainly did. She flinched. Imagine that.

"I'm waiting," he said impatiently. "What *is* it?"

Still, she gave no response. Just heavy breathing. He thrust his hands down and walked dejectedly away.

"Okay, forget it," he told her. "I'll figure it out myself. Come along, Vanessa. Let's try to find my... other friend."

"To find you," Julia snarled, droplets of saliva streaking through the air. "Those were my orders, alright? I'm here to find you, Corvid. And if you hadn't jumped, this would have been a hell of a lot easier."

"I'm sorry! Was I supposed to let the psychopath in the woods shoot me? You wanted me to just calmly get shot? Without any complaints?"

"I was just s'posed to scare you. You were the one who ran."

"Right. Sorry for the misread of the situation. I believe I've had enough of being scared, thank you. Please tell whoever gave you orders that you did your job. I was, and am indeed, very scared. So, me and Vanessa will be on our way now."

Maxwell nodded dismissively to Julia, seized Vanessa's hand, and briskly marched in the opposite direction of the way Julia was going. More to make a point, than to actually go anywhere. Vanessa mumbled an "okay, Mr. Maxwell" and seemed to go along with the idea.

"Sleepwalkers," Julia said staidly.

Maxwell whirled around and shone a gloomy chiaroscuro from his light-bulb across Julia's dirt-covered face. For once, her yellow eyes were glued to the ground, and not to him. No, not to the ground, to the thing *on* the ground. Her loathing had been redirected… for a time. He gave Vanessa a glance, willing her to stay here for a moment' as he went closer to Julia and the corpse.

"They're called Sleepwalkers," Julia said. "That's… I dunno, what I call 'em, at least."

Maxwell's eyes also now eerily drawn towards the cadaver, mutilated as it was. Somehow, its body had managed to fall in a way where he believed it would spring to life once again at any moment, and lurch at him like it had done only moments prior.

Maxwell slightly poked at the cadaver with his foot, to reassure himself that he would not revive as some sort of revenant.

"It's not the worst name, I suppose."

"I didn't ask for your opinion, Corvid."

"And I didn't ask to be stalked and shot at, but here we are."

Julia grabbed him by the collar. She lifted him ever so slightly off the ground, without a single sign of exertion. One of her nostrils flared as she made aggressive eye contact with him. Vanessa chirped.

"You've got balls, Corvid. You are *so lucky* that I have orders to keep you alive."

Now Maxwell was the one without any kind of witty comment. Julia released him. Vanessa gasped again from her hiding place over by the opposite wall.

"I'm fine, Vanessa," Maxwell said. "I'm fine, we're just wrapping up over here. Stay over there, I'll be with you in a moment."

Maxwell had a suspicion that she didn't quite believe him. Her face, all scrunched up and pouty, told him all he needed to know. After all that had happened tonight, he wasn't sure he would believe himself either, or if he really even did. Or maybe Julia had just scared her away with one of those trademark glares again. Either way, she clearly abided by the request.

"You do know what she is, don't you, Corvid?" Julia asked him.

Maxwell studied Vanessa, as she pottered about in the half-dark, just walking in circles, but not quite pacing, at least not in the usual way. Keeping herself busy, that was all it was, he supposed. Children were good at that, finding things to do. But could the child really have been related to this… this thing? The slimy gray skin, the strange yellow glow which had come from its eyes… it all seemed to match up maybe just a little too well.

"Is she…" he whispered to Julia so Vanessa hopefully could not hear. He watched Vanessa closely, making sure that there were no signs that she would be… could have been… one of those ghastly "Sleepwalkers" as Julia had called them. "Is she, y'know, one of—"

"Yes."

"But I mean, look at her! She can't be!"

Julia shot him daggers with her eyes, the same yellow eyes he had seen when she had ambushed the coach. Vanessa had the same yellow eyes. Julia wrinkled her nose yet again.

"Wait a moment," he started, taking a few steps away from Julia again. The huntress exhaled. "You have them... The yellow... I mean, you look like her... or one of..."

Julia scrounged within that big, foul-smelling trench coat she wore which smelled as if it would have been quite at home in a trench itself. He imagined her pulling out a pistol, or a shiv of some kind, and he contemplated running away. She slowly pulled something from an interior pocket, revealing it. In the light from the bulb, it sparkled like a shard of glass. She forced the sharp object into his palm.

"Don't take the high road with me, Corvid," Julia said. "After all,"

Maxwell examined the object in his hand. It was a glimmering silver shard of a mirror. It offered just enough surface area to catch a glimpse of his reflection. Maxwell couldn't remember the last time he had even looked at his own reflection. Had it been back in the coach? Back when all of this seemed like just a bad dream...

But his reflection did not stare back at him.

Maxwell turned the shard around. He rotated it around and around in his hands. It had to be an optical illusion or trick of the light.

The shard of glass reflected the face of a stranger to Maxwell. This stranger had black speckled mold on his gray-tinted skin, and perhaps a hint of Maxwell's ginger hair, or familiar facial shape. That stranger now gripped the shard of glass so tightly that blood bubbled from his hand. The shard reflected that as black, sludgy mucus.

The reflection stared through Maxwell with glowing, bright yellow eyes.

"After all, Corvid," Julia repeated, snatching the shard from him. "You're just as bad as the rest of us now."

Chapter Nine

Sleepwalking

It wasn't wrong to say that the estate reversed everything within it.

Ever since Maxwell had arrived, the world had gone topsy-turvy. Percy Crane had gone to Penny. Bad ideas had morphed into the best options. He had started to dream something he had been completely sure he had never been able to do

At the Corvid estate, right-side up was upside-down, left was right, and nothing made even the slightest semblance of sense.

It was all wrong.

All of it.

So… Not much had changed since he had left as a child.

Unless you counted the strange, moldy sludge. If anything, despite Maxwell's disdain towards all mold in general, it was just decay in the end. And the estate, like the Corvid family, had been decaying for decades.

It was nothing new.

If anything, he should have been used to it. Even the mold.

Even the roles had now been reversed. At some point, the huntress had been tailing him, and he stayed as far away from her as the estate would allow. But now, he was the one following her, creeping close behind her amidst the dark caverns, doing his best impression of her shadow.

"Mr. Maxwell?" Vanessa asked. "Are you all right? You're… shaking…"

Maxwell looked upon his own hands. Oh… He was shaking. Or was he shivering? The cave was dreadfully cold, but he hadn't really noticed that in a while. Cold became the norm, as, apparently, was decay and making all the wrong choices.

"Oh! Oh yes Vanessa," he said. "I know. I'm fine. Don't worry."

He put on the most reassuring smile he could for the girl. She tried to mimic it, but it didn't come close to the light which had crossed her face before, on their first meeting.

"It is a little cold," Julia said. "Suck it up, Corvid."

"How sweet," he replied. "Are you concerned about me, Julia?"

"Don't test me, Corvid."

Maxwell looked down at the lightbulb in his hand. That small, enigmatic, ubiquitous lightbulb. He knew what it was. But he didn't know *why* it was the way it was. Something about the light, was just beginning to become rather austere. Why was Julia unable to get it to work? Why was Vanessa not making it flicker on and off like the other one had? And just how was it even emitting a light to begin with? He turned it around and around in his hands, like it was an artifact that needed to be studied. Which it very well may have been.

"Why do you call them Sleepwalkers?" Maxwell asked, avoiding his questions about the light with questions about the things that lurked just outside of it.

Julia ignored him at first.

"I mean, that one you shot didn't seem to be asleep. Seemed pretty awake, actually."

"It's 'cus they're not in their right minds. Not anymore," Julia answered.

"What do you mean by that?"

No answer.

"Mr. Maxwell?"

He turned to Vanessa, or where he thought Vanessa had been, but she had disappeared. Maxwell waved his lightbulb as Julia growled and grumbled for him to stop. It seemed like the only time she ever tried speaking clearly was when she was insulting him.

When he finally put his eyes on Vanessa had gone into a remote corner of the cavern, into a cluster of stalagmites that blending into the backdrop almost perfectly. The glint in her eyes revealed her location.

Vanessa approached Maxwell with outstretched arms holding… a hat…

Penny's hat.

Maxwell immediately snatched it from her, despite how politely Vanessa came to give it to him. He absent-mindedly whispered sorry under his breath. Even without the obvious mold growing on it, the damp and disheveled top hat had threads pulled and ripped from it as if perhaps Penny had had a run-in with… with a Sleepwalker.

"Come on, Corvid," Julia admonished. "Keep moving."

"It's Penny's hat!" Maxwell protested.

As he had just done to Vanessa, Julia forcibly snatched the hat from his hands, like he had accidentally done to Vanessa moments earlier. Oddly, Julia sniffed the air, and then knelt, before returning the hat to Vanessa. But unlike when she spoke to him, Julia was being much more patient with the girl.

"She found it?" Julia asked him, gesturing to the girl.

"Yes. Is it a problem that she found it?"

Julia faintly mumbled the words "not bad kid" as she trudged further away into the corridor. Since he had trouble believing what he heard, he put the mild praise out of his mind and focused on catching up with their mumbling, odorous line-leader.

"Hey, kid," Julia called, suddenly stopping. Maxwell almost bumped into her. "Which way?"

They had reached a fork. Both ways looked equally dark and miserable, and Maxwell dreaded the two of them equally.

Vanessa seemed a little perplexed, as she did whenever the huntress spoke to her, tilting her head as if to ask if the brigand really was speaking to *her*. Maxwell even moved back to give her an audience with the huntress herself. Vanessa, hesitantly, pointed down the right passage. Julia took a long look down that way, exhaled sharply, and beckoned the two of them.

Vanessa, who was holding in so much nervousness, she looked like she was about to explode, exhaled through her mouth, as if she had been holding her breath underwater.

"Mr. Maxwell," she said, tugging at his sleeve again, and only once Julia was far enough in front of them to where she wouldn't hear. "I think I've met your scary friend before..."

"Really?" He asked. "How do you know my... friend... Julia?"

"I think she's a friend of my—"

"Don't be scared of me. sweetheart," Julia cut the girl off, perfectly timed as to prevent any much-needed information from passing through her lips. "If there's anyone you should be scared of, it's Corvid."

"Surprised that damn shotgun didn't give you tinnitus." He riposted bitterly, only afterwards realizing what the brigand had said. "Wait, wait, wait, hold on, me?" He tapped his chest. "Me?"

Maxwell picked up the pace until he was side-by-side with Julia. She glared at him from the sides of her eyes, not even slowing. Vanessa jogged so that she would not fall behind.

"Yes." Julia bluntly said. "You."

"Mr. Maxwell," Vanessa said. "I... I really think you should be—"

"Why should she be scared of me?" Maxwell erupted. "I've done nothing wrong!"

Julia walked faster. Maxwell matched her speed. Vanessa ran after them both.

"You've done plenty wrong, Corvid," Julia snarled like an angry dog. "Plenty. You and your whole damn family have done enough to me, and that poor girl's-

"Mr. Maxwell, please keep your—"

Oh, so this is about my dad? I'm nothing like my dad! I barely even knew the ass—"

"Mr. Maxwell!" Vanessa's voice practically shook the cave walls. "Please listen to me!" Her shouting did, indeed, cause some rocks above Maxwell's head to wiggle. He stopped.

Both of them turned around to face Vanessa. She was red-faced, or at least as flushed as her slimy-yet-ashen cheeks could be, almost hyperventilating.

Quickly, rage turned to distress. There was no other way to describe the feeling of making a child cry. Maxwell bent down and looked Vanessa in her black, goopy eyes.

"I'm sorry, I'm so, so sorry, Vanessa, I didn't mean to… I'm listening now. Go ahead."

A rare emotion flashed on Julia's face again, just barely shining through the stoney visage that the brigand had crafted for herself. It was… also, distress. As if she was worried about Vanessa, despite only meeting her a few minutes ago. As if she was mad at him, for arguing with her, and ignoring the girl's desperate cries for someone to listen to her. As if…

As if this was all *his* fault.

"Go on, Vanessa, please, I'm here to listen now."

Vanessa pressed a finger to her lips.

Rocks. Mold. Stalagmites. More rocks. It didn't look like there was anything particularly different about this part of the cave. Why was she asking them both to be quiet? The situation was no more disturbing than usual.

And then the lightbulb flickered.

It was flickering just like before, just like with the last Sleepwalker, as Julia called them. Everybody froze where they were, Julia, Vanessa, him, they stood as still as statues. The light hummed its gentle glow incoherently, as if it was buzzing in Morse code. He heard Julia quietly rustle, as she loaded two shells into the shotgun, and then quietly closed the barrel.

Julia took a creeping step forward, and then a creeping step around the corner, as quiet as he had ever seen her move. He followed her lead, clutching Vanessa's hand, he hoped, and hoped he was moving as quiet as the brigand.

"We need to turn off the light," Vanessa whispered. "They like the light. They'll know."

Maxwell looked down at her, perplexed. Julia did the same. But then, Julia's expression went through a whole array of emotions, the entire spectrum of emotions really, which was something that Julia's face was clearly not made for. And then, in the end, he sighed.

Julia gave him a nod, and then grabbed his hand, clutching it until it went numb. The light flickered, Julia held up her hand, fingers outstretched. It was five. Then, it shifted to four.

Three…

Two…

One…

Maxwell stuffed the lightbulb into his satchel. It stopped glowing.

And Maxwell was glad that it had.

Julia took three steps into the next chamber, and as she did, Maxwell heard things. Things spoken in a gargling sort of voice, vacant voices, speaking incoherently in half-formed sentences. They could speak… The Sleepwalkers could speak. Sleepwalkers plural, mind you, as there must have been thirty, forty voices, echoing around in that room.

"'Scuse me, sir… 'ave you seen my eyes? I've dropped 'em somewhere…"

"Go to sleep. Go to sleep, little baby. It is dark out, so very dark out, so very, very dark out, so very…"

"Lady Allison, I'm sorry, I… I've had enough of this dream."

Maxwell finally realized the severity of his situation.

They had stumbled into entire horde of Sleepwalkers.

Maxwell held his breath. So did Julia. Sleepwalkers surrounded them, everywhere in the darkness. The blackness stood in all directions, not even a speck of light. But somehow, some way, he could faintly feel the Sleepwalkers moving. A twitch there. A fidget here. And all around him, unintelligible nonsense, echoing off the walls and repeating.

"Vanessa," Maxwell whispered ever-so-slightly into the darkness.

Her hand gripped his. He squeezed it.

"What do we do?" he asked.

An even softer response than his initial whisper returned to him.

"I will guide you," she promised.

Vanessa inhaled deeply. Julia tightened her hold on Maxwell's free hand. A tug came on Maxwell's arm, urging him to move. He did so, despite the blinding darkness.

"Go forward, Mr. Maxwell…"

Vanessa took three steps forward, and so he did the same. Julia followed suit. Then, Vanessa stood entirely still. And soon after, the entire process repeated.

"Is someone…" the gargling voice called, "…out there?"

Maxwell swallowed, willing himself to stay still and quiet. The Sleepwalker's sulfuric breath carried on the air. It was right in front of him.

The Sleepwalker uttered something else with that distorted voice it had, and then, heard it begin to… well, in a monstrous, pelagic, snarling sort of way… He thought it was either growling or, maybe even… snoring? It was, wasn't it! It was snoring!

"Mr. Maxwell… be more careful…" Vanessa said, quiet as a mouse, tugging on his sleeve. "Turn to the left. Walk forward… please…"

He followed her directions to the letter.

If Maxwell said even a word, he would probably be torn to pieces. But if he and Julia just stood here for eternity, the Sleepwalkers would eventually wake up, or worse, simply wander into one of them. He could hear some of them moving around, squirming in the sludge, footsteps like traipsing through mud.

Speaking of Julia… where was she?

She had practically been strangling his wrist, cutting off the blood circulation. But all of the sudden, her grip had vanished.

"Roger?"

Maxwell immediately perked his ears. That… didn't sound like a Sleepwalker.

"Roger? That you?"

The voice sounded dry, gravelly even, not wet and gargling sulfiric acid in the back of their throat.

"Are you out there? Rodge?"

The voice sounded like someone who had smoked a pack a day for years. And that's when Maxwell knew, and that's when Maxwell, perhaps for the first time in his life, acted. He acted without the paralysis of overthinking.

He immediately regretted this.

Maxwell plunged into the darkness, letting go of Vanessa's hand, finding himself alone. He no longer heard the voice, the voice he swore was Penny's voice, or the choir of the nonsensical that made up the Sleepwalker's drivel.

All the Sleepwalkers had silenced. Their words, their footsteps, everything. The world stood still for a moment, as still as he was standing, as the bodies around him melted away and water submerged his body. His ears filled; any remaining sound grew muffled and distant.

Should he move? What he was feeling, it couldn't be the water left over in his ears, could it? Maxwell steeled himself. And took a step forward.

Nothing.

Maxwell stepped forward again.

Nothing happened. There was no wall, no Sleepwalker, no Penny, not even a stalagmite. Hell, the floor didn't even feel like stone anymore, it felt flat, smooth, more like glass. He took more steps forward, and more, and then even more. He was rushing now, and still no walls in sight, this… this couldn't be right? There were no walls, no… no anything. It was a void.

This place, this realm he had found himself in, was unimaginably big. So big that he felt helpless standing in it. So big that he would have rather been back in that cave. At least he knew what was out there. And at least he wouldn't be alone.

click

Then, somebody flicked on a lightbulb.

And that somebody was worse than a Sleepwalker. Much worse.

Chapter Ten

Riddles in the Dark

"HELLO... AGAIN... LITTLE BIRD..."

Maxwell almost didn't believe what he was seeing. He squinted, closed his eyes really tight, even took off his glasses despite what little they were doing for him now, hoping that when he looked again, it would be gone but... but it was right in front of him. The yellow thing, Kyrious — it was right there, towering over him, the smells of rot and sulfur so powerful Maxwell felt as if his nostrils would start to bleed. But it couldn't be real, could it?

It was a nightmare.

Kyrious was a nightmare.

It had been nothing but a nightmare... right?

It stood there, eleven, maybe even twelve feet tall, and yet its head did not brush a ceiling. In fact, Maxwell followed the lines of its tall, yellow hat, and found no ceiling at all. He only found a lightbulb hung on a string above the creature's head, gently swaying from side to side like a pendulum, illuminating Kyrious in all of its sulfuric, disgusting, moldy glory.

This... wasn't right. He had been in the cave just moments before, and now he was... here. Wherever *here* was. A dark place, bathed in a sickly golden light, and in a miasma of sicklier air. This was not the cave; this was somewhere else. Max tried to pretend like he could understand this, that he could understand what this thing was, what was happening, what any of this could mean... but his mind drew a blank. And what thoughts he did have came and went like machine gun fire.

Run. Speak. Get away. Go somewhere else. Leave. Try to reason. Run. Speak. Get away.

Despite thinking all of these things... he didn't act on any of them. And so, he stood there, frozen, and waiting.

"THE... EXPERIMENT... REACHES... THE MIDPOINT..."

"What?" Maxwell started hesitantly. As he spoke, he looked around frantically for an exit, or even just somewhere to stand away from the thing, but there was just blackness in each place that he looked. Everywhere, in all directions, the void held dominion. The thing knew he was looking too. That slithering inside his head had begun again, the creature's whispers rooting and wriggling around like worms in his mind. He tried to ignore it as he spoke. "And what does that mean, exactly? You... Never really explained it."

The monolithic thing, standing as if it was some great yellow obelisk, turned to face him, once again gifting him a look at the never-ending blackness which lay inside the space between hat and cloak. When Maxwell met the creature's gaze, which was nothing but more blankness and void. What should have displayed a terrifying visage was scariest most for its emptiness.

"TELL ME... LITTLE BIRD... HAVE... YOU... CHANGED...?"

"What do you mean 'changed?'"

Kyrious's breath rattled on the wind, as a frosty, trailing exhale snaked out of the blackness of its "face." It twisted Maxwell inside that the thing didn't even answer him. It shuddered, and what looked like a hundred veins undulated beneath that cloak, as if it was calculating his answer. Even as its cloak rippled and oscillated, as if there was a colony of woodlice beneath its skin, it was almost as if it was calculating his answer.

This had to be another dream. This could not be reality; it *could not be.*

It could not be.

And yet here it was.

"DO NOT... BE... AFRAID... LITTLE BIRD..." it said, suddenly contorting downwards. Despite never leaving its spot, Kyrious's spine twisted and bent and snapped until it was only a few inches from his face. Even this close, Maxwell did not learn anything about the thing. In fact, Kyrious only seemed to get more and more mysterious with each and every slow, shuddering breath that it took. *"I AM... MERELY... OBSERVING... I WILL... NOT... INTERFERE... WITH THE... EXPERIMENT..."*

"What experiment! You're not making any sense!"

Kyrious only recoiled from him, resuming its original stance in the center of the room.

"Well?" he asked it again.

"TELLING... THE SUBJECT... WOULD... DISCREDIT... THE... EXPERIMENT..." it said. Kyrious turned its big yellow head towards the empty space in the distance as if avoiding eye contact. Then, its body went limp, as if it was nothing but a marionette. Slow and deliberate, as it took a shambling

step towards him, its entire body about to clatter to the ground. *"NOW... MAY I... BEGIN... THE QUESTIONS... LITTLE BIRD...?"*

Despite being entirely alien, Kyrious spoke politely. It conducted itself with the language and speech patterns of a perfectly reasonable person, despite not really being a person in the first place. It was far from a brutish monster. Well, it was still a monster of course, there was no denying that. But a civilized one. Strangely, it was more civilized than anyone else he had met so far on the estate. Well, aside from Vanessa. But she was not a monstrous monster, he supposed.

"May I ask a few questions as well?"

Kyrious seemed almost irritated by that. Well, maybe it was irritation, the creature didn't really have a face for him to judge its emotions. It let out another one of those shuddering sighs, breath trailing out of the void which made up its face. Then, it inhaled, as if it was doing breathing exercises, sucking in the trail which it had just blown out.

"I... WILL ANSWER... WHAT I... AM ABLE... LITTLE BIRD..." it spoke. *"YOU MAY... PROCEED..."*

Maxwell proceeded.

"What are you?"

"I AM... KYRIOUS..."

"No, not your name, your species. What are you actually?"

The creature once again undulated, the pipes and the plumbing in its body pumping and surging whatever fluids it had, as pulsing arteries and spasming muscles popped out of its cloak as if there were a thousand worms digging tunnels through its skin. Maxwell was scared he may have said something wrong.

"NO... ANSWER..."

"You can't even tell me what you are?" Maxwell asked, confused.

No answer was returned to him.

"MY... TURN... LITTLE BIRD..."

Kyrious took another step towards him, another shuffle. The creature moved as though it didn't exactly know how to. As if even just walking was foreign to it. Maxwell took one step backwards, each time the thing moved closer. Not like it would do much, but still, distance created the illusion of safety, just like how Kyrious's appearance created the illusion of sickness.

"DO YOU... HATE... THEM... STILL...?"

"Hate who?" he asked.

Kyrious only stood there, unmoving, unflinching, not even stopping to think before it spoke again.

"PEOPLE..."

Maxwell didn't hate people. Well, he hated some people. Everybody hated some people, but he didn't hate all of them. Nobody hated *all* people.

"No." Maxwell said confidently. "No, I don't hate people, if that's what you're asking."

"NOT... THE BANKER...?"

"Well, yes, I do strongly dislike Penny sometimes, but—"

"THE... BRIGAND...?"

"Julia chased me through the woods with a shotgun, I think that's—"

"YOUR PEERS... YOUR... CLASSMATES...?"

"But they're all—"

"YOUR... FATHER...?"

Kyrious lingered on that last one for a moment.

"RESPOND..."

Maxwell didn't hate all people. He... He couldn't hate all people... Could he? He hated aspects of them, yes, but he supposed that everyone hated aspects of the people they were around, it was natural. But Maxwell did seem to hate a lot of aspects, now that he thought about it. He hated almost every aspect. Almost every single one. It was something he had been doing for years.

And it was something that his father did as well.

"RESPOND..." Kyrious repeated, in a gentle, but oddly sinister voice. Maxwell could feel the yellow thing's invasive thoughts wriggling around in the back of his head again. Max could just vaguely feel what felt like a thousand little roots slipping and sliding through the wrinkles in his brain, looking for the answer that Maxwell seemed so reluctant to give. It repeated itself. *"RESPOND... LITTLE BIRD..."*

"Well, I don't hate Vanessa... Do I?"

Kryious's wriggling in Maxwell's brain suddenly stopped.

It was then that a ghastly sound began to ring in Maxwell's ears. It was like the creaking of a door, mixed with the cackling of a hyena. The sound of rainfall, and the sound of the lightning as it struck you. Maxwell wasn't sure why he was hearing it until he realized...

Kyrious... It was laughing.

The creature's body had begun to spasm in a bizarre way that almost resembled a seizure, jerking and jolting. Kyrious's body crumpled, and it curved, and shifted and bent in strange ways that no living being was supposed to move. Maxwell didn't know what to do. He stood there, idly, watching the yellow thing look like it was being struck with invisible lightning. Laughing at him all the while.

"AND... WHY DO... YOU THINK... THAT IS...?" Kyrious said, finally containing the miserable din that made Max's insides shake. *"WHY... IS SHE... SO SPECIAL...?"*

"Isn't it my turn?" Maxwell asked it, losing patience. He didn't appreciate being laughed at, much less when the thing's voice sounded like an entire lecture hall, laughing.

The laughter stopped. Maxwell stared at the thing's empty face, and he could have sworn he saw some kind of change within the blackness. Kyrious abided by the rules of their little verbal contract. It snapped whatever bones it had broken back into place, and reeling in, until you could almost mistake it for human. If you were very far away. Then, the thing, with an aura of smugness only his father could match, ordered him to speak, like some sort of ill-mannered child.

"PROCEED... LITTLE BIRD..."

"If you won't answer what you are, then can you at least tell me where you're from?"

Kyrious seemed to wriggle a little bit in its skin after he asked that. And by skin, Max meant cloak. It almost seemed uncomfortable with the question.

"Now come on. Be honest." Maxwell cockily entreated it. Now he was the one feeling smug. "Or are you worried about ruining 'the experiment?'"

Still, the thing deliberated. The folds in its cloak tightened, its slimy, sludgy fists scrunched up into balls. The void itself began to ripple and change around it, the lightbulb flickering uncontrollably. Kyrious's one unified voice was becoming less of a voice, and more of a disorganized cacophony. The once consolidated chorus was all speaking at once, out of turn and tune. He couldn't take it... It felt as though his ears would start to bleed.

The void was coming undone. Quiet blackness broken up by unstable flickers and flits of light, tearing apart the dark before it was quickly sealed up by the ever-present shadows. Electricity charged the air. He took a step back. Kyrious took one towards him, arms limp, head staring at the floor, in an awkward, agitated dance.

Maxwell had made it angry. He had made Kyrious, very, very angry.

And then, the lightbulb burst.

Everything stopped. The cacophony of the monster's cries, the disordered voices and even the electricity, and the flickers of light. He was back in the dark again. Alone. He couldn't see a foot in front of his face anymore, but it wasn't the cave. No, it wasn't cold enough. It was too empty. He was still in the void. He had fallen *deeper* into the void.

Then, Kyrious's voice went back to normal. Unified. Together. Calm, and yet extraordinarily loud. A silent sound, and yet a booming chorus inside his mind.

"YOU... WHO STANDS... SO BLESSED... UNDER... YOUR... STARLIGHT..."

It began with only specks. Specks of vibrant color gleamed from the void like tiny stars. And soon, the stars began to grow. They began to branch outwards, like roots, tendrils of green and purple, swirling and weaving together to completely overrun the ocean of dark. Soon, the blackness, the darkness, it all melted away. It all held Maxwell mesmerized, and also perplexed, as he smelt the suspiciously fresh air.

"YOU... WHO DARES... TO REACH... FOR THOSE... VERY... SAME... STARS..."

With a blink, Maxwell found himself... outside.

It was amazing. Just like before, when he had visited Miskatonic, the dream, or whatever the dark place was, had become an almost one-to-one mirror of the real world. He breathed in the air of this place, feeling the dew that had settled amongst the grass and the reeds. Far better than the dimly-lit halls of Miskatonic University.

Maxwell stood on his very own estate. He gazed to the imperial manor in the distance, watching from its proud place on the hill above the fishing lake. Looking at his family estate now, compared to how it had looked in this dream... Nobody would have guessed they were even the same place.

Maxwell now stood at the cusp of the past. This was the estate before the small army of groundskeepers had left and before all of the trees had shriveled and died, taking his father with them. The estate was lush with color here, from the bright flamboyant lily flowers to the glittering starlight above, reflecting off of the water, which had shades of blue, purple, all amongst bright, shining stars. The estate had always had a wondrous sky. You couldn't get a sky like that in the city, with the smog and the soot. Nor could you get it at Miskatonic, despite its seclusion. No, the stars had always seemed brighter in the skies above the Corvid family estate. But that brilliance had eventually died, perhaps keeping company with Maxwell's father in the Great Beyond.

"YOU WANT... TO KNOW... WHERE I... CAME FROM... LITTLE BIRD...?"

He wasn't listening to Kyrious. He was busy taking the estate in. Or whatever this was. For this was not the Corvid estate. Not anymore. This place was from his memories. It no longer existed, and this? This was a cruel, crude, and callous approximation.

"THEN WATCH... THE... SKY..."

Maxwell did as he was told.

Maxwell stared into the beautiful sky, the familiar sky he remembered from the Corvid Estate of his youth. The rich purples and deep blues provided perfect backdrops for the glittering stars. Amidst this breathtaking scene, a trail of bright yellow streaked across the canvas.

Maxwell shivered It was like a shooting star. And then the odor hit him. Shooting stars did not smell like burning sulfur. And they certainly did not make that terrible screeching sound.

Maxwell jumped to the side, as the "comet" landed directly a few yards from him, planting into the green, verdant water rather unceremoniously with little more than a plop. Despite being about the size of his head, it did nothing but sizzle and cool down in the water for a little while, still emitting that horrible smell, the smell of rotting eggs… Maxwell watched in anticipation, as the "comet" rocked and bobbed, but still, nothing happened. Maxwell debated wading into the water to inspect the asteroid, but it was still far too hot, and his socks had finally dried anyway.

"What does any of this mean?" Maxwell asked nobody in particular, pointing to the "comet." Well, nobody around him, at least. He knew that Kyrious could still hear him, based on the voice still in his head. But the yellow thing itself was nowhere around. "You come from space? You're… what? That? The comet?"

"*NO…*"

Suddenly, the wind picked up. A warm wind. A wind which went in, and out. A wind like the breaths of the sinkhole. The world began to change again.

Maxwell's gaze washed over the strange rock as the wind kicked up, whooshing from the ground and hurtling into his ears. It was a warm wind, but not a good warm. The wind that surrounded Maxwell coated his skin with humidity, making him sticky, reminiscent of the sound the sinkhole made as it breathed… in and out, in and out.

Maxwell winced. He squinted as if trying to keep the moisture out of his eyes but as the wind whipped them open again, he saw black. At first, he closed his eyes tightly, thinking something might have gotten in them. When he opened them, blackness bled across this idyllic illusion of the Corvid Estate of Yesteryear. Before Maxwell's eyes, he stood helpless as the estate decomposed, melted, and faded until all that remained was black, slimy, white-speckled mold.

"*THIS… IS WHAT… I AM…*"

Maxwell's hand itself began to melt. Despite the disgusting spectacle, there was no pain. He was succumbing to the sludge, as it ate away at him, it ate his flesh, assimilating his palm into the tidal wave of decay, slowly swallowing the world. As his hand transformed into clumpy jelly, his finger snapped, painlessly dripping to the ground, with nothing but a slice of fingernail. He wanted to scream, but could do nothing but watch, as slowly, the black consumed it. This was of course, because the black was eating away at his throat now as well.

Maxwell raised his arm. But it wasn't *Maxwell* raising his arm. Through the mold Kyrious spread, it had spread into his body, slowly taking more and more, like a parasite. Kyrious made him raise his arm, the one missing a finger, the blackened slimy hand that had now advanced to a mold-consumed forearm and elbow. And the thing forced Maxwell to fix his eyes on the goo and the gunk and the mold.

"LITTLE BIRD... I CAME... FROM... THIS..."

Maxwell couldn't tell where he was anymore. But he knew it was black. He knew that it was incredibly, undoubtedly, unequivocally, pitch, black.

"LITTLE BIRD..."

Something touched his arm. Slimy, and balmy. It smeared across his shirt. Then, something grabbed him. Something slimy, warm and adhesive grabbed him. Maxwell couldn't tell what it was, but it certainly... felt... like some kind of person. A disgusting, slimy, rotting kind of person. But before he could finish his thought, more of those somethings grabbed him. His arms, his legs, his neck, every part of him was being grabbed and lunged for by sickly creatures in the dark. At first Maxwell thought that the somethings pawing at him in the dark, they were Sleepwalkers, they had to be...

And then, the lightbulb above, the one on the string, flicked on again.

"I CAME... FROM YOUR... KIND..."

As the light from the bulb cast its brilliance upon the void around Maxwell, he began to recognize the shadows and lumps that smeared or perhaps even constructed the walls. They were bodies. So many infinite, indiscriminate, indescribable bodies, that twisted and flowed into one another. Disfigured, misshapen masses of mold and slime, or moldy slime, or was it slimy mold... He couldn't tell. The lightbulb shone above them from the center of the room. It swayed from side to side, as they groped for it. Always just out of their reach.

Even in the light, Maxwell could not truly distinguish one form, or one being, from another, but he could tell that they were human. Maxwell could read the pain in the soup of their faces, and he could feel it too in what used to be his bones.

All human. All pain.

The void had been made within it, or of it, of them, but more importantly, of... *him.*

The void, the living void, held him, tightly, and pulled him further into his embrace the more he tried to escape. An arm would fling towards him. Then a leg would kick him and hook his ankle or press into the back of his knee. Mouths would lean into him, gently but forcefully, either purposefully without teeth or mouthing because they had no teeth. Eyes glued to his skin.

And then it all happened all at once, over and over. The disfigured, melted bodies he saw in the distance one second would smother him the next. Their sludge, or even his own, gagged him, draped into his throat like an appendage seeking to tear his guts from his chest. The decay, it filled his mouth and his nose and stung his eyes and tickled his ears. It was the same as Kyrious's embrace before, back in the supply closet. The same, awful sensation multiplied a hundred-fold.

Maxwell could no longer decipher hands or eyes or mouths or arms or even feet. Pieces of them adhered to pieces of him. The people of the void pulled segments of what he was away from him.

None of it hurt. Maxwell, if anything, felt his heart slow and his breathing lighten. His muscles relaxed as the creatures of the void claimed pieces of them. It was… relaxing, in a sense. None of it hurt, per-say, it was like… like he didn't have to try anymore. He could just go to sleep… do everything he needed to do when he woke up eventually… he deserved this.

His remaining fingers, his skin, his toes, the most intimate chunks of him were sloughed off. The fatigue, the stress of fighting, overcame him. He was tired. So, so tired. Like he hadn't slept in days. Like he hadn't slept ever, at all. And so, he closed his eyes and found his peace within the blackness.

"DO YOU… SEE NOW… LITTLE… BIR—"

"Mr. Maxwell?"

Maxwell snapped awake.

He woke flat on his back. No more living void. He had returned to the previous void, the version of black, endless nothingness where Kyrious had loomed over him. Now, Vanessa crouched over him. And Kyrious, the original, tall, yellow Kyrious, towered beyond. Maxwell and Vanessa with the lightbulb swinging in the emptiness, casting an even taller shadow. Maxwell checked his physical self. He appeared normal. Not a single injury.

"VANESSA…?"

"Mr. Maxwell, please wake up," Vanessa said, clutching his hand, tears in her eyes once more. She did her best to shake him, using what Maxwell imagined was all her strength. "Please wake up, Mr. Maxwell. Please, please wake…"

"I'm awake Vanessa, really, I am I—"

"WHAT… ARE YOU… DOING… HERE…?" Kyrious boomed. The gargantuan yellow thing bore into Vanessa. Kyrious raised its arm, aiming it towards the girl, before deciding not to strike her. *"GET… OUT…!"*

Suddenly a bright yellow light burned through the blackness of the void. Vanessa clung to Maxwell, as he embraced her, tilting his face to protect his eyes as she sobbed, profusely. The darkness and the emptiness of the void further disintegrated under the rays of light, blinding and complete.

And in the next round of chaos, Maxwell woke, with Vanessa in his arms, rousing from slumber at the same time. The air around them chilled his flesh. And the air around them smelled of… was that cigarette smoke?

"Max?" Penny's voice hissed into his ear. "Max? Maxwell, what the *fuck* are you doing? Not the time to nap!"

Chapter Eleven

"What Are You?"

"Max? Wake up for God's sake. Maxwell? Max!"

Was that Penny? Oh, Penny. He had forgotten about her, even though she happened to be the reason he was down here. With how dark it was, even with his eyes open, he felt like he was still dreaming. Like he had never left the void. He shook his head groggily.

Maxwell suddenly remembered that nodding did nothing in complete and utter darkness. "Uhm…. Hello, Penny I—"

"What the fuck do you think you're doing Corvid?" the banker hissed. Penny drew closer, her voice sharp and sputtering like oil on a hot skillet, complete with the moisture as her spit hit his face. "What the hell was that crap?"

"What did I… What… When did… I'm sorry, Penny. I really am, I—"

Maxwell stopped himself. He needed to remember that he had left the void, and now it was more than just him and Kyrious. Living down here, Sleepwalkers' hearing had probably sharpened to a dagger's point. Woozily, Maxwell stood himself up. He felt sick after that last encounter, despite however many times he assured himself it had only been a dream. Maxwell then shook the water out of his left ear. How on earth could water linger in his ear when… Oh God, it wasn't water, was it? It was… It was the sludge, wasn't it?

"Penny, I'm…" Maxwell, worried that he was facing away from her, turned in a semi-circle before finishing his sentence. "I'm sorry, but I think I found someone who could help us. Possibly. Well, I don't really know yet, she's… Well, she's a bit scary, but she knows what she's doing."

Of course, his description of Julia very well might have also applied to Vanessa. The scary part anyway. He believed that in different ways, Vanessa probably knew quite a lot. Children often did.

"Glad you finally made a friend, Maxwell. Hey, do me a favor?"

"Sure. Penny?"

"Turn that stupid thing off."

"All right, then. Glad to see you, too…Excuse me?"

"That! That thing! Turn it off!"

A dim but steady glow emanated from his satchel.

The light bulb had reignited.

"Turn it off!" Penny whispered. She leaned closer to him. Scratches and scrapes and bits of dried blood covered every exposed surface on her skin, as did an unhealthy amount of slimy black mold. Her black-lensed eyeglasses had somehow survived everything, and they now reflected the glow of the lightbulb. "Do something! Break it or—"

"I can't! We won't find our way out if we break it!"

"Mr. Maxwell?"

Out of the corner of his eye, Maxwell noticed a familiar, tear-stained, yellow-eyed face staring at him.

"Mr. Maxwell!" Vanessa exclaimed. Her face ignited with happiness, which soon dissipated upon seeing the banker beside him. "And… Mr. Maxwell's… friend? Are you… Perry?"

"Close enough," Penny mumbled. "Hey, uh, Max… Who's the kid?"

"Vanessa? Oh, sorry, Penny. This is Vanessa. Vanessa, this is my… friend, Penny."

Vanessa nodded at Penny, who dismissively scoffed, so Maxwell elbowed Penny for that. Maxwell did not care if Penny behaved rudely towards him, but even the worst people would show respect to a child. As Penny had said herself on the coach, first impressions mattered.

Vanessa pottered towards the light, drawn to it, as she smiled. Despite the seriousness of their predicament, her smiles grew more frequent.

"What… are… you…? Are… you… Va… ness… a…?"

"Kid, look out!" Penny stage-whispered. Even though, in reality, it was too late for any kind of whisper.

Vanessa walked face-first into a Sleepwalker.

"Va… ness… a…" it said. Vanessa collapsed to the floor. She quivered as the Sleepwalker placed its spindly, webbed claws atop her head. It patted her, rhythmically, creepily, and in slow rhythm to match its words. "I… like… that name… Very… pretty… name… Va… ness… a…"

"V–Vanessa?" Maxwell stuttered. "Hold on! We're going to help you, don't worry! Everything will be fine!"

And everybody knows that when an adult says, "not to worry," there is usually quite a need to worry. And that the need to worry is scaled in direct proportion to how loudly the "don't worry" was said. In addition, when somebody, especially an adult, says those four words "everything will be fine," it subsequently means that the situation will, in fact, not be fine. Au contraire. Instead, the situation will get worse, and worse, until, of course, they go astronomically, catastrophically badly.

As a child, Max had learned all of these rules.

And he supposed as smart as Vanessa was that she had learned them, too.

"Auntie Allison said I'm not supposed to- to talk to you…" Vanessa said, as the Sleepwalker lazily stroked her head, like it was trying to pet a cat. And as if things weren't unnerving enough it began to let out a guttural purring noise, from deep within the back of its phlegm-filled throat, almost as if it was the cat.

"Pretty… name… Va… ness… a…"

"S-stop it…" Vanessa pleaded. "Stop it please…"

Maxwell took a step forward. It was automatic. But before he could try to do anything-

"Corvid," Penny said. She locked eyes with him, as she grabbed his shoulder. Her black-lensed glasses slid down her nose so that her pupils stared directly into his. "Don't."

Maxwell met Penny's eyes. They peered at him with intense yellow. Had they always been yellow? Or had they turned like his? and… they hadn't always been yellow, had they? Did that mean that she was somehow connected to… to, well, the only other yellow thing which was currently plaguing him?

Maxwell was lucky Penny had grabbed his shoulder. In the place he would have been, there was now a conveniently dead Sleepwalker, along with the echoes of a gunshot and the smell of spent powder.

Julia stepped into the light. The numerous murmurs and mutterings of Sleepwalkers began to grow louder and louder, as the creatures talked amongst themselves, in their usual, rambling ways. Julia progressed further towards them; her expression unchanged from the stoicism she normally wore on her face. Penny, however, was a different story entirely. Her hands and arms flapped. Her newly yellow eyes twitched.

"What the hell was that?!" the banker whispered. Maxwell watched, with maybe a little amusement, as the brigand turned to look down towards Penny. It was at least a little funny to see with how tiny Penny was compared to the brigand.

"Good to see you." Julia grumbled.

"Why the hell did you kill him!" Penny exclaimed.

"Him?" Julia nudged the corpse with her foot. The body spasmed, jolting, despite its surely, very deadness. "*It* was a him? Did *he* have a name?"

Penny's face smoldered with the redness of rage. Vanessa clung to him. Maxwell covered her eyes.

Did Penny... know that Sleepwalker?

"Don't play dumb with me." Penny snarled, marching right up to the brigand, and poking her. "I do a lot of things, but I don't condone murder."

Vanessa crept behind Maxwell, hiding behind his legs and peeking towards the women.

"Mind filling me in on what you're talking about here. I'm not quite sure I follow, exactly..." Maxwell said.

"They are animals." Julia explained, completely ignoring him. "Sick, wounded, filthy animals. If she let me, I would shoot all of them."

"It's murder," Penny replied. "And you're a murderer."

"I'm a hunter."

"Hello?" Maxwell tried to chime in again. "Explain? Please?"

"Has he really not figured it out yet?" Julia asked the banker. Once again, they were ignoring him, and his question. He didn't appreciate it one bit.

"Max," Penny addressed him, her voice absent of any mocking subtext or sneering superiority. "You do know that the Sleepwalkers are—"

An awful inhuman blend of screeching and gibberish interrupted Penny. It reminded Maxwell of something. And soon, more joined in, a chorus of screams, of discordant voices... crying, screeching, jabbering... he had heard something like this before... hadn't he?

"All right, all right!" Penny yelled. The Sleepwalkers formed a circle around them, trapping them within their own halo of light. Better than darkness, Maxwell supposed. "Settle down, you lot! It was an accident all right? I swear!"

Maxwell took a step back but stumbled over Vanessa and froze. Penny was speaking to the Sleepwalkers. Did Penny just apologize to the monsters?

"M-M-Murd... erer..." A muffled, gargling voice spat out from the crowd. Penny whirled in the direction of the insult, as the voice continued, in the usual, slow, ambling way the Sleepwalkers liked to speak. "Murder... Mur... derer..."

One Sleepwalker pushed and squirmed its way through the tight crowd. The darkness shrouded them still.

The speaker's form was just as terrible as their gargling, scratchy voice. They were a rather slender Sleepwalker, which in this case, meant almost skeleton-thin. A slender, skeleton of a Sleepwalker with unsavory, scraggly hair sprouting from the top of its head — the first hair Maxwell had seen on one of the creatures — approached. Warts and sores grew beneath its skin like air bubbles and grew upwards. That was when Maxwell noticed that this Sleepwalker, nude as they all were, was female. The first female he had noticed.

"Oh, come on!" Penny heckled, marching towards the speaker.

Julia readied the shotgun, her finger dangerously hovering over the trigger. The sore-covered Sleepwalker took a step backwards, stumbling over her own feet, her wrinkly, featureless face somehow portraying a perfect replica of fear. At least Maxwell thought it must have been a replica. There was no way a monster like that could feel something that human.

"M-M-Murd… erer…!" The Sleepwalker shrieked, pointing a gnarled, long, finger. She was shaking so much; it was hard to tell just who she was pointing at. "M-M-M-Murderer…!"

"Stop, stop, stop," Penny said, dismissively. The Sleepwalkers moved out of the way, as Penny waded through the sea of slimy, moldy, cave-dwellers, towards the one in hysterics. Without a single hesitation, the Sleepwalker lurched towards the banker, and began to sob uncontrollably into Penny's side, like that of a widow who had just lost her husband.

"There, there," Penny said, putting on that strained customer service voice, the voice which she had used together in the coach, the voice that placated grieving relatives. "How were you related, hm?"

"H-He… was my… h-h-hus… band…" the Sleepwalker answered.

"Oh, there now, I'm sorry," Penny replied. Penny carefully extracted herself from the strained embrace. She then wiped her shirt clean of the moldy black tears. "Such, a terribly unfortunate accident. Mrs…"

"M-M-Mag… pie…" the Sleepwalker answered. "My… name… is Mrs… M-Mag… pie…"

The crowd of Sleepwalkers murmured to themselves; gibberish Maxwell couldn't understand. Vanessa, still hiding behind him, blinked with her enormous globe eyes. Some people might have called her monstrous, but she wasn't a Sleepwalker. She was strikingly different.

If somebody could mistake Vanessa for a monster, if he did at first think that Vanessa was a monster, did he also mistake the Sleepwalkers for monsters? It didn't help that he remembered a maid who had worked in his family's manor by the same name. She had been a lackluster housekeeper, always neglecting her duties to sit around and play cards with the other staff but for whatever reason, this Sleepwalker reminded him of her.

"All right," Penny reassured her, putting on that same sleazy smile from back in the coach. "Now, Mrs. Magpie, I don't suppose your husband has any insurance?"

"In… sur… ance…?"

"Yes, you see, it's quite simple. If your husband had insurance in preparation for this disaster, you would have lucked into quite a bit of money. Now I don't suppose he had been paying for any, would he?"

"I... I... I uhm... I..."

"Now, I could direct you to some high-valued insurance brands," Penny continued, still babbling on, and on. "Or, perhaps you would be interested in a package of some kind? I could—"

"I want... I want to speak... with Lady Allison!" the Sleepwalker shrieked.

All at once, the circle of Sleepwalkers shifted, the crowd ambling away, leaving no one but Maxwell, Vanessa, Julia, and Mrs. Magpie. The lightbulb dimmered. He had seen it flicker, and outright shut off but... never dim.

"You've done it now, Top Hat," the brigand said. Penny sneered back, with a look which was to say "I'd like to see you try" though, no words passed her lips.

For a moment, their chamber went silent.

Then, shoes tapped across the stone. With each tap, Vanessa quivered and which each step, Vanessa shook more and more. "Vanessa?" Maxwell whispered. "Vanessa, are you all right?"

She clapped a hand over *his* mouth.

"Mr. Maxwell," she pleaded. "Please, shhh..."

For a second he felt like fighting her on it. For a second, he felt as if this was all silly and childish, and he, a competent adult, should not be scared of sounds in the dark. But Max did as he was told. Whoever, or whatever the voice ended up being... Vanessa knew it was dangerous. And he wouldn't let it harm one gelatinous hair on her head. It was an unspoken promise between the two of them. And Maxwell would not be one of those adults who broke promises.

"Maggy, dearest," a voice asked airily from the dark.

Maxwell recognized the voice — the voice from the bushes. The Sleepwalker, Mrs. Magpie, Maggie, whatever you wanted to call her, turned to face the voice.

"Oh Maggie, come here." The voice from the bushes said sweetly. Like a caring mother. "What's the problem, Maggie dear? You sound so shaken up!"

The Sleepwalker took a fleeting glance back at Julia, who only scowled. Even Maggie herself seemed to be scared of whatever hid in that darkness. Maggie took a hesitant step into the blackness and disappeared. The echo of each one of her footsteps got quieter, and quieter, until finally...

There was a shriek. Maggie's shriek.

Julia sighed and covered her eyes. Penny jumped backwards. Vanessa looked down sullenly, as what sounded like a gruesome spectacle took place in the dark. And Maxwell, he could only look on in horror, squinting his eyes to try and make out something, anything, as the sounds of ripping flesh, tearing innards, and horrific screams, came from the dark.

Soon enough, silence returned to the caverns. Along with something else, rolling from the shadows where something horrible had just taken place, just out of view.

Maggie's bloodied head.

"See, Maggy?" the familiar voice said to a Maggie which was no longer with them. He heard Penny retch, as what remained of Maggie's maiming rolled towards them. Even Julia was quivering. But Vanessa, Vanessa seemed almost… disappointed… in the situation. Like she was used to this. The voice continued speaking, even though nobody was listening, all of them held in a state of morbid curiosity. "Now, you can join your husband. Everything's better now."

Vanessa seized Maxwell's fingers and squeezed them so hard he nearly screamed in pain. But, knowing the circumstances, he held back. He gently pulled her closer.

A narrow woman's hand in a white glove emerged from the darkness. None of them could see the body behind it. Black blood drenched the fabric. The fingers motioned towards them, curling and demanding that they come closer. As they moved, dripping echoed through the cave system. Maxwell pulled Vanessa into him, practically smothering her with his clothes. Vanessa clung onto him even tighter.

"Julia?" the woman said. "A word?"

Julia stepped forward, still shaking. She fumbled with the shotgun, trying to reload, as she took a second step. She brushed past Penny, who stood there, still gob smacked. The whole scene unfolded in slow motion. Julia lifted a foot to take her third step.

"No, Auntie, no! You can't!"

That… "woman…" in the dark was Vanessa's… auntie?

"Vanessa!" Maxwell cried.

But it was too late. Maxwell reached for Vanessa's dress, desperately grabbing at her. She was too slippery.

She rushed in front of Julia. Vanessa planted herself there and used her small fists to smash Julia's thighs. Julia and Maxwell made eye contact. They both seemed perplexed, unsure what to do next. Maxwell nodded. He wondered what the point of such a gesture was, but it had to mean… something… didn't it?

"No…" Vanessa sobbed into Julia's pant leg. "No, no, no, please, Auntie, please don't hurt her. Please, please, you said you wouldn't—"

"Kid," Julia said, getting down on one knee. The brigand patted Vanessa's head, as the girl cried quietly. "Kid, let me go speak with your Auntie Allison. She's my… friend. And friends don't do bad things to each other, yeah?"

"But- But—"

Julia, as usual, didn't respond to the girl. She merely walked off into the dark. And then the hand of "Auntie Allison" as well as the brigand, disappeared.

And so did Vanessa.

Vanessa took off blindly in the other direction, rushing past Maxwell and Penny, tears streaming down her face. Maxwell obviously took after her. And Penny, being, well, Penny, took after Maxwell, considering the light, that imaginary barrier of safety, moved with him.

"Vanessa!" he called to her. "Vanessa, wait!

Maxwell wasn't sure how long he was chasing after her, as he sprinted through chamber after chamber, tunnel after tunnel, every single one looking exactly alike. He wasn't sure how long he screamed Vanessa's name as she ran just a few paces ahead of him. He wasn't sure how long Penny was wheezing his name as she chased after them both. But eventually, there was a light up ahead. Like a crack in the void, in the black… And he watched as Vanessa crawled through it, and instinctually, without thinking, he did the same.

"Vanessa! Vanessa, stop!"

Jagged gypsum crystals scratched at his face. Bits of sharp rock snagged at his clothes. But before long, he could feel his arm make it to the other side of the gap. He squeezed his body through the jagged hole in the cave system, desperately crawling away from all the grisliness, away from the Sleepwalkers, and away from all the horrible, disgusting, mold-riddled things within, only to end up…

Outside.

Chapter Twelve

Inside Out

Maxwell was… outside again.

If you could call it an outside.

"The outside" was really nothing more than a rather large rocky shelf on the edge of the sinkhole a precarious midway between the lake at the bottom and the world at the top. Though the sinkhole went so deep that Max still couldn't see said lake. It was practically like he was still in the caves. Suddenly, the only reassurance came from the brightness of the stars, which, even with the decline of the Corvid Estate, still cast more light than stars anywhere else in the world.

"Vanessa!" he called.

Vanessa slinked and tiptoed along the ledge with an ease Maxwell could not match. Then, towards the very edge of the outcrop, Vanessa sat with her knees up and her head down, sobbing black globby tears into her dress.

"Vanessa, she'll be fine," he explained. Even though in his heart, Maxwell believed that none of them, especially not Julia, would be fine.

No response. Maybe Vanessa knew that as well.

A voice wheezed behind him in the crack between the cavern and the sinkhole. Penny's smoker's lungs had disagreed with her legs moving so fast and were currently professing their complaints *very* loudly, sending her into a coughing fit. She slithered onto the ledge and leaned, hacking into her grimy handkerchief. "Max, could you… Could you please wait a minute? Dammit…"

It was quite a spacious ledge, but still, Maxwell couldn't shake that feeling that one wrong move would send them hurtling all the way back down, ending with a great big splash.

"Max? Maxwell?" Penny said, her voice growing more insistent with each syllable. She tapped him on the shoulder. When he didn't look up, she snapped her fingers. And then, after that still didn't break his attention from Vanessa, she snapped at him instead. "Maxwell!"

"What?" Max cried.

"We have company. Listen."

Penny pointed to the crack. There was a sound coming from it. The sound of footsteps. Footsteps and dripping water. Even Vanessa stopped crying for a few moments, just so she could hear it.

Thump. Drip. Thump. Drip.

"Do you think it's... you know," Penny started, nervousness straightening her soggy and flopping tie. "Allison?"

Maxwell considered it, at first. But the footsteps sounded too heavy. And what was the dripping? Unless...

Shit.

Shit, shit, shit, shit, shit, shit, shit, shit, shit, shit, shit-

Climbing, or perhaps sliding, from the crack came Julia, the large, imposing huntress Maxwell had once thought invincible. She trudged towards them, covered in blood, before she keeled, and faceplanted into the ground.

Vanessa gasped. Penny — self-interested, self-absorbed Penny of all people — sprang into action. The banker grabbed one of Julia's arms, and haltingly attempted to drag her towards the nearest wall. Though despite the banker's best efforts, the brigand refused to move more than a few inches with each tug.

"A little help over here?" Penny called.

"Yes, of course. Sorry, Penny, uhm... Sorry."

Pulling Julia together, they eventually managed to get the brigand's broken body propped against the wall. She was barely conscious. Barely.

"She got me pretty bad this time..." Julia mumbled.

"Pretty bad" was a drastic understatement. There was a hole in Julia's stomach. A gaping, black pit the size of a dinner plate, right through her diaphragm. Entrails were twisted and ripped... but they didn't look like any human entrails he knew from textbooks. They honestly looked more like worms bursting through her chest. Blood dribbled from her mouth and her nose and dripped off of her chin. But it wasn't actually blood. Well, it was blood. But it was completely black save for a few little white flecks, like everything else on this blasted estate. It had already been rotting her from the inside out.

"Let me take a look at it," Maxwell pleaded. Julia glared at him as he spoke. "I'm a doctor. Well—"

"*Was gonna* be a doctor," Penny chimed in.

"Well— well, regardless, I can help," he responded. He didn't know why that comment hurt so much.

The brigand allowed Maxwell closer, near enough to see the stains of red which would never come out of her trench coat. Julia's breathing labored. Nervously, Penny got closer as well, huddling behind him. Vanessa, prompted by nothing but her own curiosity, nervously edged over to Julia, too, staying just out of range of her piercing yellow eyes.

Maxwell should have known what to do in a situation like this. After all, he had spent three years in the Miskatonic medical program, a quite good medical program according to the propaganda posters that covered every inch of that school. But as you may have guessed, he didn't really know the first thing about what to do. He frantically tried to remember anything, anything at all from his tests, quizzes, homework, even the consistently monotonous droning of Mr. Weaver, but nothing. He was drawing a blank. Three years of his life, and he couldn't remember one thing? How was that even possible!

He could do this. He *had* to do this. This is what he had trained for literally his entire academic career, he couldn't… he couldn't ruin it now!

"You heard him," Penny told Vanessa, scooting her back a few steps. "Stand back, kid."

He knelt and calmly removed the brigand's hand from her gaping wound. Allison — Vanessa's Auntie Allison — had done this? Julia seemed almost complacent with the gash, like this was nothing more than another day at the office.

"Penny, please take her coat off," he directed.

"Wait, so I'm a part of this now? Max, I dunno anything about—"

"Do it. Please, Penny, just… Do what I say for a change!"

Penny reluctantly, but hurriedly, removed Julia's overcoat, a little too roughly for a patient. The brigand winced, as Penny finally managed to remove the mud-stained trench coat, like she was doing that one trick with a tablecloth.

"Hang in there. You can get through this," Maxwell said, not sure if he was speaking to Julia or himself. He desperately searched for anything useful from his lessons, still desperately hoped he didn't screw anything up too badly. "Let's have a look…"

"I can get through it. This isn't the first run-in."

He could see why Julia seemed to be used to this sort of thing. Her body was like a patchwork quilt. Scars and stitches adorned her midsection like military medals, front and center and on full display, a few bullets still clearly trapped in her flesh.

With that much blood missing, Maxwell wasn't sure how much longer Julia had left. But the blood wasn't normal. It wasn't red. It was black now, like oil through her veins. He hadn't even noticed it before, but there were little clumps of mold growing on her skin and under it, too. There were these little boils and blotches like black birthmarks. Like lichen growing on a tree.

Maxwell could see it now, in the starlight. Now that he was actually looking at what his hands were doing, he was… These weren't his hands! His hands… They didn't look like this! There was… Mold was growing underneath his skin, too. Why?

Julia's eyes were slowly getting more opaque. But Maxwell forcibly held her eyelids open, and he would continue to. Vanessa had crept closer again, but Julia pushed her away using the arm not currently cradling her leaking organs.

"Don't fall asleep," he pleaded with Julia. He looked at Vanessa. Wait a moment… Maxwell thought of something, though it didn't come from any of his textbooks. "You know what? Let's play a game. Questions and answers. Alright, here we go: Who is Allison? Mind filling me in at all?"

"I'm dying, Doc… not… a kid."

"Right… That isn't really how you're supposed to play. Come on, happy thoughts! Happy thoughts…"

This was not what he had been told to do back at Miskatonic. Now he was just making things up as he went along.

"She's crazy," Julia snarled. Black stuff poured out of her mouth faster as she spoke. She looked over at Vanessa. "And… she must be the kid. Thought I knew you from somewhere. Could kinda tell by the, you know… you've got your dad's eyes."

The girl giggled at Julia's comment but stopped as the brigand coughed out blood. The girl's eyes widened, suddenly understanding the seriousness of the situation.

"But you… promised." she sniffled.

"Penny," He called out over his shoulder. "I need your lighter. Now."

"Max, why the hell would you even want—"

"Just give it!"

"No! No, that's—"

"Penny!" Maxwell said, shrill and stern. He had never taken on a tone like this before. He hadn't even meant to, but he sounded authoritative. Like a proper adult. "Give. It. Here."

Mumbling about a billion profanities under, Penny tossed the lighter at him, like she was throwing a temper tantrum after being forced to give up her toy. Luckily, he caught it. Maxwell then began to root around in his satchel.

He revealed the jacket he had found in the underground lake floating amidst the lightbulbs.

"Hey!" Penny shouted. "What the hell are you doing with that?"

"We need a bandage of some sort," Maxwell explained as he used the jacket to tie an oversized tourniquet over Julia's midsection. "This is the only thing—"

"No. No way. You are not gonna use my custom-tailored, Peacock-brand jacket for tha- "

"Penny, do everyone a favor. Shut up for literally five seconds. Please."

His order worked for about three seconds of the five he had asked for. But he was willing to accept that. After all, he had just gotten away with getting blood and entrails all over a four-thousand-pound jacket. He couldn't just tell Penny not to be angry. But really, what kind of person valued a jacket over somebody else's life?

Maxwell flicked on the lighter. He had to stop the bleeding, and he knew that cauterizing a wound this fatal with a tiny lighter was impossible, and honestly, he didn't know if cauterizing a wound like this would work at all.

"This is going to hurt," Maxwell warned. Her yellow eyes glowed glassier and more distant every second.

"Can't get much worse than this, Doc…"

"Okay, just… happy thoughts, alright? Let's keep playing our game. Do you know anything about why your… well… You've probably noticed that your blood is…"

Julia shifted, creating a ripple in the puddle of black emanating from her entrails. Maxwell now observed the damage in entirety. It was definitely more than a single, damp and barely functioning lighter would fix. But he had to try.

"Doc, don't…" Julia mumbled in exhaustion. Her eyes slowly closed. "Don't worry 'bout me. I'll… I'll come back, just like… Just like all the rest of 'em…"

She wasn't making any sense. Or maybe he just wasn't listening. Maxwell placed the flame of the lighter against the hole. It wouldn't work. But it would *have* to work.

He had once been hoping to cauterize the wound, but now that only seemed like a pleasant memory, given the size and severity of it. And it wasn't like he had anything else to use, not on this barren little speck of land, so far removed from the sane or the simple… He was losing her. What could he do to save her? What could he do? Cauterizing the wound wasn't helping, so what could he- No. Focus. The first rule of this sort of thing was…

To never let someone close their eyes…

Maxwell slapped Julia as hard as he could, his hand contacting her cheek with a brutal sting.

Maxwell had never tried to physically hurt someone. If he had, it was accident. It was what his father had taught him, though Maxwell knew now that his father wasn't exactly the greatest role model.

But did it really count as hurting someone when they were already... well...

Maxwell quivered as he placed his hand in front of him and placed it upon Julia's neck. No pulse. She didn't open her eyes. She would never open her eyes again.

He... He should have expected this. He should have known. There had been nothing he could do, missing his medical supplies and not even really being a proper doctor. He doubted even the best doctors could help someone in that state. So, really, he shouldn't have tried at all. Trying to change the impossible just led to more blood, more sweat, more tears... more disappointment.

But then why was he still feeling so... awful... inside.

"Well that's just..." Penny started. She could have been right behind him, she could have been miles away, Maxwell didn't turn around to face her. For a second it felt as though Penny was about to go off on another saleswoman rant, pitching her dad's insurance but... something different happened. "I'm going to... uh... It's been a long night, yeah? I think I'm gonna get some shut eye. You... uhm... You fine with first watch?"

Maxwell nodded over the body of his friend, though he did not hear anything the banker said. He supposed he could call Julia a friend now. After all, she had given her life to save the three of them. That was something he thought a very, very good friend might do.

"Perfect. Holler if one of those things gets through. See you in the... uh... in the morning. And I'm sorry 'bout all this."

"Mhm." Maxwell responded blankly.

The banker trod away, going off to find a particularly comfortable rock to sleep on. Maxwell wouldn't be able to sleep. He continued to stare at Julia's face. He had failed. But why had he failed? Well, he knew... he knew *why*. Lack of training, lack of materials, lack of focus, lack of proper hygiene... all of those. But *why* hadn't it worked? Even after he had tried and tried so hard, what was any of the trying even good for? Where was the point in trying when things like this could happen, and ruin everything he worked so hard for. What was the point in trying if it made him feel... like this.

Maxwell wasn't sure how much time had passed, as the world began to fade around him, little black ink spots appearing around his vision like leaks in reality. He only noticed it when Julia's face began to get eaten away by the black. He didn't respond. He knew what was happening. It had happened so many times he didn't even find it strange anymore.

"HELLO AGAIN... LITTLE... BIRD..."

Maxwell once again found himself in a void.

Chapter Thirteen

Stargazing

Sadly, Maxwell had grown accustomed to senselessness.

Normalcy, meanwhile, had become some far-off fantasy. Maxwell had found himself once again in the void, the dark place. At least it wouldn't just be him and Kyrious this time. It looked like Vanessa had joined him.

Wait, hold on… Why was Vanessa here?

He could feel the girl nearby, the cold of her hand interlocked with his own, with the smell of kippers and salt hanging in the air. She pulled him out of this place before, like some kind of lifeguard.

"Vanessa?" He asked. "Vanessa? Are you all right?"

"I… I-I think so Mr. Maxwell…"

"*LITTLE… BIRD…*" a familiar voice rang out. "*BACK… AGAIN… SO SOON…?*"

click

Just like before, complete darkness, until that single sound pierced the static, unmoving air when a bulb filled the room with gentle, golden light. Kyrious stood where the darkness had been. The hypnotic swing of the lightbulb cast a very long shadow over its visitors.

"*WHY… IS SHE… HERE… LITTLE… BIRD…?*"

Vanessa squinted and rubbed her eyes. The enormous body of Kyrious leaned, as if to inspect her. She squeaked and shuffled behind Maxwell. He didn't answer Kyrious. He could barely register he was in the void to begin with. Nothing made sense right now. It was all out of whack. Whatever Kyrious had to say… Did any of it matter if they were all going to end up like Julia anyway?

"*ANSWER… ME…*"

"I…" Maxwell started, staring at the ground.

"*…ANSWER…*"

"Why should I when—"

"*ANSWER... NOW...!*" the thing boomed.

The sound hurt. His ears were ringing. The sound was unbearable, like he had been struck with lightning, Kyrious's voice like a voltage surging through his nervous system. Maxwell staggered backwards as Vanessa did the same, whimpering, and clutching her head. She felt it, too. Kyrious didn't care if it was hurting her, did it?

"Vanessa!" Maxwell cried, trying to get through to her through her tinnitus.

"*DO NOT... ACKNOWLEDGE... THE... INTERLOPER...*" Kyrious spoke, as the light from Vanessa's eyes was quickly swallowed by the thing's nothing-filled face, the two of them looking into each other. There was a brief moment of panic as Kyrious said its next words. Even if Vanessa was still standing so close behind him, he couldn't protect her from Kyrious no matter how hard he tried. He couldn't protect her. Shit. "*SHE IS... NOT PART... OF THE... EXPERIMENT...*"

"B-B-But- B-But I'm..." Vanessa started. Her face was a patchwork of disappointment and devastation. She looked so upset that she couldn't even cry.

Kyrious raised its hand, and placed a long, gnarled finger over where Maxwell supposed its lips would be, if it had them.

"*SILENCE... VANESSA... I AM... WORKING...*"

How... how *dare* it.

"Well pardon me," Maxwell started, staring directly into Kyrious's non-face. "I can't answer if I don't understand the question. What was it again? 'Why is she here?' Rephrase it."

The thing was silent for a few moments. Maxwell couldn't tell what it was thinking. For a second, he had a plummeting feeling in his gut, as it quietly computed its answer in contemplation.

"*HOW... CAN YOU... NOT... HATE... THEM...?*"

"Hate... who?" Max asked it. It's answer was so... random. It wasn't really an answer either. And why did it care anyway? Whoever this 'them' was.

"*ALL... OF... THEM...*" it continued. It took a shuffling step forward. A step which seemed to rock the very fabric of the void itself, each movement swinging the lightbulb and shaking the shadows. "*THE BANKER... THE BRIGAND... EVEN... HER...*"

Kyrious pointed down at Vanessa. She gazed up at its gnarled, putrid finger.

Did he... hate them? He hated Penny for sure. Penny was just about everything you could hate, all wrapped up into one conveniently smoke-scented package. She had been rude on the coach, tried to sell him out not once but twice, and had been horribly reckless this entire excursion. And Julia, well, he hated her less but there was still an inkling of dislike, distrust, disillusion... What was her relationship was Vanessa's aunt? Why hadn't she told him? And why had she died! Why had she died before he even got to have a proper conversation, it was-

"*SO WHY... DID YOU... TRY... TO SAVE... HER...? IF... YOU HATE HER... SO... MUCH...?*" it inquired. It could read his thoughts. He had forgotten for a brief moment, but he knew it was still back there, doing its usual routine, slithering around the wrinkles in his brain. "*THERE WAS... NO CHANCE... AND YET... YOU STILL... TRIED...?*"

"Well... I— I don't really know it's just not— not..."

"*NOT... PROPER...?*" Kyrious asked, tilting it's head as it regurgitated his thoughts.

"Yes. Yes, it's... It's proper to try."

Something fizzled above his head. The swinging lightbulb began to flicker and buzz. The bulb in his pocket did the same, as it suddenly got very hot. Sparks jumped from his pocket, singeing his flesh as if they were little biting fireflies.

"*...WHY...?*"

The creature's voice, normally a conglomerate of booming whispers, seemed uncannily in unison. It spoke with one voice. A voice dripping with malice, discontent... and pure, unadulterated, hatred. He had never heard a voice like that before. A voice that so masterfully portrayed nothing but hate. It *hated* him. Kyrious *hated* him. And he had no idea as to why.

"*NOT... PROPER...?*" it repeated. Everything was flickering, the lightbulb, the void, Maxwell's vision, his hearing, his sense of smell. On and off, on and off. "*AM I... NOT... PROPER... ENOUGH...? IS THAT... IT...!*"

"Excuse me?" Maxwell asked it through the flickers. "I'm confused, what do you mean you're not—"

"*NOT... PROPER... NOT... PROPER...!*" it repeated. "*AND YOU... YOU ARE... PROPER... ENOUGH... IS... THAT... IT...?*"

"No, I just--

"*WHY...! WHY... ARE YOU... SO... PROPER...?*" it snarled. The lights completely cut out for a moment. "*WHEN I... AM SO... MUCH... BETTER... THAN YOU...*"

One moment, Kyrious was there, the next it was gone. In a flicker, it disappeared into the black, leaving only the echoing reverberations of its voice behind He could still smell it: the sulphur, the dust... He could... *feel it...* gliding around in the pitch-black. It was circling them. And at the same time, it was simply not there.

"WHY... DID YOU... TRY... TO SAVE... HER...?" it asked one more time. *"WHY... REALLY...?"*

"I don't... I don't really know."

"THEN... THE EXPERIMENT... HAS BEEN... A FAILURE..." it began, solemnly. Then, that solemnness faded away. *"A FAILURE...! A FAILURE...! A... FAILURE...!"*

Maxwell genuinely believed he was going to pass out. Kyrious's voice was shredding his skull from the inside out. His brain felt like it was going to explode and splatter out of his ears. He could barely move. And neither could Vanessa, clutching her head, shaking it wildly.

"JUST... ANOTHER... FAILURE... LIKE... ME...!"

"Stop it!" Maxwell screamed back. He screamed at Kyrious louder than he ever had at anyone. "Stop it! You're hurting her!"

And Kyrious... surprisingly... listened.

There was this awkward silence between everyone. Even Vanessa. Nobody wanted to speak. The light stopped flickering and returned to a calmer, more steady state. Kyrious was still nowhere to be found, and there was what felt like... guilt... in the air. Maxwell wasn't sure how he could tell, but Kyrious was... ashamed.

A long, gnarled, yellow-sleeved hand slipped from the darkness, towards Vanessa, in a frivolous attempt at an apology. She shrunk from it. She slid towards Maxwell, and he encouraged her staying as far away from the thing as possible.

"I'M... SORRY... I... I DIDN'T... MEAN TO... I..."

"Yes, you did..." Vanessa accused. "You do this all the time..."

Silence returned as the hand slithered into the infinite blackness which surrounded them on all sides.

"VANESSA... I'M... SO... SORRY..." the thing said in a quiet voice. *"WOULD YOU... LIKE HER... BACK...?"*

"Back?" he asked the thing. He turned behind to Vanessa and in his bewilderment, randomly shook her. "Vanessa, what's it talking about!"

It was in that moment however, that Maxwell realized who Kyrious was talking about. There was only one person it could be after all. If Kyrious was indeed talking about bringing someone back to life, that was. It wasn't possible, it couldn't be possible, could it?

The girl merely nodded.

"NO... MATTER.... HOW MANY... CHANCES... THEY ARE... GIFT-ED..." Kyrious responded, from somewhere in the black. *"THEY... WILL NOT... CHANGE... YOU KNOW..."*

Maxwell wanted to say something profound to challenge what Kyrious was saying. But someone else got to it first.

"People change all the time" Vanessa said confidently.

"*NOT... ME...*"

click

It was all gone. With a mere flick of some light switch out in the dark, it was all gone.

Maxwell stood on the ledge, about to fall off. The dead body of the brigand, and the sleeping body of the banker, right where they had been left.

And Vanessa... still right beside him.

Maxwell stared at the exposed moon with its veil of clouds and mist ripped away. The sky revealed many sparkling stars. You couldn't see stars like that in the city. You couldn't see stars like that at Miskatonic either. He didn't remember the last time he had seen the stars.

"Aren't they pretty?" Vanessa asked. "The stars, I mean.... aren't they just the prettiest?"

"They're very pretty, Vanessa," Maxwell replied.

In his mind, Maxwell remained dwelling in that dark place not the void from which he had just escaped but the place you hid when something bad happened.

"Auntie Allison always says that the stars have pictures inside them. Isn't that funny? She says there's a picture of a bear... and a picture of a lion... and—"

"They're... They're called constellations, Vanessa. They are called constellations."

"Right! They are called const...constee...constella—"

"Constellations. Just... Just forget I said anything, actually."

"But... I don't think the stars make very nice pictures, Mr. Maxwell... Do you?" Vanessa asked.

For once, he did not have an answer.

"Well, I... I guess not."

He had to admit that he had never really been able to see many constellations himself. Maxwell had never had much interest in the non-living. He should have probably seen many constellations, it couldn't have been that hard, it was just connecting the dots. But to him, the stars were just stars. Simple as that.

"I don't like the const-ee-lations very much either," Vanessa said, staring up at the sky again. "That's why I made my own pictures."

Vanessa reached for his satchel. After rummaging for a few moments, she materialized a piece of paper. She had retrieved her drawing, the one he had picked up in the woods.

"I made my own pictures, Mr. Maxwell. To change the things I don't like."

"Good idea, Vanessa," he said absent-mindedly.

"So why don't we change things that you don't like as well, if you'd … if you'd like to, that is…"

It did make sense. In the sort of nonsensical way a child's mind would think.

"Vanessa, it's a lot harder than it looks. Changing things."

"Well… There's nothing you can really do about it except try, is there Mr. Maxwell?"

Maxwell smiled.

"No," he said, laughing to himself. "No, I guess there really isn't, is there?"

Maxwell couldn't remember how long they both sat there, staring up at the sky. But it must have been a long time. Because by the time they finished, Vanessa was asleep, and he was quite drowsy himself. But… he had enjoyed it. Imagine that. That there were still things to enjoy in this hell of an estate.

Maxwell enjoyed their time stargazing.

And those were his last thoughts before he dozed off and went to sleep as well.

Chapter Fourteen

A Sweet for the Sweet

"Max… hey, Max." He heard Penny cough. "Maxwell! Goddammit… Kid, wake him up somehow."

"Mr. Maxwell! Mr. Maxwell, wake up!"

Something hard poked Maxwell. When he opened his eyes, he realized it was a stick. Vanessa was prodding him with a stick.

Maxwell was usually quite a light sleeper. After all, there wasn't much to go back to considering he didn't dream, so he really didn't desire any more sleep than he needed. If anything, it had always allowed him to be more productive. But he couldn't help but feel the tiniest twinge of sadness when he was finally woken up out of whatever dreamless coma he had fallen into this time.

"Mr. Maxwell?" Vanessa asked him, continuing to poke him with the stick even after his eyes had clearly opened, dislodging his glasses a little more with each time she did so. "Mr. Maxwell, the stinky ladies said to make sure you were still alive."

"Yes, I know Vanessa."

"Can I stop now then…?"

"Yes, yes you—Wait, who did you say asked you to do this?"

"You see," the banker began, "that's actually what we're trying to explain here. She's uh…"

Maxwell quickly got himself up off of the floor and adjusted the glasses which Vanessa had dislodged from his face. Without them, he thought he may have been seeing things. He looked over to where Julia's body had been leaning against the cave. It was no longer leaning. In fact, it was sitting up. She was sitting up and breathing.

"Alive," he finished.

"Yeah," Penny said. "But she was dead before. This isn't right."

Julia was… snoring. And she was shaking like a dog as she slept, her knees pulled in close, her head down. Maxwell crept over towards her, as Vanessa and Penny crept backwards. She flinched in her sleep a little as he approached and mumbled something under her breath.

"Julia…?"

"Hmm?" she murmured groggily. She rubbed her eyes, her nest of curly black hair still preventing him from seeing her face properly. Slowly, she rose up to full height. "Oh… Morning, Doc. How'd you manage to fix me up?"

"I… didn't. It wasn't me."

Maxwell watched Julia's face slowly come to the same realization that he just had. But… it wasn't exactly the face he knew anymore. Her left eye was gone. A thin layer of skin had grown over it, and possibly removed it entirely. Her right eye had had the opposite done to it, the socket growing and the eyeball itself growing loose. Her skin was pulled tight in some places, sagging in others, like she had been badly taxidermized.

Julia was a Sleepwalker.

Julia touched her own warped face, caressing the smooth space where her left eye used to be. It wasn't terrible or anything. Now she just looked like a war veteran more than she already had. If anything, it was an improvement over having her guts spilled out everywhere over the floor.

Nobody said anything. Nobody wanted to say anything. He wasn't even sure exactly how it happened; he knew it was Kyrious's doing but… What was being a Sleepwalker… like? Was she going to turn into just another mumbling, shambling… thing? Julia sighed.

"It was… bound to happen eventually, doc. Don't feel so bad 'bout it."

That was… it?

Had she been… expecting this? Had she already accepted it? Or was being a Sleepwalker not so bad? Was she even turning into a Sleepwalker or was this something entirely different?

"It's not that strange. It happened to everyone else. It was gonna happen to me, too," Julia said, trying to calm the faintly mortified expression on both his and Penny's faces. "'Sides, it's not like you're free from all the weirdness either. Look."

She pointed at him. The light bulb glowed faintly yellow from his breast pocket. He brought it out, and they all stared, mesmerized, by the luminous little mystery.

"Why's it do that?" Penny asked.

"To tell you the truth," he responded, plainly, "I have no bloody idea."

"Come on, Max," the banker retorted, snatching the lightbulb out of his hands. Immediately, it stopped glowing. "Were you chosen by the lightbulb fairies or…"

Julia left her post by the door, and so Penny timidly gave the lightbulb to her (probably still intimidated after that potential blunt-force frontal lobotomy). When, like with Penny, the lightbulb remained dormant, Julia passed the bulb to Max again. The bulb magically resumed its fervor.

"Some party trick," Julia stated.

"The word 'trick' implies I know what I'm doing," Maxwell said, tilting the lightbulb and admiring the filament within, "and I, for all intents and purposes, do not."

Maxwell instinctively handed the lightbulb to Vanessa. Nothing happened. The light for some reason stayed on.

"Wouldja look at that," Penny said, patting Vanessa on her head. Vanessa plopped onto the ground, her eyes becoming their own little lights as she stared deeply into the bulb. She shivered. While her tattered white dress did not provide enough warmth for the autumn weather of the Corvid Estate, the light gave her a joy that seemed to smother her physical discomfort. "Looks like you're special, too, kid."

Julia had sat beside Vanessa. At first the child leaned away, but then Julia draped her coat over Vanessa's shoulders.

"Kid was cold," Julia mumbled.

"Thank you, Ms. Julia…" Vanessa said softly from somewhere within the folds of muddied clothing.

"Uhm… uh, well my name's not…" Julia started. But before she could finish, she just shook her head, as she watched Vanessa's eyes droop, the girl toying with the lightbulb. "Don't mention it, kid."

"Come to think of it, what were you doing here Julia? If you don't mind me asking," Maxwell questioned. It felt like a simple response, she was a highway-woman after all, she probably just camped out here and waited for someone with too much money and even more time (like himself) to come wandering in. But after everything… There had to be more, didn't there?

"Same old, same old," Julia responded, unhelpfully. "I was trying to make a living, and your dad had money—"

"Please tell me that you were gonna rob his dad," Penny exclaimed.

"No," Julia said simply. "I was hired as security. S'posed to keep people out, keep some other stuff in. I'm s'posed to still be doing it, y'know, for Allie."

"Why would my dad need security?" Max asked. "And why are you working for… 'Allie?' My dad's the one who hired you, right?"

"He was a massive paranoid prick," Julia answered. Maxwell agreed, so the statement wasn't exactly offensive. "And have you fucking seen this place? Whatever your dad was doing, it wasn't pretty. I mean I had to deliver… You know what, fuck this. Never mind."

"No, go on." Penny said, an uneven smile slowly beginning to form on her face like a crack in a wall. "I am actually getting quite invested now. You can't stop there."

"Mind telling us something about yourself before you go prying about me?" the brigand retorted. Maybe she hadn't noticed yet, but Vanessa had actually slumped up against her shoulder, asleep. Looks like it was still past her bedtime. "How'd you end up here, you punter?"

"She's got a point there, too, Penny," he added. He wasn't exactly great at talking. But he was a pretty good listener. And if he was going to be here for the rest of his life, given they couldn't get out… He might as well learn some stuff about the people he was trapped with. It wasn't like Kyrious had turned out to be very good in conversation anyway.

"Whatta you wanna know?" Penny said her cigarette was now almost out. She lazily tipped the brim of her hat down over her face until you couldn't see her eyes beneath it. "I was only on this job because my brother couldn't do it. I'm here the same as Max. Old man Corvid kicked the bucket, and now us Cranes are cleanin' up the spill, is all. We're the janitors."

"Your dad wouldn't hire you, would he?" Julia needled her. Penny immediately shot towards her.

As Penny crossed the space between them, the light dimmed. Maxwell looked to Vanessa. She had fallen asleep.

"Of course he did! Why would I be stuck with you lot unless I had to be?"

"I mean," Julia continued, "You were pretending to be one of your brothers, and that suit ain't your size."

"Sure, okay. So he hired my brothers, not me," Penny said, disgruntled, and lighting another cigarette in a huff. "But why's that matter? I'm still stuck here now, so who gives a crap."

"Nobody." Julia said calmly.

"Probably won't even notice I left…"

"That all makes sense," Maxwell said, "but where did *she* come from?"

They turned their attention to the dozing Vanessa, wrapped in a cocoon made of an old grimy overcoat. Penny shrugged. But Julia… She averted eye contact. There was this sort of… distant closeness between the girl and the brigand.

"You don't want to find out," Julia said. Seriousness washed over her expression. "Trust me. That place is not good for anyone."

"Can't be any worse than this." Max retorted.

"Trust me. Nobody can go into that house."

"She'll die out here," he tried to reason. "We all probably will. You've survived, what... *years* in this place? How'd you do it then?"

"I had help. From Allie, I mean."

"Perfect. Then we'll deliver Vanessa to her Aunt Allis—"

"No!"

Vanessa had suddenly jolted awake. The light bulb had completely darkened, and in her immediacy, Vanessa had dropped it. Despite the lack of light, Maxwell could see the pallor and panic on her face.

"I-I'm... I'm sorry..." she whimpered, before burying her face in the folds of the overcoat, using its terribly grimy leather to wipe her bleary eyes. "I... I didn't mean to scare you all I... It's just... I don't... Nevermind..."

"The kid's right," Penny said, piping up from her corner — taking the cigarette out of her mouth to speak and exhaling the foul vapors she had been breathing in all this time. "It isn't like we can just walk her back to her grandma or whatever... You saw those things. Hell, you saw what whatever this 'auntie' thing is did to Jules over there."

"Vanessa, cover your ears," Maxwell instructed.

Vanessa peered at him, confused, but he gave her a reassuring smile. She placed her webbed little hands over her fishy ears.

"She can't just keep wasting away out here," Maxwell said.

"It isn't that simple, Corvid," Julia said. "S'all easier said than done, is all. Allie isn't the kind of person you wanna mess with... Just trust me, you just... you don't."

"Yeah," Penny chimed in, staring at the glow of her cigarette as if to avert her eyes from his own. Or maybe to avoid her eyes from Vanessa's, who was still looking quizzically at her surroundings. "Unless you feel like dying faster."

"Well, the way I see it," Max began to say. "What the hell else are we really going to do, eh? There's nothing we can really do — except try, right?"

"No," Penny said. "No, no, absolutely not. That is positively the worst logic I have ever heard, ever."

"Fuck it, Corvid. Why not?" Julia remarked.

"R-really?" Maxwell replied. asked, maybe even a little shocked himself. "I-I mean, I wasn't...I didn't mean right now, I meant maybe in the morn—"

"Yeah, we can all just sleep on it and realize how stupid of an idea this all is." Penny also remarked. However, hers wasn't nearly as remarkable as Julia's.

"What's happening?" Vanessa asked, looking around, her face confused, but still smiling. "Mr. Maxwell, what's Ms. Penny talking about?"

"We're going to take you to see your auntie, Vanessa," he replied. "Isn't that exciting?"

Maxwell watched as the gears in Vanessa's head began to turn. He watched as she processed the information, and played it over in her head, letting it echo around and ricochet. And he watched as her smile began to fade.

"W-what…?"

"No, no! Vanessa, I'm sure it's all going to be fi—"

"No! No, Mr. Maxwell! You… No… You, you can't!" the girl cried; her face more wounded than any scar her auntie had given Julia. "Mr. Maxwell, you can't! She… She'll be a-angry, and, and she… She'll yell at me, and she won't… She won't let me talk to you and… and—"

"Kid," Julia said, in a kind of soft voice that he hadn't been sure Julia was able to do and one which definitely no longer suited her face. "Do you like sweets?"

Vanessa looked at Julia's newly Sleepwalker-like face. Julia wasn't talking like a teacher. She was talking like the two of them were equals.

"A-Auntie says that… that I-I c-c-can't h-have s-sweets…"

"Well, your auntie won't have to know that, will she?" Julia said, stroking the girl's head, as the two embraced. "And tell you what, I know this amazing sweets shop back in the city. It has all different kinds, toffees, chocolates, you name it. Sounds good, doesn't it?"

"Yes…" the girl reluctantly admitted.

"I know it does," Julia said, releasing the girl from their embrace and booping Vanessa on the nose. The girl giggled for a brief moment. "How about we go see your auntie? And after that, in the morning, we can go to that sweets shop, eh? How's that for a deal?"

Vanessa's smile suddenly ignited again, and it spread through her body like pins and needles, her eyes getting brighter, all of the anger and sadness she had been experiencing before suddenly just burning away.

Julia held out her hand. And after a moment of rumination, Vanessa shook it.

"Do you… promise… we can go to the sweets shop?" Vanessa asked her.

"Promise, sweetheart."

Almost immediately after the deal was made, Julia stood up.

"All right, you lot," Julia said, stretching, as she made her way towards the crack in the wall. "Let's get a move on. Don't want to keep the lady waiting, do we?"

"Fucking ridiculous," Penny said under her breath. She pushed past Maxwell as if claiming a valuable spot in line, closest Julia. She briskly marched towards the crack, her shoulders hunched. "I'm not buying the kid everything in that store. Jules—"

"Ladies first," Julia said, gesturing. "And yes, you are."

"Fuck you."

Penny disappeared into the cavern.

Maxwell took Vanessa's hand and walked her to Julia. Vanessa continued, and made it halfway into the gap, before turning around, and realizing that Maxwell wasn't with her.

"Go ahead, Vanessa," he encouraged her. "I'll be right behind you, I promise."

Vanessa went. Only he and Julia remained.

"Something you want, Corvid?"

"How did you do that?" he asked her. "With Vanessa. How did you calm her down so well?"

"We're all just kids who've grown up, Corvid. That's all we are."

Before he could respond, Julia disappeared. And so, as he had promised Vanessa, Maxwell followed.

Maxwell Corvid took his third, penultimate step into madness.

Chapter Fifteen

Upside-Down

Maxwell had stepped back into madness, but at least the cave was so dark that he didn't have to look directly at it. That being said: the cave was very dark.

That much was obvious. Without his lightbulb, the thing would have been entirely unnavigable, and it still was difficult now. He had asked Penny, and then Julia just to confirm, but the place seemed to almost… shift. These weren't the same walls which he had once walked through, chambers were rearranged and warped since he had last seen them, the same drawings, most likely ones done by Vanessa, were seen again and again, plastered over multiple ceilings, multiple floors. Julia had been telling the truth when she had said the estate didn't want them to leave. But apparently, it didn't want them to move forward very much either. Though, even then, he couldn't be sure sometimes, it all looked the same. It was just stone, after all.

"Anybody else hear that?" Penny asked, as she huddled towards the back of the group. Julia led the way, and Vanessa fluctuated between every slot, drifting as something or another caught her attention. Most of the time, he himself somewhere in the middle. The banker scratched the back of her neck. "Because y'know, I heard it. I heard it real loud and clear."

They had walked for a long time. Penny repeated something like that every few minutes. Every drip of water, every echo of a rock hitting the floor and made Penny jump. Each time, Julia offered the same distinctly discouraging encouragement.

"It's nothing. Keep moving."

Maxwell hadn't said much on the matter, because Maxwell wasn't exactly the type of person who said things. That was more Penny's field. And he had come to realize that on the Corvid Estate, time didn't matter. The night had dragged on far, far longer than it should have. Maxwell assumed that with all the ways the estate had already broken the laws of logic, life, space, and everything else that made the universe make sense; it's take on time wasn't really that surprising.

"Kid, are we going the right way?" Julia asked. "We've been walking a while."

"Hm? Oh… uhm… Yes, Mrs. Julia, I think so…"

"Are you sure that wasn't something?" Penny asked again. Despite the chill in the caves, her brow was sweating, and she dabbed it with that overworked handkerchief. "Like, really truly sure?"

"There isn't anything back there."

"I swear to god I saw something back there…"

Maxwell held the lightbulb in his right hand, while his left hand firmly clasped Vanessa's. The bulb fizzled even brighter, with so much light that Vanessa gasped, and Penny offered another panicked jump. The group froze, except for Julia, their line leader. The brigand walked into the dark until she realized she had left her source of light behind. She returned to the others, agitated.

Maxwell thought he saw something. He noticed something twisted and warped moving beside them in the cave. But now it had vanished.

"What is it?" Julia asked.

Vanessa hurried to her, now hiding within Julia's shadow. The lightbulb warningly flickered.

"Nothing," Maxwell replied. "Just… thought I saw something."

"See!" Penny exclaimed, a rush of vindication overpowering her. "I told you there was somethin' back there!"

"Come out," Julia instructed "We know you're there. Come out."

Something reared its ugly head from the dark, pushing its gray body into the unstable light so they could all see it. It crawled on all fours at first, but then, it stood up, and towered over all of them with its long, slender frame, clawed arms falling limply to it's knees. As he and, debatably Penny had suspected, there was a Sleepwalker.

Correction, there were multiple Sleepwalkers. There were actually quite a few. As Maxwell looked around, they seemed to be emerging from every crack and crevice, from behind every stalagmite and around tight corners. Whenever he looked away, two more would appear, silently watching. Maxwell at first stood tense, as still as he could so that maybe they wouldn't notice him. That was silly of him, because they most certainly had noticed him… but they didn't exactly seem hostile. Undoubtedly creepy, but… not hostile. Just… observing.

"Lady… Va… ness… a…" one said. It pointed to her with a long, spindly, webbed finger. "Your… friends…? New… friends…?"

Vanessa didn't answer, but Julia did.

"All right, move along," Julia said, taking Vanessa's hand and beginning to walk forward, past the still-gathering crowd of Sleepwalkers. "We're just passing through here."

"Draw... me...?"

Julia wrinkled her nose and turned to Vanessa. The brigand whispered to the girl, and Vanessa nodded. Vanessa stepped forward, towards the unsightly things standing in the edges of the light. She went even closer to the line where the light ended, the line where the dark began. The Sleepwalkers gathered on the edge.

"Sorry, everyone. Not today," Vanessa announced.

A group sigh traveled through the Sleepwalkers, at least five of them that Maxwell could distinguish with what appeared as more gathering. Julia glowered at them.

"Kid, come on. Let's go," the brigand ordered. She took Vanessa's hand, causing about ten Sleepwalkers which had gathered like flies around her to scramble backwards, scattering like roaches.

"Wait, no. Hold on," Penny requested. Julia responded not with words but with a quizzical and disgruntled glance. Julia approached the gathering mass of Sleepwalkers. Like vampires faced with a cross, they pushed back into the darkness. But the more Maxwell studied them, the more he thought they were children. "You guys have been down here a while, right? Yeah?"

"Yes..." one said.

The rest nodded, a lazy murmur of "yes" going through the group. Maxwell's assumptions seemed correct– they were just a bunch of kids. Or to be more specific... Maxwell realized all of these Sleepwalkers resembled Vanessa.

"Great!" Penny said in her customer-service voice, which hid her fear and the fact that she was clearly talking out of her ass. "So can you lead us to Aunt All—"

"Don't mention her," Julia interrupted.

Penny frowned. Then, she forced that massive grin onto her face and turned to the gang. She tugged at her collar, which made the Sleepwalkers tilt their heads in collective curiosity, all at once.

"Oh, right then," Penny continued. "Thanks Jules, appreciate the heads up. We're looking for—"

"The big house, Ms. Penny."

"Yeah! The big house. Have any of you seen a big house anywhere around?"

Murmuring sounded from the darkness. Some Sleepwalkers crawled into the light but retreated once they got close to Julia. Some pointed straight ahead. Another Sleepwalked tapped Maxwell's shoulder, startling him. It mumbled an apology out in its strange, gurgly voice.

"This way..." the Sleepwalker told him, giving what looked like a wave.

"Thanks," Max replied.

The Sleepwalker beckoned him closer, and then he disappeared somewhere into the dark. The weak wattage from the lightbulb couldn't reach that far. Maxwell looked at Julia, and she gave him a nod of approval.

Some of the Sleepwalkers had managed to slip past her, and were currently ogling at Vanessa and the banker, one of which was much happier with the attention than the other. Maxwell was... well quite frankly, he was amazed. The Sleepwalkers, who he had supposed at one point were just... well, just monsters, given their appearance, may have been more polite, more civilized, and more willing to help than any of his peers at Miskatonic, let alone anybody in the city. And as they walked along the corridor, which began to open up into this huge subterranean chamber, this fact only got more and more relevant.

"Lady... Vanessa... would you... like some...?"

"Lady Vanessa... who are... your new... friends...?"

"Lady... Vanessa... you are... home?"

It was an entire city. Maxwell walked past tents made from torn white fabric, and Sleepwalkers wearing clothes made out of old tents. The light from the lightbulb washed over little patches of green growing over the moldering stone walls, moss which the Sleepwalkers must have been eating to survive. Dish-shaped rocks were placed under stalactites, as water dripped down into them.

Julia ignored the sights. But the Sleepwalkers were also ignoring her. They must have thought that she was one of them. That's why they weren't attacking!

"Vanessa," Maxwell asked her. "Are they... Well, do you live here? While... while you were missing from your auntie, I mean. They seem to like you a lot."

"Yes..." she mumbled, as she halfheartedly waved to one of the Sleepwalkers furtively skulking by. "They... they like me... They like me because Auntie tells them to..."

"Why would your auntie tell them to like you?" Max asked. "Everyone likes you just fine, don't they?"

"Not my Auntie..."

"Vanessa...?" a Sleepwalker cut in, tapping her on the shoulder. Maxwell could just barely see an eyeless face staring out at him from the dark. "Would... your... friends... like to... join... us... tonight...? In... prayer...?"

"Prayer?" Maxwell asked. But before Vanessa could respond, her particular Sleepwalker friend had vanished into a crowd of the things. They pushed and shoved past him, every single Sleepwalker dropping whatever it was they were doing to join the horde. There were so many that he and Vanessa were forced to follow the will of the crowd, integrating into the sea of Sleepwalkers and walking with them to their destination. "Vanessa, what are they doing?"

A murmur filled the chamber. An incoherent jumble of voices, all so different, and yet all so unified. It sounded like… Well, it sounded like the voices which he had heard in the dark place, the voices he had heard coming from Kyrious. It sounded almost exactly alike, only calmer. All the Sleepwalkers were simultaneously gathering near a particular wall of the grotto. And they were all beginning to kneel, heads hung low, as each and every Sleepwalker began to emit a low hum. A low, electrical, lightbulb-like hum.

"What the hell…? he said to himself, and to Vanessa beside him.

"Shut up," Julia told him. "Leave 'em. They get upset if you interrupt 'em."

On the wall of the cave, there was a drawing. A mural, in fact. Maxwell moved towards it, but he almost tripped over one of the Sleepwalker's bodies. They had bent in what looked like prayer, prostrating themselves before the art. The mural might have depicted some kind of God. It showed two figures in a cloud of black scribbling.

One, a more feminine shape with her hand outstretched.

And the other, the other shape he knew. Large, imposing, standing straight, in a long, flowing coat.

The second figure was drawn in yellow paint.

Vanessa averted her eyes from the mural. Maxwell looked to it again. To the left, away from the other two, a smaller figure was drawn outside of the black cloud. The drawing was tiny, and crude, and resembled Vanessa's own drawings. It was… well, he didn't want to make assumptions, but it was… or may have been… her.

"Oh… Lady Allison…" one of the Sleepwalkers said. The murmuring ceased as it spoke.

"Oh… Lady Allison…" the rest repeated in total synchronicity.

Maxwell, unsure of his own motivation, took a step closer. And then another. And another.

"Max, what are you doing?" Penny chastised from the sidelines.

"Mr. Maxwell," Vanessa whispered. Maxwell was nose-to-nose against the mural's wall. The Sleepwalkers, amidst their ritual, did not notice. He placed his palm against the painting. The cold wall of the cave was contrasted by an unnatural warmth of the lightbulb's light, as he squinted his eyes at the mural, and placed his fingers upon one line and traced it. It stopped, and resumed, and as Maxwell followed the shapes, he realized — what he had perceived as mindless doodles were actually… letters. They were names. And some names… he recognized.

"Felix… Finch," he read aloud.

"Yes… Lady… Allison…?" a Sleepwalker called.

He read aloud another name, one he recognized from his childhood, one of his father's friends who came to parties all the time.

"Ian Woodcock," Maxwell announced.

"Lady… Allison…?" a voice replied. "Lady… Allison… is… that… you…?"

"Danica Dunlin."

"Present…"

"Leondre Pesquet." Maxwell continued to read.

"Allison…? Are… you… there…?"

Maxwell pulled away from the wall and scanned the crowd praying at his feet. These were people he had known. The Sleepwalkers were people his father had known, housekeepers and aristocrats. This was where they had been the whole time, everyone on the estate, everyone reduced to… this. Just a mass of mindless drones, finishing their prayer, and pottering onto whatever else they had been doing before he had even the slightest chance to ask a question.

"I know these people," Maxwell said, half to himself, half to anybody who could hear.

"About time," Penny said snarkily. "This is your property after all, ain't it?"

"This… way…" a Sleepwalker said from up ahead, already scampering off to the closest corridor, formed out of the stone. "This… way… everyone…"

"What was that?" He asked Julia, and considering she was so close, Vanessa as well.

"I thought we went over this Corvid," Julia mumbled. "They're people. All of 'em. Or, well… They're not people anymore. They changed."

"No, no, not that," Maxwell said, although he felt as though he did need the reminder. "I… gathered. I was more so talking about the prayer."

"They were praying for us, Corvid." Julia said, as the group turned the corner. "After all… Nobody ever goes to see Allie and comes out."

"We're… here…" the Sleepwalker at the head of the line said. "This… is… as far… as we… can… take… you… Take… care…"

The Sleepwalkers parted, revealing a downward staircase chiseled out of the rock foundation of the caves…. At the bottom, Maxwell squinted. The oppressive darkness he was so accustomed was broken by a firefly-like flurry of lights. And those lights illuminated a rather familiar shape.

Well, familiar to him, at least.

Two elegant towers, gazing imperiously from their perches, both now half-collapsing and broken down into disarray. The roof of the manor was ruined, a massive hole in the ceiling's center, the shingles sliding right in or dangling haphazardly above an expansive leak. The wooden walls were rotting, and what little plants were left now lay dead or deliquescing, covered by a black mucus, just like everything else. The smell of mold and mildew suddenly hung in the air, and even if it was a nasty smell… it was a smell he recognized. A smell he had memories of, both good and bad.

Maxwell didn't know whether to smile or grimace.

He was home at last.

Chapter Sixteen

Home, Sweet Home

The Corvid family manor had never been in the best shape. Though you could say that in reference to the entire Corvid estate in general. The cost of upkeep was much too high, especially considering how much money Maxwell's father had borrowed, the cost of the effort to maintain it was a much more likely culprit as to why the entire house had fallen into such disrepair over the span of its lifetime. To Maxwell's surprise however, the manor had survived its fall into the depths pretty well… even if where it had landed made no sense geographically.

The walls had crumbled, and yes, the manor had somehow fallen into a cavern with an enclosed ceiling, but despite the logical inconsistencies, it was surprisingly still in good shape. And the vibrant lighting showed that its electricity had not suffered.

Maxwell knew that the old family house had turned from a place of luxurious decadence to one of decrepitude and decay over the years. The caretakers hardly knew where to start. And in his older years, his father's unnamed personal experiments had drained the family fortune, and with the lack of pay, there came a terrible illness spreading amongst the staff, one that caused extensive lethargy and rancorously rude behaviors. And since the house's degradation had started long before its fall down here… not much had changed. Maxwell's family manor felt as if it had been almost untouched by the insanity of the estate around it. Or maybe, it was the cause.

The house was the thing that broke the silence between all of them, as it creaked, and groaned in the distance. Vanessa backed away. He gave her a look of encouragement, but that didn't seem to work at all. Anything repeated enough times would lose its effectiveness.

"Mr. Maxwell…" Vanessa whimpered. "I-I don't want to go anymore… Can we go back…? Please?"

Before he could respond, Julia responded for him.

"Kid," Julia said. "Don't worry about it. Think of the sweets shop, yeah? All those sweets, just waiting. Just waiting for top hat to buy 'em for us."

"Hey!" Penny called out. "I never agreed—"

"Just think of it," Julia said more insistently, slowly turning to Penny. "Think real hard."

"Yeah kid," Penny said, her tune changing quicker than flicking a radio dial. "Just think of that, okay? We're gonna be uh… quick."

Vanessa nodded solemnly. Maxwell figured she would walk along with them, but… not because she wanted to. Probably not because of the sweets shop either.

Julia was the first to try and descend down the stairs to the unnaturally bright house. Little light bulbs lined each stair, glowing with each footfall. Maxwell was sure this looked much worse than it was. That Vanessa was just exaggerating, and that her aunt Allison would be just as reasonable as any other grownup. The bright side. He just had to think of the bright side.

"Everything's going to be alright Vanessa. You do know that don't you?"

"You've said that before, and it still doesn't make me feel any better, Mr. Maxwell…"

Hm. Not the response he was hoping for.

They had all reached the bottom of the steps now. Julia turned towards him.

"You first, Corvid," Julia said. "It was your idea. You knock."

"Wouldn't it be better to have you, do it? I mean, Allison, you know her—

"Knock, Corvid."

"I'm just a little nerv—"

Three knocks suddenly pierced the stagnant air. Three heavy knocks on the large, wooden door. Maxwell looked at Vanessa, who had silently crept under the house's front awning, in front of its two massive front doors. She did not look back at him.

A terrible silence hung between them, the only sounds were the creaking wood, dripping water, and sporadic coughs from Penny.

Finally, without the advanced warning of footsteps or any sign of life behind the frosted glass of the front door, the house let out a robust creak not too unlike a human scream.

And the door opened.

Opening the door was a gateway to a world of mold and mildew, a palpable and overbearing odor of rot overtaking the surroundings. It was terribly bright inside, but it was that false light again. That uninviting light, which conjured no warmth.

But it wasn't what was in the house that caught his attention. It was more of… who.

"Oh, hello there, darlings!"

A woman stood in front of them. A woman with pale white skin, long white hair, and a flowing, if ripped and torn, white sundress. A woman with a smiling face, and a cheery voice, which did not match the situation. The woman who Maxwell had dreaded meeting all this time.

And — it was remarkably anticlimactic.

"Hello, Auntie…" Vanessa said, dutifully and without enthusiasm. Though the creature who he assumed was "Auntie Allison" quickly darted past her, almost entirely disinterested in what she had to say, not even giving a passing glance to her niece.

"Oh, let me get a good look at you, darling!" Allison gasped, ignoring her niece. Allison instead rushed towards Maxwell and placed a slimy hand over one of his cheeks, looking directly at him with her… approximation of a face. Twisted into a permanent smile, it was almost two-dimensional: no other features except two black eyes, and a line curved upwards for her mouth. "You're so much bigger than I expected! Ah, how much you've grown!"

"I'm sorry, Lady Allison," he said as she pulled and pinched the skin on his face. "You may be thinking of someone else. I don't believe we've met befo—"

"Oh, but we have!" she exclaimed, thrusting her arms to the sky. All three of them. A third arm emerged from behind her right shoulder as she danced and twirled, he now noticed that she moved on three legs. He didn't even have time to react before his attention was taken away from them though, as she daintily leaned against the doorway. "You see Malcolm, I—"

"My name's Max—"

"Don't bother, Corvid," Julia said close to his ear. "She's absolutely dotty."

"Yes, thank you, Julia!" Allison said, giving Julia a wave with her third arm, the other two crossed. "I knew you when you were just a child, Matthew, just an itty-bitty child! I remember you used to love playing doctor. Do you remember that? Playing doctor?"

"Well, actually—"

"How silly of me!" Allison said. Allison made eye contact with Penny, hiding behind Julia and somehow suppressing her smoker's lung. Allison scuttled to her like a spider, and Penny, lacking her charismatic confidence, shakily held out her hand. Allison took it, rather enthusiastically, whipping Penny's arm up and down. "Marcel, you forgot to introduce me to your friend! She smells rather lovely, like firewood!" She released Penny's arm. Penny massaged her shoulder. "I see you've met Julia! I hope that she was hospitable to you both."

"Actually, ma'am," Maxwell said. Allison quickly jerked around, like an animal noticing it had been spotted by a predator, and then gave a little laugh, as if it was some kind of inside joke, he didn't quite get yet. "We're actually here to return your niece to you. Don't you see her? I'm sure you've been worried sick about her, right?"

Vanessa's face reddened deeply when he mentioned her, and quickly began a staring contest with the ground, rather than looking at her auntie. Allison glanced right through her.

"Who?" Allison asked.

Did Maxwell… hear that correctly?

"Vanessa. Your niece," he repeated. The blankest smile he had ever seen took over Allison's face. "Your niece? Your niece who has been missing for… for who knows how long? That's who."

"Ohhhhh!" Allison giggled. "You mean Vivian. No, Vivian has been right here. Isn't that right, Vivian?"

"Yes, Auntie Allison."

"Now, come, come. We have much to talk about–so, so much!" Allison declared, as she whirled around quickly, and started a trek down the main hall: once again almost entirely disregarding Vanessa, before popping her head back out of the doorway. "Follow me, Mason!" she sang. "The party is this way!"

Maxwell took Vanessa's hand and entered the manor. Julia followed, with Penny dragging behind.

"I do hope some of the renovations I've made to the place since you've been gone aren't too shocking, Mattias, but I simply had to make changes! The house was dreadfully dull and felt like it could use a little light."

Their hostess wasn't kidding about the changes. The dirt and the debris from the roof he could ignore. But it was not the dirt or the dust that he was shocked about. But everything—absolutely everything — had been covered head to toe in lightbulbs from the ornate banister of the stairway to strings of them wound around the frames of oil paintings. He had lived with such little light for so very long that he had to squint to make anything out.

"Has it… always looked like this Max?" Penny asked from the back of the line. Julia quickly, and quietly, elbowed the banker to the side. Then, Penny wheezed something under her breath, which luckily, none of them, including Allison, managed to hear.

"Always," Vanessa responded for him. "It's always looked like this, Ms. Penny."

"Not when I lived here," he responded to Penny's previous question. "But I must say, the decor certainly has uhm… brightened the place up a bit, Lady Allison."

"I'm so glad!" Allison responded while continuing into the house. "I thought it may have been too much, maybe a bit too overbearing, but voila! I knew you'd have great taste, Martin! Your family always does. Your father did, and now you do, too!"

"You knew my father?"

"Oh yes, and he was an awful, awful man, Manuel! No good! He deserved the charred, fiery depths of..." Their arrival ended her statement. "Ah, here we are!"

She had brought them to the lounge, perhaps once his favorite place in the house. He recognized the four stained and torn armchairs he would climb into and read in as a child, though almost everything else was foreign. The books he used to read no longer stood proudly on the ornate bookcases but lay scattered on the floor, an unsightly mass of ruined volumes and crumbled pages. And the chandelier rested crumpled and destroyed atop the central coffee table, probably where it had haphazardly fallen during the descent into the sinkhole. Allison gently, but quickly, tiptoed her way around the books, took a seat in an armchair, and crossed her three legs.

"Sit, sit! We must catch up!" Allison said. A kettle whistled and Allison immediately flicked her head to Julia. "Oh, Julia, be a dear and go get the kettle, I've been making tea. I *love* tea parties, don't you?"

"Yes, Auntie Allison," Vanessa said robotically.

"I quite enjoy them, yes," Maxwell replied, though he didn't take his seat quite yet. He wasn't sure how he was supposed to traverse the mountain of books strewn across the floor.

"I'm more of a coffee person," Penny said, most likely jokingly.

Allison, head tilted to the side, silently stared at Penny. Julia glared at Penny, too, as did Vanessa. Penny patted her still-sweating brow with the handkerchief, coughing awkwardly. Then, delicately, Allison spoke.

"Julia. The tea, if you would."

Julia obliged, and like some kind of butler, began briskly walking to where he thought the kitchen still remained, following the hiss of the kettle.

Vanessa, who had been standing back from the group, waded gloomily through the sea of books towards one of the four armchairs. But the moment that the girl sat down, Allison quickly flicked her head to her instead. It reminded him of an insect, when she did that. A massive, twitching, six-limbed spider, sitting atop her web of discarded literature. And that made Vanessa the fly.

"Oh no. Oh no, no, no, no. Victoria, go play upstairs. The adults are talking."

"But I——-"

"Vienna, go to your room. I'll call you for supper."

"Yes, Auntie Allison."

"Good girl."

Vanessa dejectedly walked out of the room and went through to the right of the lounge and up the staircase. Then, he watched through the bars on the banister as she ascended the stairs, carefully making sure not to step on those which were falling apart. And then, it was just him, Penny, and Allison.

"Come, come! Sit! I'd love to get to know you better, Matthias. It's been so long since… Oh, and your friend! What did you say your name was?"

Penny and Maxwell took seats opposite one another as far away from Allison as they could get. Unfortunately, that wasn't very far as Maxwell ended up seated directly next to her.

"Sorry, ma'am," Penny said, "had something caught in my throat, is all. I'm Penny, Penny Crane."

"Ah, you must be Otto's girl!" Allison said, clapping all three of her hands together. "You know, Otto had much to say about you! Lots to say indeed."

"Really?" Penny asked, seemingly snapping out of character for a moment, her smile dropping for just a moment before she quickly corrected her mistake. "What'd… what'd he have to say 'bout me?"

"Oh darling, it was so funny! We laughed and laughed about it for hours!" Allison responded, shimmying in her seat. "Otto told me, you, a tiny girl, wanted to become head of the family business! Hilarious!"

Penny grimaced. She removed her hat, turning it in her hands. Allison's unexpected comment had stung even Maxwell, so he could only imagine Penny's pain.

"I mean, I guess it was sort of a pipe dream, wasn't it? But I mean, I'm still gettin' closer to it. Day by day, gotta keep moving," Penny said with the empty facade of a smile behind her words.

"Tea's here." Julia said, emerging from the doorway.

Amid the creaks and groans and banging pipes of the old house, Julia had reentered the room without anyone noticing. The brigand placed the charred bottom of the kettle down onto the table, and a tray of four china teacups with matching saucers. And then, as if she was house staff, poured the tea.

"Ah, thank you, Julia! Is this the usual kind of tea? Oh, do tell me it is! I just love that kind. What did you call it again?"

"Chamomile, Allie."

"Oh yes, chameleon. Chameleon, that's its name," Allison repeated, as she took the teacup and sipped. Julia did also, and Maxwell was surprised she was doing it with proper etiquette. He could not say the same for Penny, who noisily slurped her tea like she didn't know the meaning of the word manners. Allsion glared, aiming her eyes towards Penny, and Julia gazed uncomfortably at their traveling companion. "Oh, Persephone, is that how the Crane's drink tea? Or are you just completely classless?"

"Sorry, ma'am. Like I said, more of a coffee person."

The terrible silence resumed. A silence where Allison leered at Penny who held her teacup in front of her face as if the tiny china vessel could make her disappear. Maxwell hated the silence, and he wished Vanessa were still here.

"May I possibly use the restroom?" Maxwell asked.

Allison whirled towards him and inspected him with those terrible blank eyes on that terrible blank face. Then, her posture relaxed.

"Of course you may, Miles! You know where they are! Take the stairs, to the right? Go on, be fast or your tea will get cold!"

The upstairs seemed to be just as ruined as the downstairs, the damage preluded by the hole-filled state of the staircase. The hallway had almost nothing in it, stripped bare of all its tacky decorations which his father had loved so much. The walls were so bare now that he wasn't sure they had ever known plaster, the rotting wooden muscular system of the house now exposed. The only thing left in the hallway were those rows and rows of lightbulbs. Allison really seemed to like those.

Maxwell walked right past the lavatory peeking instead into the other rooms of the house. Guest room. Guest room. Music room. Smoking lounge. Where was she… where was the door to *her* room? He was halfway to the end of the hall now, and he still couldn't find her…

"Mr. Maxwell?" a familiar voice called out of nowhere.

"Vanessa!"

Vanessa was peeking through a crack in one of the doorways, the doorway at the end of the hall. The doorway to his own childhood room. Maxwell could just make out a yellow eye peering out at him, the structural foundations of the house wobbling with each step he took towards it. When he did in fact reach the door though, her eye disappeared, and it quickly closed shut on him.

"Mr. Maxwell, what are you doing?" she whispered, her voice muffled from the other side of the door. "You'll get us in trouble! Auntie won't like y-y-you and she'll… she'll—"

"I'm perfectly aware of what she might do," he said. She hesitantly creaked open the door with the loudest creaking sound he had ever heard. He continued to speak through the half-closed door. "But this was a mistake, and it's no home for you. We'll find somewhere else to go. Come along."

"Mr. Maxwell, she'll hurt you," Vanessa said, now just her eye peering out again.

"That's a risk I'm willing to take, Vanessa."

"Shame..."

It was Allison's voice. Maxwell shuddered, as a horribly cold hand rested on his shoulder. Then, two more did the same. He slowly turned around, and stared into her cold, blank face, as she smiled that hollow, unflinching smile.

"It's an awful shame..." Allison chastised, her voice sickly sweet and airy, yet lined with something disgusting and hateful. "Marshall, have my niece's bad manners have rubbed off on you?"

"We're leaving," he announced, as he brushed Vanessa safely behind him.

Before he finished the statement or could explain himself, Allison's face rippled as if thousands of maggots wriggled beneath her flesh. Each bump of movement turned deeper black below her pallor. Her veins transformed into mycolic tendrils, squirming and rooting deeper through her skin, the strings keeping her together figuratively and literally unravelling.

"She's not going anywhere." Allison whispered pointedly. "Violet, come over here darling. Away from that awful man."

Vanessa shook her head.

"N-No, Auntie."

"What was that, Veronica?" Allison replied. She pushed past Maxwell and grabbed the door with all three of her hands, her talon-like fingernails pushing into the wood. Vanessa gasped and tried to close it shut, but Allison's three arms were much stronger than her own two.

"No!" Vanessa screamed.

"Get off of her!" Maxwell shouted. He shoved Allison away from the door with all of his might. She recoiled for just a moment, letting go of the door long enough for Vanessa to slam it shut, though Allison regained her three-legged balance quickly after. For a moment, Maxwell's stomach dropped.

For quite a few moments, Allison stared with her static, unmoving face, up at the moldering ceiling. The lights around her began to flicker. Maxwell took a step backwards.

"Ah..." Allison said, gazing upwards like she was speaking to an angel. The lights were now flickering on and off so frequently that he could only vaguely see her. "I'm sorry sweetie, did we wake you up? We didn't mean to... I just have to teach these unruly children some manners is all... We'll call you down for supper when we're done. I'm making your favorite!"

There was this stench that was invading his nostrils. An awful stench. Like that of rotting eggs. No, like that of sulfur. And there was dust, so much dust, hanging in the air. Or... wait. They were spores. The spores of mold. No. No, no, no, no, not now, please, any time but now.

"Are you... talking to Vanessa?" Maxwell asked Allison. No answer was returned to him. Well, at least not one from Allison. "Who- Who are you talking to?"

"ISN'T... IT... OBVIOUS... LITTLE... BIRD...?"

The lightbulbs went out. And the world went black.

Chapter Seventeen

Family Legacy

Of course it had to be now. Of course, it had to be when he was in danger. Of course, it had to be when *Vanessa* was in danger. He had to say that these repeated visits were nothing more than a chore now. And he was now rather fed up with the yellow thing's dramatics.

"Turn on the lights already," Maxwell said aloud, to the infinite blackness which stared him down on all sides. "I know you're there. You always are. Cut the theatrics already."

Kyrious obliged.

click

The lights came on without much of a peep from the jaundiced host of this repeated nightmare. Though these lights were quite different from the ones he had been accustomed to. The single lightbulb illuminating all the inglorious nothing no longer remained above his head.

No, instead what surrounded him was… well, his room. Or his childhood room. The same room which he had been standing in front of moments earlier, although less tarnished by the ravages of time, and much more well-furnished. Though, still not terribly furnished. He had a bed, a toy box, a bookshelf, a reading light… not much else. And there was something else which surrounded him, too. Distant, but it was everywhere. The sound of… music. Of laughter. The sound of a party.

"What are you going to show me this time?" he asked.

While he lay here dreaming, or at least that's what he assumed was happening, Allison was probably turning his body into mincemeat pies. Maxwell opened the door and went into the hallway. The house that Maxwell explored now was free of degradation or decrepitude. The hallway displayed red wallpaper, a minute tear here or there but nothing like the present-day manor. Portraits of past Corvid family members decorated the walls. The wood banisters, the railings and the floorboards shined with polished perfection. As Maxwell rounded his way to the stairs, the laughter and the scratching and music from the phonograph grew wildly terrific.

Maxwell gravitated towards an equally terrific light at the bottom of the stairs. At this point, all Maxwell wanted to do was see what Kyrious wanted him to see or experience whatever Kyrious wanted him to experience or learn whatever Kyrious wanted him to learn so that he could finally just wake the hell up. The sooner he found the object of the exercise, the sooner he could return to his life, instead of dreaming about it.

When he reached the bottom of the stairs, Maxwell entered a masquerade ball. He walked into a familiar but forgotten time, the time before the estate had warped his perceptions. The men and the women wore luxurious silks, jacquards and velvets, in exquisite colors, and covered their faces with the most elaborate of masks, feathers and headbands and bold blocks of jester-like patterns Women in gowns span on the arms of smoothly dancing men in the reflected spotlight of the glittering champagne flutes and fruit that sparkled on silver trays.

Maverick Corvid loved to throw a good party, but Maxwell bristled at the thought. He wove through the guests and slid between dancing couples seeking out his father who always needed to be at the center of it all. Maxwell checked the phonograph, the door to the wine cellar, even the dining room table, amidst the freshly hunted meats and the lavish sugary goods that smelled of sugar and Madagascar vanilla. Maxwell could not locate his father. He started asking guests, but no one would respond to his inquiries. He tugged at elbows and tapped on shoulders, but no one would acknowledge him. He was strictly an observer, not an active participant at this event. And he would gladly play the role. Unlike his dad, Maxwell wasn't much for parties.

"What is this?" he bellowed. Maxwell wanted Kyrious's attention. If he couldn't find his father, he needed to find the faceless creature in yellow. "Excuse me? Hello? Isn't something shocking supposed to happen? That's usually how these things go, isn't it?"

Once again, no response. Maxwell would have been a little upset after being ignored by this nightmare's host, if he hadn't gotten distracted by the figure twirling past him.

"Allison?" he asked.

A small, fair-skinned, blond socialite fluttered by him, wearing a blindingly red dress adorned with circles of black sequins. Instead of a mask, she wore a big red floppy sunhat with black felt circles sewn to the ribbon. It was the same dress Allison had been wearing in present reality, although not bleached. This dress was clearly bright red instead of pale white. And most importantly, she had an actual human face, not whatever twisted approximation of one she was sporting now.

Maxwell followed her as she moved from the crowd, not even pausing to speak with anyone, just crossing in and out of the partygoers.

"C'mere, Allison!"

Standing at the base of the stairs, a very short, very wide man with dark skin called for her. A familiar grin tore across his face, dividing beady eyes from double chin. And Allison immediately went to the man and hugged him. Maxwell studied the smile and the suit and the man's top hat.

"I'm bored of this party already, Otto," she whined, their difference in heights making it so that she was practically using him as something to lean on. Was that man Otto Crane? "Let's go somewhere else."

"Eh, Ladybug's right," Otto said, obviously gesturing to Allison's costume. They were both bugs, though Otto's antennae headband was only just visible beneath his top hat he had apparently refused to take off. Maybe he was a firefly? Otto turned to someone else nearby and Maxwell had to change his position in the crowd to see him. "Your brother's got shit taste, you know that?"

Otto addressed a man beside the hatrack, a man so freakishly tall and thin that he, at a quick glance, could be mistaken *for* said hatrack. But once Maxwell noticed him, he noticed the man wore his silver beard long, almost to his lower neck, and he wore epaulets, perhaps as his costume. Even before Maxwell met the man's eyes, he recognized him. It was his uncle Alexander, the man with whom Maxwell had lived for most of his life and the man who had sent him to the estate.

"My brother is the only person in our family who's ever thrown a party that I've liked. Maybe it's your taste that isn't refined enough, Otto," Alexander Corvid said. He took a sip of champagne.

"What's that s'posed to mean, Alex?"

"Who's this strapping specimen?" Allison purred to Alexander who stood at attention. The man never could really relax, not after his days in the war. "My, my! Aren't you the tall one? A veteran, too!"

"Hey! Red, whatta you doin'? Don't talk to him!" Otto exclaimed.

"Madam," Alexander said, his eyes not wandering from his drink. Maxwell also recalled that the man had never had much interest in romance either. "You must be Otto's latest paramour. Keeping the little oaf on a leash?"

"Fuck. You. Corvid," Otto said bitterly, downing the rest of his champagne glass.

"I try to, Mr. Corvid," Allison answered, snaking around his uncle, admiring the man from all angles. "I was told that this party was going to be exciting, and yet I'm halfway bored to death! What does Maverick have planned? You must tell me."

Otto stomped away in a huff, possibly to go get a new paramour, after his previous one had spoken so ill of him. Max's uncle sighed.

"I'm afraid I have no idea what my brother has planned," Alexander said. "But, Lady Allison, if you are so intrigued about my brother, would you like to meet the man himself?"

"I would love nothing more, Alex, if you would be so kind."

The two of them locked arms and strode away through the crowd. Maxwell moved one foot forward to follow them, but the party suddenly faded.

click

The lovely music, the exotic costumes, everything… with the mere clicking sound of a light switch, it was suddenly all gone. Replaced only by the blackness of the dark place.

"So, what happens next?" Maxwell asked. "How did she… get like what she is now?"

"*SHHHHHH…*" the yellow thing said from the dark. "*WATCH…*"

click

The lights flickered to life again. Maxwell was suddenly standing in a different room again. A new room. Or, well, an old room, of which he didn't have the greatest memory. He found himself in his father's study, bookshelves on all sides, old artifacts and curios, taxidermy and shrunken heads propped on pedestals, the Corvid family's personal museum. The party continued downstairs. Maxwell remembered the song, and the din of the guests had not changed.

And of course, his father's study couldn't be complete without the man himself.

The door to the study suddenly opened. Warm air surged into the cold room — which ignited a strange tactile memory in Maxwell. The study had always been horribly, uncomfortable frigid. As the music washed over the room and the figures in the doorway moved from shadow into light, Maxwell recognized the newcomers, Uncle Alexander and Lady Allison.

"Alex," Maverick Corvid said from behind his large ebony desk. He didn't smile. His father never smiled. He also did not make eye contact with Allison. "For what do I owe the pleasure, dear brother?"

Alexander unclasped Allison's arm and released her. She airily moved towards the desk, pausing to admire a most certainly fake, taxidermized jackalope from within its glass case. Then she planted her eyes firmly on Maxwell's father.

"This young lady wanted to see you," Alexander said as he backed his way to the door. "She's Otto's new inamorata, so to speak."

"The young and beautiful Allison Swan!" Max's father said, still not smiling despite his pleasant tone. Maxwell hated it when the man tried to sound pleasant. "Alex, I do hope that Otto isn't too angry about this. He can be a tad possessive of his new toys sometimes. You didn't hurt his feelings, did you, madam? We need the Cranes for funding."

"You need them for funding, Maverick," Alexander replied gruffly. "I want no part of it. I was on my way up to see your boy. Lady Allison just caught me at the right time."

This was the night. This was the night Alexander had taken him from his father. Maxwell had forgotten a lot of the details. After all, he had only been a child. Yet, he remembered that Alexander had come up into his room. Alexander had seen him there, lying sick in bed with the mold poisoning and… Well, the rest was history.

"Yes, yes, carry on Alex," his father answered. "Make amends with Otto, if you can. It would be quite useful to the family if we were to keep our relationship with the Cranes."

Alexander closed the door. That left Allison and his father.

"Mr. Corvid, I have to grant it to you, you do throw an excellent party!" Allison said, contradicting her earlier statement. The dainty, girlish tone in her voice suggested that she might be trying to seduce his father. Maxwell had to hold his abdomen for a moment as his guts twisted at the thought. "You really are as marvelous as the rumors!"

Next, his father did something that Maxwell had never known his father to do. The man smiled. He smiled an awkward, somewhat terrible, and yet completely genuine smile.

His father walked over to the windowsill, where a bottle of bourbon waited along with two glasses. Maverick poured the first normally, but on the second… Maxwell studied the reflection in the window. His father took a small white bag from his jacket's breast pocket. He poured something *else* into Allison's drink.

"Care for a drink, madam?"

"I would love nothing more," Allison said, taking the glass. "Mr. Corv—"

"If there must be a mister, call me Mr. Maverick."

"Delighted, Mr. Maverick."

Maxwell dashed forward about to scream at them, to warn her, when the ground disappeared beneath him.

click

"What did he do?" Maxwell screamed into the darkness, the ever-present, all-swallowing darkness. "You have to tell me what he did! You need to!"

"IN... GOOD... TIME..." Kyrious spoke from the shadows. *"YOU... WILL KNOW..."*

For the third, and hopefully the final time, the lights flicked in the dark place.

click

Maxwell once again stood in the study, but the study stood in disarray. The glass boxes that had housed curios and artifacts had broken, a puddle of indecipherable liquid with an alcohol smell stained one of the bookcases to the right. Behind his father's desk, one of the bookshelves had been moved. The shifted bookcase revealed a door, moldering and black.

"PROCEED..." the familiar voice of Kyrious spoke from nowhere.

Morning had blessed the estate with first light and the delicate pinks of morning., a morning in the early months of spring, pussy willows tightly clasped and expressing their willingness to bud. A parade of carriages and hungover socialites drove away from the house. Maxwell stood at the study window, facing the door, the door that reeked of mildew and mold.

"PROCEED..."

"Down there? I'm not going down there unless you tell me why."

There was a long silence which gave him no answer.

"PROCEED..."

Maxwell stepped into the doorway. Foul air filled his lungs and nose. He found himself at the top of a set of ancient stairs. They could crumble at any moment. It was also incredibly dark. At that moment, the lightbulb in his pocket decided to glow. Maxwell hoped it would offer him answers or guidance, or reassurance. It did not. Seeing the filth, the fuzzy blackness only made the experience worse.

The staircase just went down, down, downwards. Never ending, almost. Just like mold. That disgusting slimy mold, so much of it, everywhere, all around, stinking like sulfur, and so thick it felt like mud, its spores choking the air. And all of it glimmering like stars. A stairway going down, down, directly down, into the glittering, abyssal cosmos itself. A cosmos made of nothing but filth, disease, and ancient mold.

"What is this place?"

"YOU MUST... PROCEED..."

Maxwell abided and continued proceeding. He believed himself to be getting nowhere. The stairs went on for eternity. There was no light at the bottom. They shifted from wood to stone, and then from stone to something spongy and squelching, possibly mold packed so tightly that it created a solid surface. He continued walking. And walking... and walking.

Until he heard the music.

And then, the scream.

At first, it was faint. Maxwell thought he was hearing things. But no… no, the deeper he went, the louder it was. The music. This terrible, gaudy, happy ragtime music, played at the right volume to camouflage the screams of a woman.

Maxwell walked faster down the staircase. He listened, hoping he was wrong, but he thought he recognized the scream. A faint light appeared at the bottom of the stairs. The music became louder. A light accompanied by a song which was so morbidly happy, despite the screams of agony improvised into its tempo, a song which sounded nothing like the wondrous music of yesterday's party, despite it probably playing there. Maxwell moved so fast he almost tripped. All the while, her screams grew louder… and louder… and louder.

Allison's screams.

More morbid vocalizations to fit a morbidly sadistic tune, such as this one.

"What is he doing to her? What is he doing, please, you have to tell me, what is he—"

"DO YOU… SEE IT… NOW…?"

Maxwell drew closer to the light. A terrible, yellow light emanated from the bottom of the stairs, hidden stairs to the hidden room in this hellish, horror-filled house.

And he found… Julia?

Maxwell waved his hand in front of a younger Julia waiting at the bottom of the stairs. As expected, she gazed right through him. She wore a brand-new trench coat and carried a brand-new shotgun. This Julia seemed troubled by the screaming, but she was also clearly scared to enter the door, this ancient-looking door of rusting metal and ancient wood. The door from which Allison's screams escaped.

Maxwell didn't want to open it either.

So, out of what he could only assume was some morbid curiosity, Julia opened it for him.

"LOOK… LITTLE BIRD… DO YOU… SEE IT…?"

"Everything all right in here?" the younger Julia asked.

Julia entered the room, showing genuine concern on her younger face. And as she looked deeper inside the chamber, that concern turned to panic. A feeling which Maxwell shared. Anybody would. It was awful. The only word for it: awful. Pure awfulness.

Maxwell could see it. On the masonry floor, Maxwell could see ritual circles drawn, sigils of blood and salt, circles of black powder and spice. The phonograph played in the corner, endlessly looping a single song. He recognized that the mold held dominion here, squirming, squelching, spreading.

Then, Maxwell saw Allison. Poor Allison. Restraints strapped her to a filthy floor, where she squirmed and struggled, all the while screaming. Tears rolled down her face, reflected in the single lightbulb, that single fucking incandescent lightbulb which hung above her head on a string. That bulb provided all the light, all the hope she had.

"What is this…?" Maxwell asked Kyrious.

Julia also had questions, but she didn't ask them in the same direction Maxwell did.

"Boss?" she asked loudly, avoiding eye-contact with the subject of the morbid spectacle. "What, what in the hell is this? I didn't… I didn't sign up for—"

"What do you plan to do to me?" Allison screamed at Julia. At least, that's what Maxwell thought at first. But somebody stood behind Julia. And so, Maxwell looked behind, and he saw his father's silhouette, standing in the doorway with younger Julia. Allison struggled more which made her restraints tighter. "Just tell me! Tell me, please!"

"Back to your post," his father callously commanded Julia while Allison whimpered and cried.

"Corvid, sir, this wasn't in the contract. You said—"

"Every second you stay within this room, a room which I specifically instructed you to never enter, your pay will be docked. Wait. Outside. Like a good guard dog."

"Yes, sir."

Julia took one last look at Allison on the floor. She hesitated, but Maxwell saw in her eyes that she wanted to do something to save Allison. As did he. But Maxwell also knew he wasn't even there. Not really. And so, Julia left and closed the door.

"Now, now dear," Maverick Corvid cooed as if Allison were a distressed child or a baby that did not want to sleep. Maxwell retreated to the corner of the room as if Kyrious might let him escape this torture. "Quiet down. You will be part of my most interesting experiment to date. What I have planned for you Lady Allison is best experienced, not spoken about."

Maverick Corvid turned off the light, leaving the room eerily consumed with candlelight. Despite Allison's continued screams and panicked pleas, Maverick left and locked the door behind him. As the candles burned lower, Maxwell noticed something moist and textured cascading from the ceiling, spinning into tendrils, tiny limbs of black-speckled cosmic pigment draped in yellow.

"*NOW…LITTLE BIRD…*" Kyrious said from the dark. "*DO… YOU… SEE… IT…?*"

Everything inside Maxwell twisted upward into his esophagus, into his throat, as his body retched and desperately wanted the relief of vomiting. Tears poured from his own eyes, and he turned to Kyrious, begging him to please remove him from this place. He pleaded with Kyrious to erase the memory of that awful place in time and that horrible behavior from his father. The happy song on the phonograph continued to play.

And Kyrious listened.

All of a sudden, the wailing stopped, but the music continued. That terrible music, going around and around in his ears. The smell of kippers invaded his nostrils… Vanessa's smell. He covered his eyes, and blindly reached around for her, so that she wouldn't have to see his father's abominable performance.

"Vanessa!" he screamed out. It was completely black now. He wasn't sure if he was in the void or not. He still could have been in that tiny room, where the music continued. But he was sure Vanessa was nearby. "Do what you did before… please… please do what you did before and get me out of here, I've- I've had enough of this dream!"

"*DO… YOU… SEE IT… NOW… MAX… WELL…?*"

The lights came on. Maxwell peeked from between his shaking fingers. No Vanessa.

"I don't see anything. Please, what has this all been about!"

"*DO YOU SEE… HER…?*"

Allison's corpse lay on the ground. Or at least, Maxwell thought it was her corpse, bloodied and broken, practically unrecognizable, a twisted smile twitching on her face. Allison then reared and seized, renewed wailing and screaming until mold surrounded the last of her vocal cords and choked her throat.

And then, something ripped through Allison's chest.

Something with yellow eyes. Something with gray skin. Something with strange ears. Something with webbed feet. Something which was crying and wailing profusely.

Something which smelled terribly of kippers.

"*DO YOU SEE IT…?*" Kyrious asked again.

And this time, although he wished he could, Maxwell could not deny what he saw.

"Oh God…" he whispered.

"*YOUR… FAMILY… LEGACY…*"

Maxwell wasn't sure where the dream ended and the waking world began. Something forcefully pulled him from the darkness and into someplace terribly bright. And amid the brightness, the song on the phonograph continued to play. It continued even though Maxwell found himself seated at the dining room table, thick nautical rope bunding him to his seat. Penny struggled against similar confines in her seat as Julia remained knocked out cold across from them.

The horrible rag-time happy song continued to play in the waking world and in his head. And it played on the same phonograph now in the corner of the dining room. The same tune played from the same record. Maxwell gazed with groggy eyes towards Allison, their captor, who airily ambled around the table.

"I just love this song!" she said in a voice that at once sounded happy and sinister…

Maxwell did not agree.

It was a terrible, terrible song.

Chapter Eighteen

The Afterparty

Once upon a time, Maxwell Corvid had never had dreams. In fact, he had been jealous of those who could dream. He had been jealous of those whose imagination could conjure such things, take them away into a land of slumbering escapism, even for just a few hours.

But now, he no longer wanted them.

In fact, after seeing what he had just seen, Maxwell Corvid didn't think he would ever sleep again.

The first thing Maxwell noticed upon his waking, if you wanted to call it that, was the lingering music. Maxwell thought he had to still be asleep, he felt asleep, especially since he still heard that terrible song. It just went round, and round, forever.

"Oh Marcel! You're awake!"

Maxwell stared at the plate of rotting food before him as Allison hummed along to that music, continuing endlessly, stuck in a loop.

And even if he did want to eat what Allison presented as her cooking, he could not reach for his silverware. His hands had been bound to the back of his chair. The smell definitely resembled something in the midst of decay, palpable enough to make his throat seize and his eyes water. Maxwell wished he were still unconscious. Which was a lie, because at this point, he still didn't want to go to sleep ever again.

"I'm so glad that you're awake! So glad!" Allison exclaimed from somewhere in another room. "Did he give you a stern talking to? He said he would. So, what did he show you?"

"'Him'? What do you mean 'him'?"

"Silly, silly Mackerel! You are a laugh! My husband! Which dream did he show you? The one about our honeymoon? Oh, I do love that one!"

Penny rocked her chair back and forth. Maxwell supposed she was trying to free herself, but in actuality all that would do is knock the chair over and draw Allison's attention. Julia still hadn't recovered yet, so she remained slumped like a drunk.

"Glad you could join us Max," Penny said, leaning over her mound of slop. "Tea was drugged, shoulda figured."

Julia roused, but remained entirely silent. She stared, limp-necked, at her food.

Whatever had happened to Allison, it had shuffled and rearranged the contents of her brain. Remade her. Perhaps that was why Vanessa called her "Auntie." Because, despite what it looked like, the Allison who had given birth to Vanessa no longer existed.

And this Allison, this inhuman approximation of Allison, was merely the leftovers of a woman violated by his father and by Kyrious. Another victim of this place, just another nohr above the Corvid family fireplace. Allison returned to her seat, elegantly cutting into the rotten food on her plate.

"So, what did my darling husband show you, Mr. Marcus? Please, tell me all about it. Tonight is a special occasion! A party! I even saved some of the food from the last party I attended. Here in this house. Would you believe it?"

"I'd rather not speak of it actually."

Penny shot him daggers with her eyes.

"Oh?" Allison asked.

The corners of her smiling mouth drooped before she propped them up with her hand. She looked more and more like she was rotting along with the food.

"Are you sure?" Allison asked, gripping the sides of the tabletop.

She crawled over her food and onto the table, though her feet never truly left the ground. Somehow, she had managed to get into Max's face and glare at him with those soulless, sagging black eyes. She reminded Maxwell of a rotting fruit, with bruises and bad spots staining her face, oozing black mold from every orifice. "He didn't show you anything you'd like to talk about. Nothing at all?"

"Well, uhm..." he muttered.

"Max," Penny hissed under her breath. "Tell the crazy bitch what you saw!"

If only she knew.

Allison made another shuddering exhale as she fought to hide the rage fuming within her. It clearly wasn't working. Penny avoided her glare, so Allison turned her attention to Maxwell. Her facial muscles, if you could even call it a face, tensed.

"Let's go back to you, Mr. Maxwell. Maybe——-"

"He saw you and your husband. First time you met."

Maxwell released a massive breath he did not know he was holding. Julia. Julia had answered Allison. Julia had woken just in time to save them from this nightmare.

"Well?" Allison said, flicking back to him in that cockroach-esque way. "Is she right, Marley? Because I love that dream! I get it all the time!"

"Yes… in the basement," Maxwell painfully remembered aloud. "He was, he was doing something to you—"

"So, he did show you that one? I hoped he would. He always knows just what to do."

"I'm sorry, Lady Allison," Maxwell began. "But… didn't your husband… didn't he…"

The lights flickered. Lightbulbs wound around everything within the manor, glimmering off the moldering wallpaper. The lights which Allison must have set up herself.

"Oh, hold on! One second, Maxwell, dear," Allison said, shushing him with a bony finger being pressed over his lips. She offered her complete attention to the ceiling, to the flickering lights. Lights he now gathered were used to communicate with her "husband." "What is it. darling? We were just talking about you…. Oh, I'll be right there!"

And in this rare moment where Allison wasn't looking, something caught Maxwell's eye.

Something waiting for him at the top of the stairs.

Max wasn't sure how long she had been watching the rest of the group, trapped in their crude imitation of a family dinner. The moment he met eyes with her, she looked away from him. And even that was only for a split second, having to turn to Allison as she sputtered back to life from her transfixed state.

"Oh, yes dear?" Allison asked the air. The lights pulsed. Their own marital code. On and off. On. On. Off. On. Off. "Come now, come down. Your supper's getting cold!"

Max looked at Vanessa. She still couldn't meet eyes with him. Of course she couldn't. After all, he was the one who had dragged her to this terrible place, to her terrible aunt. He was the one who hadn't listened to her obvious hints and worries about returning. He was the one who had gotten them all into this mess. He hoped that she already had made the decision to stay safe, to get away from Allison, from the estate, from anything a Corvid had touched… And he hoped that she had decided to stay far, far away from him, too.

"You finish your work down there, dear!" Allison called to nobody. Vanessa hid behind one of the balustrades. It didn't necessarily hide her very well, though Allison was so dotty, and the walls so moldy and gray, that she didn't notice. "Allow me to tend to our guests. Magnus? Magnus, what are you looking at?"

"Nothing, Lady Allison."

"I should think not. People should engage in conversations over dinner!"

As the lights stopped flickering, Maxwell noticed Allison discreetly picking up the gleaming carving knife with her third arm. The candles that she had lit on the table, despite all the bulbs, leisurely danced and reflected their light gently off of the blade.

"I'll have your meal prepared shortly, my dear," Allison said to the numerous lights above. And he gathered, that they all were the dinner.

He riskily looked back up the stairway at Vanessa. She was retreating back up the stairs sullenly, face glued to the ground. He didn't want it to end like this. With her hating him for a mistake. He had to try something, anything. It wouldn't work, he knew that it probably wouldn't work but… he had to try it. That was what she had told him, right? That he had to try.

He had to listen to her this time.

"W-Wait! Wait, hold on!" Maxwell cried. "Hold on one minute! …Please."

Allison slowly turned to him, her entire body twitching again, in her terrible buggish way. Out of the corner of his eye, Max could see the glint of Vanessa's yellow eyes look up at him one last time.

There was nothing he could do now but try.

"Please, don't… don't do that," he started. "Don't do what you're thinking… Please!"

There was just one problem, a problem which was so easily solved, and yet a problem he seemed to run into quite often:

He didn't have the slightest idea as to what to say.

"I… I know that I didn't listen to you," he said, taking fleeting glances to the stairs whenever he was able. Allison's murky gaze still bore into him, and he could feel what little patience she had dripping away with each twitch of her eye, each twirl of the carving knife. He was speaking to both of them now. "And I'm sorry for that. I truly am."

"You should be," Allison hissed back. She stabbed the knife into the table. He flinched, as it slid through the wood like butter. And then Allison gracefully removed it, flipping it in between her fingers. "*Children* are supposed to do as they are *told*. I've spared the rod for too long, you know, *far* too long."

"I know." Maxwell said, avoiding eye contact with his hateful hostess. He looked at Vanessa. She was looking at him now. Looking right at him. "But could you find it in your heart to… to well, forgive me one last time? Because, well… I am trying. And that's all I can do, and you have to trust me but… I'm trying. Promise."

Allison stabbed the knife into the center of the table. Vanessa's large yellow eyes were quickly replaced by Allison's pale face as she grabbed his face with one of her gloved hands. All he could see was her plastered smile, smeared across her featureless visage.

"You have had… *so many chances,*" She snarled at him, spitting spatters of black gooey saliva onto his face. "So many chances to do what was right… to be proper, to be good… and in all of those chances, not once have you done the right thing… Not once!"

He wasn't sure who she was talking to. It sounded almost like she was talking to Vanessa now, instead of him.

"I… I know." He replied, now avoiding Allison's and her niece's eyes simultaneously. "But all I can do is try. You just need to keep trying, until-

"Until you run out of chances. And that was your last one."

The carving knife had been removed from the table sometime in their conversation. Allison was getting ready to stab him. He managed to crane his neck around his hostess, peeking at the stairs. Vanessa wasn't there anymore. He really was out of chances…

"But I-

"But nothing! No more tries, Maverick!" Allison snarled. "You did this to yourself! Now just where did I put that knife…"

Allison wasn't talking to Vanessa. She wasn't talking to Maxwell either. She was speaking to his father. She meant to say Maverick. She got it right that time. Allison was speaking to some half-remembered remnant, trapped within the walls of this dying house and within her dying mind. Wherever he was now, Allison had addressed Maxwell's father.

And Maxwell was not his father.

"Stay still, Mr. Maxwell…"

Ah. So that's where Vanessa had gone.

Maxwell stared straight ahead, as somebody behind him began to use the missing carving knife from the table to saw the bindings which strapped him to his seat. Someone who he couldn't see, but who smelled quite strongly of kippers.

"I'm sorry Vanessa," Maxwell whispered. In that moment, it was all he could really think of saying. "I'm so, so sorry I didn't listen—"

"Mr. Maxwell, please be quiet…"

Maxwell listened.

"Veronica?" Allison burst out. "I can see you… What are you doing?"

Maxwell felt a feeling of panic rise in his chest. Oh god. Oh god she had been found out. Shit. Shit! Vanessa began to saw faster through the ropes, but no matter how fast she did, it wouldn't be fast enough.

"Valencia…" Allison said, the words dripping from her mouth, drenched with malice. Vanessa did not run. She froze. Allison turned her head slowly and peered at her niece's now tear-filled eyes. "Why are you downstairs? You know not to come downstairs when auntie has guests over, don't you?"

"Auntie, I—"

"No. No, you don't have to talk back." Allison said with anger and force reverberating in her voice. "Go upstairs to your room, and I will deal with you later."

Vanessa stood there.

"*Now*, Vienna."

Vanessa didn't respond.

"I said go upstairs you, disrespectful little brat!" Allison shrieked. "Can't you see that your auntie is very, very busy right now? Can't you?"

Allison moved with the velocity of a bullet, about to strike Vanessa across the face with one of her hands, one with a razor-like claw. Maxwell threw himself against the loosened ropes, his temper — the one he never showed in everyday life — fueled him in ways he never thought it could. A spark of terror shining through Vanessa's eyes. Putrid rage lit Allison's.

And he saw both parties' mortified reactions as Allison walked into her own blade, Vanessa accidentally driving the carving knife into her Aunt Allison's side.

Allison screamed, as blackened, moldering blood squirted from the wound, the blade sliding through flesh with almost no effort. Vanessa must have hit an artery of some sort, a vital one, one that would get her to scream like this. She screamed almost loud enough to disguise the horrible song.

"Auntie! Auntie I— Auntie please, I didn't— Auntie I'm sorry, I—"

"You! You… you…" Allison tittered madly as she sputtered black bile from her plastered lips.

Allison removed the knife and staggered, three legs shaking, like a spider that had just been squashed. "You… little… *monster.*"

"Auntie…?" Vanessa asked her aunt in vain. "Auntie? Please don't… Please don't… leave me… Please don't leave me again…"

Allison keeled over onto the floor, lying flat on her back, muscles twitching, gazing up as the lights began to flicker. The lights danced, and danced before finally, dimming. Slowly but surely, the lights went out, one by one, and the house was left in complete darkness. And in that darkness, a single phrase sputtered out of Allison's mouth.

"Vanessa… That was your name… wasn't it? Vanessa… That's a pretty name…"

Maxwell wasn't sure what gave him the strength to wriggle through the rest of the ropes. But as the lightbulb in his pocket began to glow, he forgot all about his colleagues still trapped in their seats. He forgot all about his father and the yellow thing, and that horrible nightmare.

All that mattered was trying to make Vanessa hurt less.

It was what doctors did, after all.

"There, there," Maxwell said. Vanessa ran towards him. He embraced her. "Everything's better now… It'll all be okay… I promise. I promise you, Vanessa. It'll all be okay."

He doubted it, of course. He doubted anything was okay. He knew Vanessa probably doubted it, too.

They could try their best to make everything okay again.

Trying, as he had come to learn, was the important bit.

Chapter Nineteen

Where the Heart is

Maxwell knew exactly what to do in a situation like this.

He didn't know how or when he had learned those skills over the course of the night, but it seemed he most certainly had. And there wasn't really a whole lot to it. He now knew exactly what to do when somebody was crying. Or well, he knew what to do when Vanessa was crying. Maybe if it were anybody else, things would be a slightly different story.

"I-I-I didn't m-mean to…" Vanessa sniffled in the dark. The lightbulb was practically burning through his pocket, but he didn't care. As long as it gave her a warmth and a little light, he couldn't care less what it felt like.

"I know, I know," he reassured her. It must have been minutes since she had begun sobbing. In that time, Maxwell had not looked back at the others still tied around the table, and they had not interrupted. "You were very brave. The bravest person I've ever met. And good things always happen to the brave."

"But she's…"

Vanessa couldn't finish her sentence before bursting into more tears.

"You did good, sweetheart," Julia said from her place at the table.

"Yeah, fishstick, you…" Penny began. She paused, not sure what she really wanted to say, as being genuine was not her strong suit. "You did good. Real damn good."

"Thank you, Ms. P-P-Penny," she said between sobs.

Maxwell and Vanessa sat there in the quiet and the dark for a while longer. He didn't know how long. Until Vanessa wiped her eyes.

"How about we go and untie them, yeah?" Max asked her, still holding her hand.

"O-Okay…"

The ropes proved no worry, although something was clearly different now. Penny thanked him under her breath when she got out of her restraints but lacked any sneering remarks or smart aleck comments. And Julia, well, she seemed… Well, to start with, she had been crying, too. But when he and Vanessa undid her restraints, she didn't even stand up, she just… sat there. She sat there, the silence of the room echoing around her.

"So, what now?" Penny finally asked.

Maxwell had anticipated it would be Penny who broke the spell.

We leave," Julia said, she looked to all of them, her face red, tears in her yellowed eyes. "We leave, and we never come back. There isn't a reason to anymore."

"Hold on, we can't go back out, can we?" Penny said to nobody in particular. "We turn into those monsters if we stay here long enough, right?"

"Yeah, that's how it works." Julia confirmed. "Ain't nothin' else we can do."

"Wait," Maxwell said.

Julia and Penny jerked towards him, their brows furrowed as they processed his objection. Vanessa wiped her nose on her dress.

"We can't leave," he announced. "I can't leave. I think there's… There's some stuff I still have to do or try to do."

His lightbulb in his hand flickered. In that spark something spoke to him, something in the light offered a faint sense of confirmation.

"What'd you have in mind, Corvid?" Julia asked.

Penny shrugged.

"Mr. M-M-Maxwell?"

"It's upstairs," he said to everyone. "I saw it before… There's this room in the study."

"I'll stay with the kid," Julia said, placing a hand on Vanessa's shoulder. Vanessa's face lightened.

"No, Ms. Julia," Vanessa said, smiling up at him. "I think we should go. I'd like to try," she added.

"That's all any of us can do," Maxwell told her.

And with that little exchange, Corvid Manor suddenly felt more like a home than it ever had.

The four of them mounted the staircase, maneuvering slowly as to not put the wrong amount of weight on the wrong rotting stair. The same was repeated for the dilapidated hallway at the top of the stairs, now completely shrouded in the gloomy chiaroscuro cast by the lightbulb. Though both of these were a trivial worriment.

It was what waited for him in his father's study that worried him.

Maxwell approached the third door on the right of the hallway, and while it looked the same as every other door in the manor, he hesitated to grab the doorknob.

"Go ahead, Mr. Maxwell," Vanessa said.

He finally forced himself to touch the cool brass, hoping maybe all the answers — as uncomfortable as they might be — rested on the other side of the threshold.

It was locked.

"Figures," Maxwell mumbled. He jiggled the knob, pushed on the door, and nothing budged. Of course, his father had locked his study. "Can anybody lockpick?"

"Step aside, Max," Penny said, grinning proudly ear to ear, stretching and cracking her knuckles. "Anybody have a… I don't know, a pin or something?"

Julia reluctantly passed her a bobby pin she pulled from her nest of ratty hair.

"Thank you. Now, watch the master at work."

"Why would a banker need to know how to pick a lock?" Julia asked.

"You ever heard of a deposit box?" Penny returned, taking her hat off and placing it on the floor. Julia nodded. "Well, notice I didn't call 'em *safe* deposit boxes, yeah?"

Penny bent over the lock. Maxwell, Julia and Vanessa leaned against the wall on the opposite side of the hall. The jimmying of the lock groaned and clattered with the same spooky tones of the settling walls of the manor.

"Max," Julia muttered. She didn't look at him as she spoke. She was completely focused on that doorway. "I know what's in there. I don't know why it showed you any of that, but… I'm sorry. About helping your dad do all—"

"Don't worry," he cut her off. "It's all in the past now anyway."

"Because come on. You're the girl's favorite anyway. It just… felt right. Doesn't matter."

"We are talking about what happens if Max dies?" Penny asked, as she maneuvered the pin. "Could I take the house?"

Well, Maxwell supposed he didn't want it, even if it didn't die, and there probably wouldn't be any other buyers interested in a decaying cursed house at the bottom of a sinkhole…

"You know what? Fuck it! Penny, you can have the whole bloody estate for all I care."

"Good one, Max," Penny muttered with a small guffaw.

"You have that handkerchief? And a pen?" he asked. The banker paused and rooted through her pockets. She retrieved the two items. Maxwell licked the nib of the ornate gold and black fountain pen.

He passed Vanessa the light bulb, before carefully leaning on the rotting wooden wall and signing his name on the disease-ridden scrap of cloth, the ink just barely clinging to it.

"In the event of my death, I Maxwell Corvid, being of sound mind and body, grant Penny Crane all mortal possessions on the Corvid family estate."

It wasn't official by any means, but Penny was the executor. She would figure something out. She always did.

"You're serious?" Penny said. "Are you uh… sure? It's a nice house y'know, and it's been in your family for generations—"

"You'll do a whole lot more with it than I will. Besides, you actually have the money to renovate it, fix it up. I'm technically a broke college student, remember?"

Penny took the handkerchief, and stared at his signature, bleeding through the fabric but recognizable. And then, she stuffed it in her pocket. Penny then returned to her work.

"Thanks, Max," she said. "Yeah, thanks a lot."

Even when receiving a gift, Penny sounded jaded. But he expected that.

"Aha!" Penny cried triumphantly, quickly changing the subject.

clink

The door opened lazily; dust puffed out like a swarm of locusts. They all coughed, and Penny theatrically handed Julia her bobby pin.

The study, like the rest of the house, was irreparably damaged. Books lay strewn across the floor, ancient, one-of-a-kind books written in forgotten languages by forgotten authors. And there was no sign of any of the various curios or keepsakes which his father had collected throughout various chapters in Corvid history. Even the ornate desk was ruined, the mold transforming the hand-carved piece of history into nothing but rot.

And of course, there was the door.

It glowered from behind the broken desk, the corridor it led to, black as pitch. He had only taken one step within the room, and already he could feel that immense feeling of misery emanating from his father's study. And it all came from whatever was down, beyond that gloaming doorway.

Vanessa broke her longstanding connection to Maxwell and moved towards the outside of the room. Julia lingered there, so Vanessa tethered to her instead.

"Max?" Penny asked him tremulously. "What's uh… What's down there? Last I checked, not even the Corvids owned a private portal to hell."

"I don't quite know," he replied. "But I need to find out."

"You sure you know what you're doing, Corvid?" Julia protested. "I don't want the kid to go down there with—"

"We should all stay with Mr. Maxwell," Vanessa proclaimed.

They all looked at Vanessa, despite her strange fish-like appearance her innocence overshadowed. And so, they moved closer to the doorway. And reluctantly, closer to Maxwell.

Maxwell Corvid then took a step beyond all of the madness.

The passage looked almost the same as it had in his dream. It was so dark that the lightbulb could barely illuminate the next stair, let alone the rest of the passage. Maxwell entered first, but Vanessa squeezed by to lead the way. Julia clodded heavily behind them, and Penny brought up the rear.

"Julia, what do you know?" Maxwell asked her. Vanessa hopped down the stairs ahead of them at ease in the meandering turns. "What haven't you told us?"

"Where do I start? Your father was a piece of sh—"

"No, no," Maxwell interrupted. "About this place. About her father." He tilted his head ever so slightly towards Vanessa and stared pointedly for emphasis. "About Kyrious."

"Not much. Except that thing… Well, you saw what it did to Allie. And I know it hated what it did. And I know it hates me, because I… Well, I helped your dad do everything."

Julia stopped speaking. Maxwell thought it best to leave the conversation there.

"Sorry to cut your little *tête-à-tête* short," Penny asked from the back. "But is anybody else noticing the floor? No? Just me?"

Penny was right. Something had changed about the steps. They had been going down for quite a long time now, much longer than they should have. And not only had they still not reached the bottom, but the very staircase itself had changed.

No stone remained beneath his feet, nor wood, nor any other sort of reasonable material. Instead, there was squirming, squelching, mold. The entire staircase was made of it now.

"Mr. Maxwell?" Vanessa tugged at his sleeve. She stopped tottering down the steps, which caused the rest of them in the single-file line to stop as well. "What is that?"

Something else had changed as well. It was this… light. A faint, yellow light, at the end of the passage, glowing steadily from down below, at the bottom of the stairs. A light which would pulse steadily… like a heartbeat. Faint, but steady, weak, but rhythmic and measured.

And then, the light began to speak.

"THE… EXPERIMENT… WAS AN… UTTER… FAILURE…"

The voice of Kyrious droned and echoed. In the darkness one of Maxwell's companions stumbled. He turned, and he froze when he read the fear on Julia's face. The brigand had shuffled backwards and bumped into Penny. Maxwell's lightbulb flashed. Soon, it joined in the rhythm of the other light, the light that swirled from the unseen bottom to greet them.

"I don't want to…" Julia muttered. "Down there—"

"Daddy," Vanessa whispered. She reached into the light as if she might catch it and pull it towards herself. "Auntie said this is where my daddy lives."

"If you don't want to go, Julia," Maxwell said sincerely. "You don't have to."

Julia's respirations accelerated and Maxwell could imagine the speed at which her heart pounded. Vanessa reached for her hand, and the child wrapped her webbed fingers over Julia's shaking ones to still them.

"It's going to be okay, Ms. Julia," she said.

When an adult reassures a child, that reassurance comes off as an outright lie. But it seemed, when a child reassured an adult… That was quite a different story.

Vanessa hugged Julia. She only came up to the tall woman's waist. Then, Julia's pulse began to slow. Her hand began to firmly grasp Vanessa's, as she stopped shaking. And then, the brigand's breathing went back to normal. And before long… Julia was fine again. Or, as fine as she could be, in a place like this.

"Ms. Penny?" Vanessa asked, looking at the banker. "Will you buy Ms. Julia a sweet when we get back?"

"Thank you, sweetheart," Julia said shakily. With Vanessa at her side, she stepped forward to rejoin the group, looking backwards at Penny. "I'm sure she will."

"RESULTS… HAVE PROVED… INCONCLUSIVE…"

Kyrious's voice was so much louder down here. The voice got inside Maxwell's head and resonated, rebounding off of the walls of his skull, each time echoing louder and louder. And yet, as always, it sounded only like a whisper in their ear, a deafening, overwhelming whisper which drowned the rest of the world out.

Maxwell hesitantly continued down the passage. Each pulse of the light seemed only to further distort the walls. The passage melted and swayed. Maxwell's feet were unsteady, as the ground moved and pulsed, the ceiling dripping with decay, everything *rotting*.

"SUBJECTS…" Kyrious began. It paused for a longer time than normal, as if lost in thought. *"I… SUPPOSE… IT DOES… NOT… MATTER… IN… THE END…"*

He looked back at Vanessa. She gave a bright smile, so, so much warmer than the cold light at the end of the passage. Whatever happened he would make sure that her smile remained on her face. It had to. It was the last bit of dying light in this world which he cared about now.

"SUBJECTS… ARE INCORRECT…"

Maxwell reached the bottom of the stairs and the rusted metal door Julia had guarded in his dream. In the cracks, that yellow light continued its constant, rhythmic discharge. When Maxwell touched the door handle his hair rose until it stood on end. Vanessa approached, drawn to the energy of the handle. When she touched it, she giggled. Maxwell, observing the mirth in her reaction to this occurrence, smiled. Vanessa smiled back.

"SUBJECTS... WILL BE... PREPARED... FOR... TERMINATION..."

Maxwell wasn't afraid of what lay behind the other side of the door. He... he wasn't quite sure what he was. It was a bright feeling though, as bright as a freshly struck match, contrasted even better down there, in the darkest depths of the world.

"YOU MAY..."

Maxwell looked at Vanessa who still held the knob, her hair now standing and reaching into the strange light. Vanessa's dancing hair brought a nervous laugh from Penny and a snort from Julia.

"PROCEED..."

Maxwell and Vanessa opened the door. Together. The way things should be.

"MY... LITTLE... BIRDS..."

Despite its age, the door swung open easily. The rusty metal didn't squeak or cry.

The room within was not unfamiliar to Maxwell. In fact, he knew this place quite well. It was a place he had visited many times tonight. The place where reality and dreams were blurred and muddled, a place which was impossibly empty and impossibly dark. Except of course, for a single lightbulb, hanging down from a string, gently pulsing with light.

And standing under the swinging, pendulum-like light, there was something tall and towering, head hung low. Something which should not have been there. Something he had only ever seen in his nightmarish "dreams."

Something wearing a yellow cloak.

Chapter Twenty

Two Little Birds

"HELLO... LITTLE... BIRD..."

Maxwell no longer knew what classified as a dream. He had puzzled over that question since arriving on the estate and now he wondered if he would even recognize the real world.

"HAVE YOU... SEEN IT... YET... MAXWELL...?"

Kyrious stood in the center of the room: tall, motionless, monolithic, staring out to something beyond which the rest of them could not see amidst the dim light of the lightbulb.

The thing shifted. Nothing but blackness lurked beneath its hat.

"All this time, you've been asking me that, and I still don't know what I'm supposed to be looking at," Maxwell said. "I clearly don't see anything."

"HOW... DISGUSTING... IT ALL... IS...?"

"I don't see that at all."

Kyrious jittered. It angrily spasmed beneath its cloak, veins and bumps appearing and shifting and twitching and throbbing. It turned around fully, twisting as if it were rooted to the ground by roots digging into the nothing below. It must have been frustrated.

"REALLY...?" it asked. *"YOU... DO NOT... SEE... THIS WORLD'S... TUMORS...?"*

"I don't. I don't see it anywhere around."

Maxwell approached the thing. Kyrious did not retreat, or even flinch. It just peered at him from its empty face, staring in solemn, empty silence.

"YOU... USED... TO SEE... IT..." Kyrious replied. *"WHY... WHY ARE... YOUR EYES... CLOSED... NOW...?"*

Maxwell didn't think that his eyes were closed. In fact, he thought they had opened. Yes, there were some bad parts about the world, parts which he was all too familiar with but, there was also plenty of good, he had come to realize. He glanced at Vanessa.

There was goodness all over the estate, if you chose to look.

"You made this place!" Maxwell told it. "You control everything here, the Sleepwalkers, the lights, and you still think everything is awful?"

"*MOLD... ONLY SPREADS...*"Kyrious droned. "*I... CANNOT... HELP... SOMETHING... THAT IS... ALREADY... ROTTING...*"

"Well... What about Vanessa? Is she rotting?"

Maxwell pointed to Vanessa. He gestured for Vanessa to come closer, but she only shuffled backwards and shook her head.

"It's okay, Vanessa. It won't hurt you," Maxwell told her, reassuringly. "I *know* that it won't."

Maxwell enunciated that last phrase.

Vanessa crept forward. Kyrious, seemingly instinctually, reached her but quickly withdrew its limp, vaguely human hand. It avoided the girl's eyes.

"*SHE... WAS A... MISTAKE...*" it said. "*SHE IS... A PRODUCT... OF... THIS... FOUL... ROTTING... WORLD...*"

The creature twisted its spine, bending impossibly to stare at Maxwell, the abyss in its face staring at him. He stared back. Neither of them flinched. Vanessa trembled but she also remained strong and tall.

"*UNFORTUNATELY... SHE IS... A SYMPTOM... OF THIS... WORLD'S... DISEASE... AND... IT'S—*"

"She's *fucking* wonderful," Maxwell told it. Kyrious recoiled. The abyss had flinched first. "And if you think otherwise, if you think it of your own daughter... you're just as bad as *him*."

"*I... AM... **NOT**...!*"

The entire void around them rumbled. The lightbulb flickered uncontrollably, strobing into the darkness. The thing's scream made his head pound and his legs unsteady, as the world went out of focus for a minute. But by the time Kyrious was done, by the time that the terrible sensation had ended... The outburst was almost sad, rather than threatening. A child's tantrum.

"*DO NOT... COMPARE ME... TO... **HIM**...*" it spat. "*I... AM... **NOTH-ING**... LIKE... THAT MAN...*"

"If you're better than him, then act like it!" Maxwell shouted. "Because you lock yourself down here and ignore the family you have! Sounds an awful lot to me—"

"*TRYING... TO FIX... THINGS...*" Kyrious interrupted. "*IT... WOULD CHANGE... NOTHING...*"

"Speaking from experience, it would change everything."

Electricity crackled, as the light stabilized, and there was no yellow thing with them. Maxwell could still hear it, they all could. It had gone into hiding, somewhere in the dark.

"*WHY… TRY… WHEN YOU… CAN DREAM…?*"

The void above them crackled. Sparks of golden electricity transformed the black void into a thunderous sky on some distant, alien planet. The lightning extended on forever, the lightbulb fizzling as it did so.

"*DREAMS ARE… OFTEN… SUPERIOR… TO… REALITY…*" it said from somewhere within the nowhere. "*I WAS… GIFTED… NO BODY… NO SENSES… NO… ANYTHING… TO CALL… MY OWN… AND SO…*"

The lightning crackled again above them, thousands and thousands of lightning strikes, illuminating a sky of emptiness.

"*I… DREAM…*"

The voice went from bitter and hateful, to calm and serene, from a tsunami to a gentle tide going in and out.

"*I DREAM… I CAN… FEEL… THE RAINDROPS…*" it said, little droplets of water sprinkling down from above, amidst the lightning storm. The droplets ceased as soon as they had appeared. "*I DREAM… I CAN… MAKE LOVE… I SNAP… MY FINGERS… AND…*"

A silence echoed through the dark place.

"*EXCEPT… I CANNOT… SNAP… MY FINGERS… CAN I… LITTLE… BIRD…?*"

"What are you talking about?" Maxwell asked. "Of course you can! Of course you can snap your fingers!"

"*DREAMS… ARE OFTEN… SUPERIOR… TO REALITY…*"

Maxwell thought he… almost… understood it. Kyrious only existed in dreams, and even down here in the dark place, the line between dream and reality was drawn tenuously thin. It couldn't really… *live*. It could only dream about living.

"*YOU…*" it said, its voice so… jealous. Imagine that. A being, capable of powers that could remake reality… being jealous. Being jealous of someone like him, who could barely dream at all. "*YOU ALL… GET… TO LIVE… IN… REALITY…*"

Kyrious moved and Maxwell sensed its head against his ear. He could feel its breath, as it took shuddering inhales and exhales. It reeked of brimstone.

"*AND YOU… YOU ALL… HAVE MADE… A… NIGHTMARE… OF IT…*"

"But you can try to fix—"

"*YOU… ARE A… DOCTOR… LITTLE… BIRD…*" it said.

Maxwell clutched Vanessa's hand tighter.

"*YOU… SHOULD KNOW… IT IS… BEST… TO CUT… OUT… THE CANCER…*"

"Like what you did with Allison?" he asked. "I mean, that was the only way she could still be alive in that state, right? After what you——"

"**QUIET**…!" it bellowed. The void shook again. Maxwell's head rattled along with it, lightning striking his nerves and coursing through his head. "*I… DID… **NOTHING**… BUT LISTEN… TO **YOUR**… FATHER…*"

"I know what my father did to you was awful, but you have——"

"*AND WHY… SHOULD I… **EVER**… LISTEN… TO ONE… OF YOU… AGAIN…?*"

The thing waited for his response. It waited… and it waited… and it waited. It waited with glowering animosity, it waited, already entirely unimpressed with his hypothetical answer. Kyrious would never listen to him. It had made up its mind a long time ago, in fact, he doubted that there was any merit to the experiment Kyrious had supposedly been running this whole time. This had just been an excuse for it to torture them out of hate. A private tour through the diseased and the tumorous parts of the world, highlighted in golden yellow lights.

Maxwell had no answer.

Luckily, Vanessa did.

"Because Mr. Maxwell is good."

Maxwell and Kyrious turned their attention to her. The towering yellow monstrosity and Maxwell Corvid both stared at the girl in perplexion and pride, respectively.

"*STAY… OUT… OF THIS… VANESSA… I AM… SPEAKING—*"

"No!" she shouted. The void shook. Kyrious winced. "Mr. Maxwell is a good person! You just don't see it, because… because you hate him! You hate everything!"

Kyrious released an indescribable growl, halfway between the crackling of electricity and a thousand voices whispering just out of earshot. The yellow thing glowered at Vanessa, shifting its hateful spotlight of a gaze. And Vanessa stayed beneath it and weathered the creature's loathing. Kyrious warped its posture, taking an imperial pose. It studied her.

"*NO… I DON'T… YOU——*"

"Yes, you do!" she yelled at it again. There was this glow in her eyes of determination which he had never seen before in anyone, much less in a child. A glint which shone through the tears she was holding back and outshined everything else. It was no longer a spark in her face. It was a fire. "You hate him, and you hate me, and you hate yourself!"

Imagine that. A child, reducing something like Kyrious to silence. It felt like something that could only happen in the most absurd and nonsensical of dreams.

"*HATE…?*" Kyrious hissed. Each movement Kyrious made was calculated, each gesticulation premeditated, each undulation measured. "*YES… I HATE… YOU… LITTLE… BIRDS…*"

The lightbulb weakened again. In a blink, Kyrious disappeared again. Kyrious was no longer hiding behind any veneers, any facades of experiments or blame.

"Max? Hey, Max! Fishstick! Quick, Jules, it's over here!"

A familiar, cigarette-tarnished voice called from the darkness. Penny and Julia appeared; Julia's face slashed with wrinkles of worry. Vanessa ran towards them and when she reached Julia hugged her tightly. Julia returned the hug as both of them faltered between smiles and tears. Penny, meanwhile, merely walked to Maxwell and slapped him on the back.

"Glad you're okay, Max," Penny said dryly. "For a second there, I thought I was gonna get your whole bloody house!"

"*WHAT… A NICE… LITTLE… FAMILY… REUNION…*" Kyrious said from somewhere out in the black. Maxwell could smell the rancid way the thing said "family." Like the word tasted of rot and maggots. "*TOO BAD… IT ALL… HAS TO… END…*"

Maxwell could only vaguely view the silhouette of the monster, the monster in the yellow cloak, as it shambled towards them all. One step. Two. With each one, the void rippled.

"*YES… THE EXPERIMENT… WAS… BIASED…*"

A single gnarled, crooked finger emerged, as Kyrious began to point at them. No. At *him*. And an equally crooked monster was not far behind it.

"*TRUTHFULLY… I DO… HATE… YOU… ALL…*"

Kyrious returned from the depths of the darkness. It shuffled and limped. Maxwell moved closer to Julia and Vanessa. Then, Kyrious laughed.

"*I HATE… THE BRIGAND… FOR HER… COWARDICE…*" it said, the very air itself was charged by Kyrious's spiteful words. "*I HATE… THE BANK-ER… FOR THROWING… HER LIFE… AWAY… PUFF… BY… PUFF…*"

Kyrious pointed at Vanessa.

"*I HATE… HER…*"

And then Kyrious pointed at him.

"*FOR WHAT… HIS… FATHER… DID…*"

"She didn't do anything to—"

"*I HATE… ALL… OF YOU…*"

Maxwell finally got a look at Kyrious clearly. It looked like it was… melting. Melting like candlewax, cloak and creature becoming the same… no, not melting. Kyrious was… decaying. Decomposing, its own mold eating it alive, overtaking everything on its body. The mold slowly crawled out of the void in its face, and slowly dyed the yellow thing black.

"IN MY… SITUATION… WHO… WOULDN'T…?"

Kyrious paused with another one of those hissing, crackling, indeterminable laughs. It's new, moldering body was jittering and gyrating, almost like it was in pain, and yet it was laughing…

"AND I… WILL SIMPLY… HAVE TO… SHOW… YOU… THE LIGHT…"

The thing moved like lightning. One moment, Kyrious had been in front of him, and the next it was suddenly behind him. The lightbulb flickered madly, as Kyrious twisted out of the very void itself. It reached out towards Vanessa. She was too paralyzed to move.

Maxwell was not.

Maxwell wasn't particularly sure why he did it. Or if he had even meant to. It all happened so fast, a million times faster than the stagecoach crash, or Penny's hat coming off for the first time, or when Julia had shot that first Sleepwalker, or when Allison had attacked the for the first time, or… or anything. It happened faster than anything, as he dove for Vanessa and pushed her aside, the yellow thing grabbing him in a grip of gnarled, blighted, festering fingers.

"Mr. Maxwell!" Vanessa shrieked. She ran to the yellow thing stood and pounded on its cloak, only to have no impact other than scathing silence. Julia followed, reaching for Vanessa, pulling her back. "Mr. Maxwell! Please, please! Don't! Please, don't hurt him! Don't hurt Mr. Maxwell, please!"

Kyrious examined Maxwell, like it had so many countless times. The thing tightened its grip around him, squeezing his rib cage until he could feel it splintering, shards of bone lodging into the sides of compressed organs. It hurt. It hurt a lot. He coughed something up. Something that used to be red, but that the mold had turned black.

Maxwell looked at Vanessa, still kicking and screaming in Julia's arms, as the brigand tried to get as far away from Kyrious as possible. He put on the most reassuring smile he could.

"It's going to be okay," Maxwell said to her. "I promise it will."

And for the first time ever, when he said it… it sounded sincere.

"NONESENSE… THAT… IS… NONSENSE…" Kyrious said. *"YOU… KNOW… THAT IS… ALL… NONSENSE… DON'T YOU… LITTLE… BIRD…?"*

Maxwell watched as something began to… happen… to Kyrious. The blackness which had made up its visage, the shadow which that hat cast over its face, it was beginning to… leak. The shadow the mold which had crawled out of Kyrious's face, it slowly slithered and writhed towards him, extending like a proboscis. It slowly crept up his mouth, his nose, everything, tendrils of rot extending into his body until he was suffocating on the spores.

But before everything went black, before the little tentacles of black entirely swallowed his vision… he heard one last little glimmer out the outside world. The faint little spark of a voice…

"It's going to be okay, too, Mr. Maxwell."

And Maxwell believed her.

But after that there was… nothing. Literally nothing. Everything faded to silence and… that was it. Maxwell at first, thought that he must have been dead.

There was no other way to explain it really. The outside world had well and truly vanished. There were no distractions… No feeling… No… anything. It was like a void, within a void. And he floated in it.

Was this… Hell? Limbo? Heaven?

He supposed this was it.

No, no this couldn't be it!

This wasn't what death was like, was it?

If it was, it was rather anticlimactic. But what else could this be?

He kept falling… falling… falling…

Wait… What was that?

There was a… lightbulb.

A little farther in the void, Maxwell spotted a tiny lightbulb, making its own descent along with him. The very same lightbulb which had guided him through the whole miserable estate. He moved his arms as if he might swim towards it. Eventually, Maxwell even grabbed it. And when Maxwell gathered it into his hands, it shined rather brightly.

Really bright. Too brightly, actually. It burned and melted the void until all that was left was… was… was…

A pair of windows.

Maxwell's eyes focused within the brightness and deciphered familiar curios. He recognized the sunlight streaming in through the sparkling clean windows and illuminating the dust which drifted from old books, neatly shelved and categorized. A fresh autumn chill carried in the air, a chill that seeped into old wooden walls and floors unable to keep it out. Everything was so neat and tidy and… pleasant. He could have never imagined a place for such a terrible man could be this pleasant.

This was the study. All that was left… was his father's study.

And… Well, Maxwell knew there couldn't be a study, not this version of the study, without…

"Maxwell? Maxwell, my son, is that… you?"

"Dad?"

Chapter Twenty-One

Reunion

After everything Maxwell Corvid had been through... After everything that he had done, everything he had seen, everything he had experienced, this whole time...

Maverick Corvid had just been sitting here. Wherever *here* was.

It was strange not seeing his father as some kind of boogeyman, twisted into existence by the estate, but well... a man again. Once, a man who had stood with an arrogant stride in his step, and an imperious glint in his eye... but now, a man who could not step at all, his frail body confined to a wiry wheelchair, that glint hidden beneath the layers of bandages across his eyes.

Maxwell studied the figure in the wheelchair and silently took a step towards him. The eyes behind the bandages did not land on him. They did not follow Maxwell's movement. He waved an arm, gestured obscenely, but nothing. Max's father was completely blind. Blind and immobile.

Maxwell couldn't answer. He couldn't sort the words and the reactions, so he didn't quite know *how* to answer. And a part of him wanted to let his father suffer in silence, because that part of him never wanted to speak to Maverick Corvid ever again...

...but a part of him also wanted to respond.

"Yes, Dad, it's um... it's me."

"O-Oh my God..." Maverick said, in a strained way, like invisible hands were wringing his shriveled neck. "Is it really you? I didn't think... P-Please come over here, I..."

His father reached for him. Even if he wasn't close enough to touch his dad, Maxwell still backed away, as Maverick shakily waved his arms in the air around him, slowly inching his iron wheelchair across the hardwood floor. Despite his father's apparent feebleness, a tenseness gripped Maxwell's heart and guided his feet backwards. Even blind, even bound to a wheelchair, Maxwell would not embrace that man. He still believed that everything his father touched, just rotted away.

"Ah… I suppose you've seen it then…" his father said, calmly. Far too calmly after everything he had done.

"Yes. Yes, I have, dad."

"I figured you would see it all one day."

"Dad, you owe me answers. Lots of answers."

"Son…" Maverick said, gazing down at the floor. "I don't have them."

The nerve.

The absolute *fucking* nerve.

"What do you mean you don't have them!" Maxwell screamed. Max marched towards him, fist coiled and about to strike the man's wrinkled, rotten face. But he restrained himself. He had never had to stop himself in such a way. Ever. But Maxwell knew he was better than violence. He was better than his father. "You… You did all of this! You have to have answers!"

"You're right," Maverick said, laughing to himself dryly, a creaky laugh rattled the squeaking wheelchair. "It really does make no sense, does it? And yet, here we are."

Maverick was… laughing. Maverick Corvid was laughing at all of it, at everything he had done. Did he… seriously not have any answers? How? How could he not have answers?

"But if I had to guess…" Maverick began, gazing (or more accurately, not gazing) off into the opposite direction. "It was probably because I was bored. That's why all experiments happen in the first place Maxwell."

"You are disgusting," Maxwell spat. It wasn't a good enough answer. Not at all.

"Everyone is. Everyone and everything is, at its core."

That was wrong. All of what his father was saying was wrong. The man didn't deserve this place. He didn't deserve this calm, serene little plot of hell he had found himself in.

"Do you even know what this place is?" Maxwell asked his father, staring out a sunlit window, interior dust dancing in the air like dandelion fluff. Outside no birds chirped. No wind blew. No life… lived. On this beautiful spring morning, the courtyard of the manor remained completely static. "This isn't the real thing… is it?"

"That is by design," Maverick replied. "Our friend in yellow wants me to suffer, that's all it wants. It took away everything except my voice, just because it liked hearing me scream. And my ears, of course."

So that's what had happened to his father's eyes. Kyrious had taken them.

"So, this… this is another dream?" Maxwell asked, still desperately trying to get something that resembled and answer out of his father. "Another one of Kyrious's nightmares?"

"I have no idea for certain what this place is." Maverick said, still gazing longingly out the window. "But… I have a theory. This is *its* dream."

"Its dream?" Maxwell asked. "As in… Kyrious's dream?"

"Kyrious, it can exist only through our dreams," Maverick explained what Maxwell already knew. "But I think we're a part of it now, a part of its dream. And for you to end up here Maxwell, it must have been dreaming about you quite a lot."

"So… I'm a dream?"

"Dream, reality, in the end what difference does it make? We're here, aren't we?"

"Prove it."

"Fine then. Close your eyes." Maverick instructed. Maxwell obliged, if only for a second.

Almost immediately, he was met with the indescribable. Instead of eigengrau, he was met with a horrible array of sights, sounds, smells, like he was suddenly everywhere all at once. From Sleepwalkers to plants and animals, he was viewing everything, from every living thing on the estate. This was what Kyrious was able to do. Infiltrate others' minds.

Maxwell staggered backwards, opening his eyes once again, blinking to make sure he was still him, and not someone else.

"You can focus on the one person," Maverick lectured. "If you try hard enough."

"Don't talk to me about trying harder." Maxwell spat, closing his eyes once more. He knew who his *one person* was going to be almost instinctually.

He thought of the first time he entered the cave gallery decorated by drawings and drawings of Sleepwalkers. He recalled the first time he handed her the lightbulb, on the little ledge. He remembered how proud of her he was, when she finally stood up to her terrible aunt Allison and then to her terrible, yellow-draped father.

And then…

Maxwell recognized the smell the scent of mold and sulfur once more. He suddenly found himself in the dark place again, eye level strangely lower than it should have been. There was a panic in his chest as he scanned the room, searching for someone, frantically searching for himself… He was doing exactly what Kyrious had said it had to do… It was like he was dreaming about someone else's life.

Kyrious stood in the center of the room, head held down limply. But something was wrong with it. It looked frozen, stiff, still in the same position it had been in when it had grabbed Maxwell but the blackness in its face was gone. Instead, there was light. Light was pouring out of the space between Kyrious's hat, and its robe, a blinding yellow light. Maxwell realized the lightbulb had fallen into Kyrious with him. The lightbulb which glowed hot when it was near him…

"Kid!" Penny yelled, peering down at Vanessa, her glasses not masking her worry. The light of the void sputtered and crackled — and that's when Maxwell realized it wasn't the dancing light of the bulb but the heat of a fire. A fire that was beginning to burn down the walls of the dark place. A fire that was emanating from within Kyrious itself, judging from the smoke that was pouring out of its face now and its burning yellow robes, as the thing spasmed around, beginning to burn from the inside out. "Kid, we gotta get outta here! Now!"

"But Mr. M-Maxw-w-well…" she stuttered. The walls of the void itself melted into a black tar around them.

"Sweetheart, you heard him, he'll be… fine. Let's move."

Vanessa ran.

Maxwell thrashed open his eyes. He couldn't stand to watch it any longer, it was too much, between the indescribable screaming of Kyrious's still flailing carcass, to Julia's vice grip around Vanessa's hand as the brigand tugged the girl away against her will, to the overbearing smell of smoke. The feeling of sunlight on his eyelids came back, as did the scent of dust. He had returned to the study.

The smell of smoke, however, did not disappear.

"Maxwell? Maxwell, son, do you… smell smoke?"

There was a strong odor of smoke that was filling the study. Little trails of black began to drift lazily from underneath the floorboards. Maxwell watched as a tiny little flame flickered into existence on the edge of the curtains where Maverick's wheelchair sat. His father couldn't stamp it out of course, and so Maxwell did the stamping. But as he did, another pocket of flame appeared. And further, another flame materialized on the other curtain. Maxwell tried to smother that one, too, but they kept coming, hotter and faster and striking not only the curtains but the throw rugs and the upholstery on the chairs.

"Do something!" Maxwell shouted at his father, as Maverick sat there complacently, the flame spreading to the walls around the windows. "Help me put it out!"

"Dreams can't put out fires." Maverick muttered bitterly under his breath.

"Dreams can at least try!" Maxwell shouted at him.

Maverick Corvid sighed. And then, *stood* and stepped out of his wheelchair.

"Enough, Maxwell," his father said. Wobbling, his legs beginning to crumple under his own weight, he then sat. "I've been here for who knows how long. There's no way out of this room, which means there's no way out of the fire! It's over. You can stop trying."

The fire had spread throughout the room. Everything was engulfed in flames now, everything, from the floorboards to the ceiling. There was nothing left to do now. The fire raged on, as burning pages from books and little charred scraps of yellow fabric began to dance through the air, in time with the intense rhythm that the crackling made. Even the dust in the air burnt. All of it, smelling overbearingly of smoke.

"Maxwell…" his father began. "I just want you to know that, wherever we wake up next… If we wake up… This will all just seem like a bad dream."

"For your sake." Maxwell replied.

Everything was melting now, it was all melting like a clock in a Dali painting, the books, the windows, the sunlight, even… even their faces. He looked down at his hands and noticed that his fingers were fusing together. But it didn't… hurt. His clothes were on fire now as well, but it didn't feel like he was burning alive. It just felt… warm.

His father was on fire, too. Maverick Corvid retched and spewed forth a black pile of mush. Maverick's jawbone dropped off of his melting his face and shattered onto the ground. The bandages shot up in flames as Maverick's eyes turned to mush in their sockets. Maverick's fingers snapped free.

"Sweet dreams, Maxwell," his dad somehow managed to still say in a gargling, Sleepwalker-esque voice.

"You, too, Dad."

And, probably to Kyrious's great disappointment, Maverick Corvid did not scream as he disintegrated into a pile of ash and mold.

He closed his eyes once again. He returned to his thoughts about Vanessa.

Through Vanessa, Maxwell witnessed a sunrise. Vanessa was on the surface somehow. But… she was staring at the sun, as the night finally came to an end… But maybe, since the night was finally over, and Kyrious was… well… Maybe she would be allowed to leave.

Despite the chilly morning autumn air, the sunrise turned the sky all shades warm of oranges and pinks. She should have been elated, this would have been her first trip to the surface, and what a beautiful surface it was. Vanessa basked in the warmth of a sunbeam. Maxwell felt it on his face too, that pleasant warmth. It seemed that for the moment, she had forgotten all about him. But that didn't matter. She was happy. That's all he wanted now.

Vanessa sniffled and wiped tears from her eyes.

"Why are you crying, sweetheart?" Julia asked, kneeling down and squeezing Vanessa with everything that she had. "You heard Mr. Maxwell... He'll be... fine."

"I know what he said, Ms. Julia..." Vanessa began. She looked at the sunrise again. "I... I don't know why I'm crying..."

Vanessa didn't know why, because they weren't really her tears.

They were Maxwell's.

Maxwell could feel everything, everything around him, melting. Soon, the coach crash, the yellow thing, his unfinished assignments at Miskatonic, the Sleepwalkers, Vanessa's auntie Allison, his father... none of it would matter. Maybe he would just... wake up from it all. It was like waking up. Yes, that's how he had to think about it. It was just like waking up in the morning, from a wonderful, terrifying, exhilarating... miraculous... dream.

Maxwell Corvid didn't dream. That was all there was to it, or so he had once believed. At one time, he had thought there was no changing it, and that it was the way things were. That trying to change it wasn't worth the effort. That there wouldn't be anything worth remembering. And that to try was nothing but a waste of time.

But... he supposed this dream, this waking nightmare, for all its bad and its good. One thing was for certain: He hadn't felt this awake in years. Maxwell closed his eyes.

He was... he was so tired. He hadn't truly slept in ages. He had napped, but he hadn't... slept. And he was so tired, even now...

Maxwell Corvid drifted off rather peacefully, into his rest.

Because this experience, it had been one dream that was well *worth* remembering.